A QUESTIONABLE SHAPE

a novel by

BENNETT SIMS

TWO DOLLAR RADIO
Books too loud to ignore.

TWO DOLLAR RADIO is a family-run outfit founded in 2005 with the mission to reaffirm the cultural and artistic spirit of the publishing industry.

We aim to do this by presenting bold works of literary merit, each book, individually and collectively, providing a sonic progression that we believe to be too loud to ignore.

TWO DOLLAR RADIO
Books too loud to ignore.
www.TwoDollarRadio.com
twodollar@TwoDollarRadio.com

For Dave

I hastily left the narrow street at the next turning. However, after wandering about for some time without asking the way, I suddenly found myself back in the same street, where my presence began to attract attention. Once more I hurried away, only to return there again by a different route. I was now seized by a feeling that I can only describe as uncanny. Other situations share this feature of the unintentional return. One comes back again and again to the same spot. To many people the acme of the uncanny is represented by death, dead bodies, revenants… The return of the dead.

Sigmund Freud, 'The Uncanny'

Human love is implicated with death, because it implies either resurrecting the beloved or following the spouse into the death realm. It is fitting that *the lost one* is a synonym for *the dead one*, since the dead are lost *de jure* and one loses them *de facto* in the labyrinth. Marriage requires the spouse to follow his wife into the labyrinthine realm of death… To follow them into undeath, as Orpheus did. Orpheus is the model spouse.

Jalal Toufic, *Undying Love, or Love Dies*

MONDAY

WHAT WE KNOW ABOUT THE UNDEAD SO FAR IS this: they return to the familiar. They'll wander to nostalgically charged sites from their former lives, and you can somewhat reliably find an undead in the same places you might have found it beforehand. Its house, its office, the bikelanes circling the lake, the bar. 'Haunts.' The undead will return to the neighborhood grocery store and shuffle down its aisles, as if shopping. They will climb into their own cars and sit dumbly at the wheel, staring out the windshield into nothing. A man bitten, infected, and reanimated fifty miles from home will find his way back, staggering over diverse terrain—which, probably, he wouldn't have recognized or been able to navigate in his mortal life—in order to stand vacantly on a familiar lawn. No one knows how they do it—whether by tracking or instinct or some latent mnemocartography—nor why, but it's an observable phenomenon. In fact, what it calls to mind are those homing pigeons, the ones famous and fascinating for the particles of magnetite in their skulls: bits of mineral sensitive to electromagnetic pulls and capable of directing the pigeons, like the needle of a compass, homeward over vast and alien distances. It is as if the undead are capable of 'homing' in this way.[1]

---

[1] Sometimes I wonder whether we, the living, are constantly generating the magnetoreceptive memory pellets that will guide us in undeath. Could it be that each time a place leaves a powerful impression on us, it deposits into our unconscious these mineral flecks of nostalgic energy? Eventually, over the course of a lifetime, these might accrete and calcify into little lodestones in our minds: geospatial anamnestic kernels, capable of leading us back to places, but activated, for whatever reason, only in undeath. In that case, the undead mind would really just be a chaff cloud

At seven this morning, an hour before Mazoch usually arrives, I sit down with a sheet of loose leaf to write out some of the sites where we'll be searching for his father today. The list is for Rachel, who's still asleep. I'll leave it on the coffee table by our copy of *FIGHT THE BITE*, the infection-awareness pamphlet that the Louisiana Center for Disease Control doled out back in May, at the beginning of the outbreak (chapter titles include '1. A Bite's Never Alright [sic],' '5. A Knock To The Head Will Stop 'Em Dead,' et cetera). Recently Rachel has been requesting a list of those places 'you two go every day,' so that, if I'm worryingly late coming home, she'll at least be able to tell the police where to start looking. She's right, of course. At the heading of the sheet, first item on our itinerary, I write down Mr. Mazoch's old address.

He went missing from his house in Denham Springs several weeks ago, and Matt emailed me shortly afterward to enlist my help. We gave ourselves the month of July, just before hurricane season hits, setting this Friday as our deadline. Assuming that Mr. Mazoch hasn't been detained, quarantined, or put down already, he might still be wandering, compelled, toward his remembered places. We figured it was only a matter of determining what places these would be, staking them out each day, and waiting for our routes to overlap. If our trip to his house in Denham coincides with Mr. Mazoch's, then he and Matt will be reunited. To inspire us each morning, Matt copied out two Thomas Hardy quotations on separate post-it notes and taped them to

---

of remembrance, this mass of pellets causing sharp pain as it shifted magnetically in the direction of various homes. And the undead wouldn't remember memories so much as be shepherded by them, tugged by headaches toward recalled geographies. (It occurs to me on clear nights that the Pleiades, clustered like buckshot in Taurus's thigh, might be like memory pellets of this type. When the Pleiades shift, the bull's thigh aches in that direction, and it is a kind of homesickness that leads him sinking beneath the horizon.)

the dashboard of his car: 'My spirit will not haunt the mound/ Above my grave,/But travel, memory-possessed,/To where my tremulous being found/Life largest, best./My phantom-footed shape[1] will go/When nightfall grays/Hither and thither along the ways/I and another used to know' from 'My Spirit Will Not Haunt the Mound,' and, 'Yes: I have entered your old haunts at last;/Through the years, through the dead scenes I have tracked you;/What have you now to say of our past—/Scanned across the dark space wherein I have lacked you?' from 'After a Journey.' Each poem seems to speak to the other across the inch of dashboard leather that divides them, just as I imagine Mr. Mazoch letting out an unearthly moan, and Matt humming out the open window to keep awake as he drives, and that moaning and that humming speaking to one another across Baton Rouge's fields and highways, across all the remembered and misremembered suburbs that separate Mazoch from his father.

I place the list on the coffee table and check my cell phone for the time. 7:15. Matt is no doubt doing his morning pushups right about now. He completes sets of a hundred before setting out each day, and always manages to arrive at eight sharp, giving his familiar, hearty knock at the door. With equal regularity he manages to drop me off by four, and—if Rachel and I

---

[1] I like the phrase 'phantom-footed' because I've often imagined the footprints of the undead phosphorescing beneath moonlight, as if ectoplasmically, such that they glow in determined trails toward particular houses, restaurants, live oaks… wherever that undead had found life 'largest, best.' It would be like reading a map of remembering to look down on all the ectoplasmic paths glimmering through the city at night. Like Hardy's spirit, our 'walking dead' don't simply walk: anytime an undead is walking, what it's really doing is remembering. It's retracing steps from its former life and moving blindly along a vector of memory. In this way, the tracks that it leaves (of rainwater, of dirt across a carpet, of blood) record more than a physical path: they also materialize a line of thought, the path of that remembering.

don't invite him over for dinner—goes home to read his 'book a night.' He's been this way since undergrad: a mesomorphic litterateur, who keeps his square jaw clean-shaven and his blond hair buzzed close, like a wrestler, and who's succeeded, too, in cultivating a wrestler's physique (the perfect inverse pyramid of his back; the chest like a breastplate; the forearms thick as my calves), even though he's never grappled with anything bigger than an OED. Back when he was LSU's model English major, the bodybuilding always struck me—a stereotypically scrawny philosophy student—as a waste of his time: something that he would grow out of eventually, or else replace with a new routine. But not even the outbreak has altered his regimen. In the living room of his apartment a used bench press abuts a floor-to-ceiling bookcase, brimming with paperbacks, while in the doorway of his bedroom a pull-up bar is installed, with a fifty-pound weight belt coiled beneath it. It is this same self-discipline and rigor that Matt has been bringing to bear on the search for his father.

In his initial emails to me, he compiled a brief assortment of some of Mr. Mazoch's likely haunts. Since starting the search, we've made surprisingly few additions to that list. There's the house in Denham, which is my first item for Rachel, plus a number of other places that Mr. Mazoch would have frequented: the Freedom Fuel gas station; Louie's Café; the grocery store, auction house, and antiques mall; the plumbing warehouse where he reported every morning for forty years (even into his sixties, when finally a debilitating heart attack forced him to retire). I write all of these down, in a column beneath the house's entry. Then I add some of the fast-food restaurants—McDonald's, Taco Bell, Jack-in-the-Box—where Mr. Mazoch took his lunch breaks every day (causing him to accumulate weight ruinously in later life, ending it, according to Matt, near three hundred pounds). The Goodwill, the Salvation Army, where he bought the used boots and ripped jeans he worked in. These businesses are all boarded up by now, but they're still places where his father might be. Places where Matt's sensitivity and agitation reach a kind of peak, where he holds his breath at the appearance in the distance of every undead silhouette, trying to determine by the height and breadth of its fatherly shape whether it's worth lifting the binoculars for.[1]

Mr. Mazoch was sixty-four when he went missing. From what little Matt's told me about his life, I gather that the man ordered his adult existence almost exclusively around these spaces: never worked another job than plumbing; only ever lived with Mrs. Mazoch, spending his last decades alone in that one house in Denham; and had as his single hobby (his only reason for traveling elsewhere) 'antiquing,' i.e., driving to garage sales at dawn on the weekends and buying up refuse from families' attics, which he could then put on display in his own home or sell for a profit to dealers. Not an avid traveler, not a sampler of novelties: just a workhorse who lived and loved at a few addresses, where even now he might be found. Where, at any rate, Matt still expects to run into him.

At each of the sites, Matt's MO is to case the perimeter, looking for traces that Mr. Mazoch might have left there. But in the past three weeks we've turned up nothing. Day after day the premises remain undisturbed and blank. That is how thoroughly the police have been patrolling the streets: any remaining strays are quickly apprehended and sent to the quarantines. When Matt first emailed me (when I-10 was still jammed with mass-exodus car wrecks), it was impossible to imagine conditions ever stabilizing to this degree. But now we really are learning to live

---

[1] A far-off infected usually constitutes our great excitement for the day: Matt will peer at it awhile through the windshield, then—shaking his head—pass on the binoculars to me (though I still haven't worked up the nerve to look through them. I've only ever seen one undead in person—up close I mean—and it was eerie enough from two blocks away, by the naked eye).

with undeath. The federal government has standardized its plan for handling the epidemic, and Louisiana has been faring no more or less poorly than any other plague state. Though most schools, businesses, and malls remain closed for decontamination, FEMA has begun providing relief in the form of refugee shelters and welfare checks. It's FEMA relief that is funding Matt's search, in fact, and funding the shelter where Rachel volunteers every day. The worst that's going to happen appears to have already happened, and life in the city is returning to some version of normal.

Other than the quarantines—which Matt and I visit on Fridays—I'm not sure what else to include on Rachel's list. There are a few extra sites, but none that we bother to check on our rounds: Matt inspects his apartment himself, and he also visits his mom's house (the one that she won in the divorce, and raised him in). Now, as we're heading into the final week, he's begun suggesting that we revise our itinerary. Maybe stake out some new sites. For instance, there are places from his own childhood that he's brought up before: like his elementary school, where Mr. Mazoch had to wait in carpool for him, or Highland Road Park, where he used to take Matt to play chess on those weekends when he had custody. I add these to the list with asterisks, in the event that we end up going, then explain in a footnote[1] that they're provisional.

One site that Matt has mentioned in a passing way is Tunica Hills, a pine-forested park up near St. Francisville, with hiking trails winding along red-clay cliffs and down through precipitous

---

[1] Since the outbreak, I have often reflected that the footnote is the typographic mark most emblematic of undeath. By opening up a subjacent space on the page, the footnote digs a grave in the text, an underworld in the text. The words that are banished there are like thoughts that the text has repressed, pushed down into its unconscious. But they go on disturbing it from beneath, such that if the text were ever infected, they are the words that would guide it. Footnotes are a text's phantom feet.

waterfalls. He and Mr. Mazoch had gone on day trips there when Matt was a kid, and they always remembered the hikes fondly together, promising they'd do it again sometime. But once Matt was grown, Mr. Mazoch was already too out of shape—his back too wracked from manual labor—to attempt anything so physically strenuous. Then, after the heart attack, it was out of the question forever. So Tunica may well be a site on Mr. Mazoch's radar, a locus of nostalgia and regret. Matt's said that he might expect himself to wander there, eventually, if he were undead. I doubt we could actually go—it's a three-hour drive; the area's too large to feasibly locate one body in; and, because of the travel ban that's been enforced, we'd have to circumvent border guards simply to leave Baton Rouge—but it's nice to talk about.

I myself remember Tunica fondly (even though I've been only once), and could almost be guaranteed to return undead to it, so strong a pull does it exert over my memory. Rachel and I went on one of our best dates there, late last summer. Like Matt and Mr. Mazoch, we hiked along the cliff trails, and at the end of one steep uphill slog we rewarded ourselves by splashing around and otherwise disporting in the algid waters of a wading pool, and by showering beneath the thundering brainfreeze of its waterfall. We must have stayed in that same place for hours, passing the entire afternoon—or at least this is how I remember it—kissing and smiling goofily at one another. In fact, I find that most of the frames of this memory are just of Rachel's smiling face: her jagged blond hair plastered wetly against her cheeks, her green eyes gleaming as I cradle her head in my hands. Everything's shot through with a burnished yellow light, as if there were actually lens flares in my memory. I've discussed this effect with Rachel—the color saturation of my memory of that day, its emphasis on amber—and she says that she experiences the same thing, that what she can recall of Tunica is more like a music video than a memory. She thinks that it's a result of our having paid such close attention to the quality of light in the park. On our hike, she kept stopping to admire the sun's suffusion in the air, pointing out the way that it punched through the pine branches in great gold shafts, so like the conical tractor beams of hovering UFOs that all those backlit motes of dust, which were in fact being circulated in every direction, seemed to float only upward, in abducted currents. Given the level of attention we paid to scenes like that, it's possible that our memory is a little sundrunk, Rachel said. The moment that even now, a year afterward, we still recall to one another is the one when Rachel cupped her hands beneath the waterfall and withdrew them, holding them up so that a scattering of sunlight was reflected there, between her hands, lambent in the water and over the skin of her palms. The sun was diffracted into a dozen small spots of glare, wriggling white oblongs, like larvae of light. We stared at them for a full minute, delighted. Because they were caught in her handful of water, Rachel was able to slosh them around, and to make them appear to sift through the creases between her opening fingers, and finally to make an offering of them: to extend her hands to me, the way the moon rises, and proffer her handful of the sun's light. As she ladled it over my head, I didn't shiver, or feel reinvigorated by solar forces, but I pretended to.

A few weeks into the outbreak, Rachel wrote me an email reminding me of this afternoon—as if I needed to be reminded—in which she referred to the lights in her hands as 'Bethlehem stars' (I knew at once what she had in mind, but to me those slivers of brilliance had always seemed, all wriggling whitely in her hands, more like lampyrid maggots than stars). She asked me whether I remembered Tunica, and specifically whether I recalled the constellation that she had caught, 'as bright as Bethlehem stars.' Of course I did. The entire day was—to adopt a photic vocabulary—'seared' into my memory, and it was this episode especially, the quiet magic and mad happiness of watching sunlight play on each other's bodies, that

Rachel and I had incorporated into the mythos of our courtship. We always referred back to it with semi-tragic nostalgia, as if for a prelapsarian period in our love. We might ask, in the middle of a fight say, why things couldn't be now as they were then, or remark, in acute distress, that we hadn't watched light together in weeks. That was the rhetorical strategy of this particular email, which exhorted the two of us—this was after a string of nasty fights, induced in part by the cabin fever of our staying inside the boarded-up apartment for days—to exhibit only our best selves: to try getting out and going on a sunset walk together; to recuperate the love we'd displayed at Tunica, when we spent whole minutes staring patiently into her hands, into the lights there, as if stargazing. A bath of Edenic goldness, a trace of our best selves: it is this kind of life that that afternoon has taken on in our imaginations. And because neither of us has been able to visit Tunica Hills since, we both, if we were infected I mean, might be expected to head straight there, bypassing other sites (our crappy apartment even) in search of this one memory. Following, as it were, our Bethlehem stars.[1]

After some hesitation, I decide to write 'Tunica Hills*' at the bottom of Rachel's list. We won't be going there today—or any other, for that matter—but I suspect that Rachel will appreciate its presence on the page. At the very least she'll savor the coincidence of our sharing the site with the Mazochs. Of course, it's unlikely that the hills hold the same significance in Matt and his dad's relationship as they do in hers and mine, or that Mr. Mazoch could be expected to wander so far afield. But maybe they do, and maybe he could, in which case Matt might devise

---

[1] All that Rachel meant by the phrase when she first wrote it—little was known at that point about the homing of the undead—was that the lights were brilliant and beautiful. It's a happy coincidence that these Bethlehem stars happen also to have matured in our memories in the way that they have, and that they might serve—like the Pleiades, like memory pellets— as the guiding lights that will shepherd our undead bodies.

a way of driving up there after all. Probably, though, we'll just keep visiting the same handful of sites, until we find Mr. Mazoch or until Mr. Mazoch finds us. Or, failing that, until Friday arrives, and Matt abandons this search and gives up.

TODAY, AS ON EVERY OTHER, MAZOCH AND I BEGIN the search at his father's house, which—recessed at the end of a dirt driveway, its aluminum siding gone faded and dun, with tar-colored gaps showing between its shingles—is more of a squalid shack than a home, and not a place where (personally) I think we're likely to find the man. But earlier this morning, while casing the perimeter, Matt discovered a broken window out back. Now, emboldened by the discovery (and despite my objections), he's looking inside the house. I keep watch in the car, gripping a wooden baseball bat between my legs.[1]

This is the one time since the first day of the search that he's insisted on going inside, and it was in vain that I tried to talk him out of it. The house *had* to be empty, I told him. The window wasn't even a point of ingress, just a pane in the rear door's fanlight. Even if an infected did reach up to punch a hole there (and why would it?), there was no way it could get in. But Matt was adamant: he had to check. So for the past half hour, as he has been patrolling his father's rooms, I've been glancing from window to window and mirror to mirror in a state of nervy surveillance. It's reassuring to see that the area is as deserted as ever. The houses on either side of Mr. Mazoch's are both still

---

[1] We bring these bats with us everywhere, but we've never yet had to use them. Technically speaking it would be illegal to: it's considered murder to murder the undead. Only in self-defense, in close-quartered combat, are you supposed to follow *FIGHT THE BITE*'s concussion instructions ('A Knock to the Head Will Stop 'Em Dead'). Otherwise, the infected are to be quarantined, since they possess roughly the same citizen status and legal rights as, say, coma patients or the mentally ill. (In this respect, it's noteworthy that *FIGHT THE BITE* rarely ever refers to the infected as 'undead,' which is considered dysphemistic and dehumanizing.)

boarded up and unvandalized. Down the block the Freedom Fuel gas station is empty: all of the pumping stations have been removed from beneath its porte-cochere. There are no undead silhouettes. It's 9:05. Matt has been inside for an unusually long time now—close to half an hour. What's he doing in there? I imagine him grappling with a random infected, or staunching a bite wound over the bathroom sink. But no. He's probably just taking his time. Reminiscing. It's been weeks since he's seen the place, and he might be using this opportunity to sit in the empty living room, meditating among Mr. Mazoch's antiques. I study the front door in the rearview,[1] waiting for him to reemerge.

---

[1] Matt backed into the driveway for getaway purposes, so I had to fiddle with the rearview mirror to bring Mr. Mazoch's house into frame. As I was doing so my thumb smudged the glass, leaving a whitish smear of finger oil on its surface. Now, whenever I glance up at the mirror, I see that cyclopean smudge, as milky and white as an undead eyeball: it mars the glass like a cataract, distorting whatever reflections lie behind it. Currently it's hovering over the house's façade, forming a scotomatous opacity in the aluminum siding, which looks erased somehow. Whereas everything else in the reflection is pristine, this one patch of Being has been rendered otherworldly and blurred. Is that how it is to be undead, I wonder? Is *everything* blurred like this, when seen through undead eyes? I try to imagine what Mr. Mazoch might be seeing, wherever he is right now: whether the whole world is otherworldly to him, on the other side of the smudge. (What I have in mind here is Hans Holbein the Younger's *The Ambassadors*. This portrait features two 16th-century French dignitaries posing in a parlor beside a globe and an astrolabe. Meanwhile, distorting the foreground, is a gash-like diagonal pancake of bone-white blur. Only when you approach the painting from the side does this blur resolve itself, clarifying into the image of a skull... with the result, however, of distorting the *rest* of the painting. So the portrait, looked at from one angle, has a small blur where the death's head's hid; then, once you reveal this skull, it's everything else that becomes as blurry as death is. As if to really see Death requires blinding yourself to Being, and vice versa: either you can see the skull as the ambassadors see it; or you can see the ambassadors as the skull is seeing *them*. This optical illusion is precisely how I've been imagining that the

That one time we went inside together, on the first day of the search, it occurred to me that maybe his father hadn't wanted to survive, or at the very least that he had been waiting for death with a kind of patience. None of his windows had been boarded, nor the flimsy wooden doors. The scene surrounding the bloodstains in the living room carpet was so legible, forensically speaking, that reading it took a matter of seconds: the front door hanging open and left unlocked; a bright, uncovered lamp (the bulbs still glowing, Matt says, when he got there) situated in direct view of the street; no weapon—not a rifle, a kitchen knife, even a baseball bat—lying on the floor. The man was totally defenseless, and, what's worse, he was broadcasting that defenselessness by leaving his windows unboarded. It's surprising that he wasn't attacked and infected earlier on in the outbreak, though I suppose his living in a satellite town, in such a sparsely populated area, gave him a survivor's edge over city dwellers. Although, again, my impression of Matt's father is that 'survivor' would have been the worst wrong word to describe him.

I don't just mean that the windows aren't boarded.[1] There's

smudge in Mr. Mazoch's house would operate. When I'm able to contain the distortion within one spot of the bone-white siding, and keep everything else coherent, it's as if I remain—optically—on the side of the ambassadors. But when Mr. Mazoch, undead, sees the blur all over, it's because he's entered the skull's side of his life. [What was the name of this painting technique, anyway? Rachel would know. I'll have to ask Rachel when I get home. She was the one who introduced me to Holbein in the first place: my resident art-history major.])

[1] Though this is literally one of the first pieces of advice in *FIGHT THE BITE*: 'Ch. 2. Fight the Bite: Hide Your Light!' Fitting the window frames with iron bars would certainly deter the undead, but it would do nothing to prevent catching their attention and attracting crowds of them. Even with curtains drawn, the warmth of each window would serve as a beacon. Mr. Mazoch's carelessness here—with regard to his lamp—is tantamount

also the fact that the house itself, a dingy rental, doesn't much seem like a place where the sixty-four-year-old Mr. Mazoch would have found life 'largest, best.' Subsisting on disability checks after his near-fatal heart attack, Matt's father evidently didn't know what to do with himself in retirement. He lived alone here, half an hour from anyone he loved enough to want to see, and if he went out at all he did so only to eat, or to attend an occasional garage sale or auction. Most afternoons he stayed inside and watched daytime television (Antiques Roadshow, Storage Wars). I know all that because Matt told me, but I could have guessed it—it was forensically legible—from the hermitic, indifferent disarray in which the house was kept. Mr. Mazoch seemed not to have minded sleeping on an unsheeted mattress; or heaping his soiled clothes at the end of the hallway and piling clean clothes at the foot of his bed; or letting scum develop in the bathroom, and his toiletries crowd all over the sink, and letting the tiles of the floor dislodge, uprooted from their grout; or ignoring a leak in the roof until a water stain spread gangrenously down the wall; or abandoning weeks of dirty dishes in the sink, and storing cardboard boxes of dinner plates on a dusty stovetop, and keeping a refrigerator stocked with nothing

---

to the air-raid lapse of a lit-up attic. He would have been a bull's-eye in some ghoul's eyes. (Whenever I step outside in the morning, and see the boards that Rachel and I installed in our own windows, I feel a strange rush of proprietary pride. The first place we rented together, this apartment was merely the cheapest we could find, a one-bedroom unit in the cinderblock Chateau Dijon complex [or Mustard Castle, as Matt calls it], which we moved into last summer with zero plans to renew the lease. But once the epidemic erupted, we were forced to fortify our hovel overnight: nailing plywood to the window frames, and shifting makeshift barricades—bookcases, sofas, the refrigerator—in front of them. Just like that, our starter apartment had become our end-times apartment, doubling as both a domicile and a citadel. And suddenly it felt—for the first time in a year—like home. We had protected it, and it was protecting us. It was what was keeping the bad things outside. What a beautiful apartment!)

but that garish light, forcing him to eat out every meal (which of course he did at those restaurants Matt and I visit daily now, all notorious purveyors of cheap, greasy, disheartening foods); or dropping newspapers and plastic bags and empty take-out containers just on the floor, wherever he was done with them; or accumulating so many antiques (lamps, sofas and chairs, vintage high-school yearbooks, vitrines still filled with pharmaceutical paraphernalia, tin coffee cans, streetlight fixtures, radon-painted wristwatches, illuminated anatomy maps, heavy Coca Cola signs, stuffed wildlife and wall-mounted shark jaws, immovable marble gravestones, a faux-marble bust of Caesar, old stamps, state plates, the guts of a stock ticker in a plastic dome, gorgeously filigreed headphones, et cetera), accumulating so many of these and like items, in such a bachelor's hoard of disorganized piles, that only a narrow, barely navigable path could be made from the living room to the bedroom. So not a 'survivor,' exactly, so much as a man who had very little left to anticipate. A visit with Matt once a month, another disability check. The opening of his eyes another morning: sunlight on the ceiling, this breathing again. If he had expected regular guests, he might have kept the house presentable; if he had expected to live long enough to justify cultivating a pleasant space, he might not have let the house crowd so cartonnage-like around him. As it stood, he had contented himself to lead, for the past few years anyway, a moribund life, a deathbed life, lying alone and complacent at the center of a massing decay. The outbreak must have seemed to him, like the flood of a hurricane, or a wreck at an intersection, or a second heart attack, as fitting an end as any, not to be resisted when it came.

Why would a man, released into undeath, return to a house like this one? It seems unreasonable to expect to find him here, and yet it—arguably the *least* probable stop on the itinerary of the undead Mr. Mazoch's nostos—is our first stop every morning. While I wait outside in the car, Matt cases the perimeter, peering in through each window like an orphan at Christmas, trying to get a good look at his father's rooms.[1] And each morning he rounds the corner, shaking his head no to me, a blankness on his face. Thus our days begin, exactly as inauspicious as this.

---

[1] I can only imagine what it might be costing Matt right now, to actually linger inside those rooms. I picture him taking long, sommelieran drafts of his father's shirt collars, which might still smell faintly of his father. One of Rachel's most potent flashbacks to her own father was brought on by a scent memory like this. She told me how one morning, when she went to unlock her street-parked car, she saw that a burglar had—by all appearances just the night before—broken into it. This would have been a few years ago, before we were dating. Sitting in her driver's seat that morning, and feeling very violated and unsafe because the burglar had made a mess of the CDs in the center console and of the insurance papers in the dash, she caught the sharp odor of smoke from a cigarette, which the burglar must have been smoking. Sunk deep into the upholstery, the smoke was recognizable as a particular brand, the brand that her father had smoked and the brand that had killed him. This scent memory (its suddenness, the instantaneousness of the association) put her powerfully in mind of the man, she said, and part of her felt that her father was there in the car with her: she was half-prepared to hear his voice from behind, as if it weren't a stranger's cigarette smoke but the very presence of her father's ghost that her body—at the level of the subconscious, at the level of the limbic system—was picking up signals from and being flooded with automatic responses of familiarity and warmth with regard to. She felt so grateful, she told me, to be reminded like this of the man (to be transported bodily to the precinct of his memory) that, almost involuntarily, she composed a mental prayer of thanksgiving to the burglar, for breaking into her car and smoking a cigarette the night before, like some St. Pavlov, St. Proust, some St. saving synapse from out of her past. It wouldn't surprise me if Matt eventually confessed that this is the real reason he went inside this morning: not because he actually expected to find Mr. Mazoch, but because he wanted to smell his father where he lay. Because there are certain memories accessible only by that smell. Because—if later on this afternoon he was going to have to confront the corpse of the man, and be repelled by its dead fetor—he wanted to begin the day with just a little of his human scent.

Then again, I might be wrong about Matt's father. It's possible that I have mischaracterized him: that in fact the man was a survivor; that he fought through his heart attack tenaciously; that, despite appearances, he lived for his accumulation of antiques and for his breakfasts out at McDonald's. That he didn't welcome the undead that attacked him, as one swallows a willing lungful of water, but tried energetically to fend it off. What little I know or think I know of the man's character was gleaned from what Mazoch told me and from spending a single afternoon in his house. So perhaps this house, comprising as it does the final years of his life, is denser with nostalgic energy than I've been giving it credit for. Perhaps one day—even today!—Mazoch will find his father standing in the shower stall after all, hot water running down the length of his body, darkening the denim of his jeans. Perhaps Mazoch is finding him in there right now.

Still watching the front door in the rearview, I reach for the mirror and tilt it upward slightly, bringing the finger-oil whorl to head height in the threshold. The smudge hovers right where Mazoch's face will be reflected. When he opens that door, he'll walk face-first into the blur. The second he steps outside, he really will have a blankness on his face. A Holbein blankness, a death's-head blankness: the face his father would see.

MATT AND I ARE PLAYING CHESS IN HIGHLAND Road Park, deep in a deserted picnic field. This was Matt's idea: both the hike into the field, and the game of chess (he keeps a board in his trunk). Whether he associates the game with this place from his childhood outings with Mr. Mazoch, and just likes to play when he comes here; or whether he had hoped that by reassembling enough of the props of one memory—himself, the grass, the beige and black plastic of the figurines—his father would arrive as if bidden to complete the scene; or whether his desire to play was more subconsciously motivated than that… were questions that interested me for precisely four moves into the first game, at which point Matt captured a pawn of mine so unexpectedly as to sting my pride, and I resolved to focus entirely on the match. In the end I lost, though it was very (indeed, frustratingly) close, as was the second match that I lost. In each case the balance tipped in Mazoch's favor only late into the middlegame, when a deadlocked block of our pieces—one of those nasty mires in which any given piece threatens three others and is defiladed in three directions by comrades ready to counterattack, and which develop on the board like (it always seems to me) that scene at the end of action movies, when the hero draws a gun on the villain, only to have a gun drawn on him by a henchman, who is surprised to have a gun drawn on him by the hero's newly arrived sidekick, himself now compromised by the gun being drawn by a second henchman, et cetera, et cetera—finally dissolved in such a way that I was put on the defensive, masterfully pursued, and ruthlessly checkmated. Needless to say, I am determined to win one match before we leave.

When we first got here, pulling into the parking lot, I assumed we'd be surveying the area from the car. But Matt surprised me by stepping outside. What was I waiting for, he asked. Wasn't I coming with him? Obviously I refused. The grounds of the park, which has been closed to the public since the first weeks of the outbreak, haven't been tended to in months, and the weeds have risen far above our knees. Overgrown and deserted like this, the place has a kind of sunken, shipwrecked look, as I can recall it did anytime hurricane rains flooded the valleys between its hills. Standing beside the car, Mazoch pointed across the field toward three far live oaks, separated from us by a sprawling waste of waist-high grass.[1]

'Are you kidding?' I asked. 'An abandoned house isn't enough for you?' I told him that we'd already taken enough risks today, without trudging through jungle. Matt waved off my concerns. He reminded me that the infected would have been rounded up as comprehensively here as everywhere else in the city. Then he cited, from this morning's paper, what was meant to be a mollifying statistic: there had been only two attacks in Baton Rouge this past week. Statistically speaking, he said, we were more likely to be mauled by sharks, in the shallows of some Florida beach, than be ambushed here. Which was all that I could think about, naturally, as I followed behind him into the tall grass. Wading through the overgrowth, unable to see my feet, I felt exactly like

---

[1]After Katrina, this area of the park was heavily flooded, to the point that the hilltops just barely emerged from out of that sheet of black, practically lacustrine rainwater. I can remember that the trees that breached the surface of the water seemed to float there like verdant boats, and that boats, in fact, were actually taken out for sheer novelty on the water, trawling slow wakes across a space where, a week ago, birds might have flown and where, but for fear of water moccasins, one could swim down through the frigid water, all the way to the grass on the ground, lowering oneself along a ladder of underwater branches. That is how high the weeds look now: Matt may as well have been suggesting that we swim.

a selachophobe in dark ocean: each step seemed to bring my ankle nearer to the gray hand that would grip it, tripping then dragging me beneath the surface, to be fed upon like chum.

Midway into the field, Mazoch stopped suddenly, cocking his head to squint at something to our left. I spotted a short shrub, nondescript, then watched as he knelt beside it. After a moment he called me over, and I saw what had caught his attention: in the thorns of the thin branches, there was a blue scrap of tattered plaid cloth. There was no telling how old it was. It could have preceded the epidemic, even, left here by some Ultimate Frisbee player, foraging for his disc. But as I watched him pore over the plaid—with a kind of Sherlockian scrupulosity, as if searching it for prints—an absurd thought occurred to me. When he looked up, his face was bloodless: 'I know it sounds crazy.' 'So don't say it.' 'Would you believe me if I told you my dad had a shirt like this?' 'I would believe you if you told me *I* have a shirt like this. It's generic plaid. *Everybody* has this shirt.' 'I know, I know. It's probably nothing. But weird, right? First the window, then this? Two traces in the same day. It's like we're closing in.' Closing in on what, I did not ask him. I simply nodded and asked what he wanted to do. Set up camp, he said. Stake the site out.

We quickly stamped down a clearing of flattened stalks, like a protective ring, for about ten feet around ourselves, and we have been playing chess here for the past two hours. Standing, we can scan the horizon for any silhouettes; sitting, out of sight, we can concentrate safely on our games, listening for disturbances in the rim of the grass. It's been forty minutes since either of us has bothered to take a periscopic survey of the park. The sun has risen higher overhead, basting us both with sweat. I doubt we'll wait much longer beyond the close of this game.

Of which it's still Matt's move. He's lying across from me, propped up on one elbow and studying his configuration of units. When he extends his free hand to hover it over a knight, I sit up and watch him deliberate. Two of my pawns are divided in such a way that he could place the knight on a square equidistant from them, forking both at once and forcing me to sacrifice one over the other. He lifts the knight in question, then lets the piece hang tentatively in the air, between his fingers, like a junkyard car from one of those crane magnets. 'Ready now?' I ask. He places the knight back on the square where he found it. 'Hold your horses, Vermaelen.' 'Move yours.' He smiles: 'When I'm ready.'

I close my eyes and begin to massage them. When he's ready. For a quiet moment there is phosphene-less dark against my eyelids, until I thumb a pressure cloud of electric blue into vision. One of the conversations we've been having off and on all day, in between moves in our matches, is about what being undead would be like. It's a topic I've been meaning to raise with Mazoch lately, and today it came up while we were flattening out our playing area. As we marched around in a wide circle, making a spectacle of ourselves, I stopped to peer across the field. 'Do you think any infected could see us out here?' I asked him. Matt shook his head. They were just corpses, he said. Rotting as they walked. Their eyeballs were glaucomatic and clouded and white. How well could they possibly see? If he had to guess, he'd say they were close to blind. I was surprised to hear this,[1] and I told Matt that he had touched on a topic of particular fascination for me. As we finished stamping down the grass and started setting up the chessboard, I asked him how he thought the undead navigated, if not by sight.[2] Oh, he'd read the usual studies, he

---

[1] My own longstanding suspicion—which I did not share with him—is that the undead *do* see: it's just that the way in which they see is so different from human vision that it would be misleading to call it seeing. That they're really seeing something else (a Holbein blur, a death's head, the skull's side of their life) when they see.

[2] It was at this point in our conversation that I began to wonder specifically about Mr. Mazoch. If he couldn't see, then how did Matt expect him to find his way back to the park? Maybe that is why he brought the game

said: lab tests suggested that reanimated eyeballs, critically compromised, were possibly over-reliant on motion and light. But he had his doubts that they could perceive visual data at all. He went on to speculate—after making his opening gambit—that the undead probably can't see consciously, no matter how well their eyeballs are functioning. So even when the undead seem to 'see' an object in the distance, they must actually—Matt felt sure of this—just be seeing it in the way that a robot with sensors sees, or the way in which a sleepwalker maneuvers through an environment: by processing and responding to brute stimuli. Automatically, unreflectively, beneath the threshold of awareness. Rather than seeing in the mind's eye way that he and I can see—when we appreciate the greenness of this grass around us, or the blueness of this sky—the undead must be all dark inside, he said. Consciously blind while physically sighted.

Matt's response distressed me at the time, and not only because it allowed him—by capitalizing on my distraction—to take my pawn. Rather, I found his dogmatism in the debate unsettling. No matter what, he refused to believe that the undead were conscious.[1] This seemed like the secular equivalent

---

along, I thought: less as a chessboard than a Ouija board, inviting the blind Mr. Mazoch to join us (as if the high hats of the regal pieces—the crowns and tiaras and miters that all terminate in small crosses—could, like antennae, actually broadcast signals of distress, activating the relevant pellets in the chaff cloud of Mr. Mazoch's remembering, and guiding him reliably down Highland Road).

[1] Indeed, he seemed to be thinking of them more or less as zombies, those hypothetical thought-experimental monsters from mind-body philosophy. For they, too, are defined as lacking conscious experience, with no interior appreciation for the greenness of green. As David Chalmers puts it in *The Conscious Mind*, the zombie has 'no phenomenal feel. There is nothing it is like to be a zombie.' It is—in Chalmers' phrase—'all dark inside.' Is that what Matt thinks it would be like to be undead, I asked myself? *Nothing*? Or is he imagining a more mundane—a less metaphysical—brand of

of denying that they had souls—a dualist way of dehumanizing them—and it made me wonder how far he would go in denying their subjectivity. Such questions interested me precisely until he announced 'Checkmate,' at which point I did my best to push these thoughts out of mind. But as I sit here now (rubbing my closed lids, massaging phosphenes into my eyeballs), it has begun to bother me all over again.

'Hey,' I say, opening my eyes. Matt is reaching for his knight when he looks up at me. 'What did you mean by "all dark inside"? How do you even visualize it?'

I half-expect him to quote Chalmers, or, knowing Matt, to quote Homer or Milton or some other blind poet. But after a moment he responds that what he always visualizes—what the blindness of undeath reminds him of—are the black graphics in videogames. 'Like kill screens,' he says, 'when a character dies. Or like the sidewalls of a platformer, the boundary lines you can't cross.' In videogames, he explains, this darkness signifies death, or the void, or the unknowable, and it always has the same unnerving texture: completely flat and black, without depth. 'That's what I mean when I say "all dark inside,"' he says.

Again I want to ask him about Mr. Mazoch—whether he thinks of his father this way, as nothing more than a brain-dead game-over screen—but what I hear myself asking instead

---

blindness? (E.g., blindsight, the technical term for the kind of vision that he seemed to be describing: 'consciously blind while physically sighted.' In the neuroscientific literature, there are plenty of case studies of *living* patients who perceive in this way. Although they're cortically blind, their brains are still able to respond to certain visual stimuli—edges, borders, motion, light—without consciously 'seeing' any of it. In *Phantoms in the Brain*, V.S. Ramachandran even compares this ability to the philosopher's zombie, explaining how one blindsight patient can reach out her hand and snatch a pencil with unerring dexterity: 'You'd never have guessed she was blind,' he writes. 'It was as if some person—an unconscious zombie inside her—had guided her actions.')

is what games he has in mind. '*Goldeneye*,' he says. Whenever he lies in bed at night, and tries to imagine the advance of the epidemic (how far and fast its blindness's vectors are spreading; how that darkness is encroaching on the globe), he says that he pictures it as a worldwide game of *Goldeneye*. When four people play this first-person shooter at once, the television has to be divided into quadrants, mini-screens that accommodate each character's point of view. Once a player is shot dead, his POV runs red with blood before shutting darkly off. And while the other three quadrants continue to televise the POV of their respective players (framing the rifles or Moonraker Lasers in their hands, the corridors they're jogging down), there remains in one corner of the TV this black box, the kill screen, where the dead player's eyes have closed. With each character who dies, obviously, another quadrant winks out. 'That's what I always think of at night,' Matt says. He visualizes the epidemic as a global agglomeration of kill screens. Because if there were billions more players, he says—if you multiplied the mini-screens a billionfold—the TV would eventually be honeycombed with these black cells. Assuming that all the POV in the world were arranged on an analogous master screen, with 'live feeds' televising mortal sightlines and 'kill screens' representing undeath, a viewer could measure the progress of the epidemic just by watching the cells black out across the grid. The screen would build in blackness like a hive of blindness, he says, until finally—when its entire surface was covered—the visible world would be replaced by this monochrome plane of unseeing.

'I don't see it,' I say. I ask him how this master screen would distinguish undeath from just plain death: wouldn't these 'live feeds' go dark no matter what? No matter whether it was a bullet, or a brain injury, or a bite wound that extinguished them? 'If you want a videogame to model the epidemic, you need to find a better example.'

'I've thought of that too,' Matt says. And he confesses

that, while lying in bed at night, he has also tried visualizing the epidemic in other ways. He asks me to imagine the scrolling levels from *Super Mario Brothers*, the ones in which all the scenery onscreen drifts steadily backward, as if on a conveyor belt, forcing Mario to run ever forward, lest the lefthand side of the screen, which swallows the scenery as it goes, swallow him as well. This black limit of the screen, he says, this onrushing apocalyptic line, like a tidal wave of dark water,[1] drowning all of the trees and clouds and Goombas that have backslid into the oblivion of the out-of-frame: what could better convey the urgency and inexorability of the infection, the way that it seems to sweep over the land? What could better model the submersion of mortal eyes in the undead depths of phenomenological blackness?

'Almost anything else,' I tell him. In truth, I'm horrified that Matt has made even Mario a nightmare for himself. If his model has to be a videogame, why can't it be *Tetris* or *Bubble Bobble* or something? I don't tell him this, of course. I just find ways of picking apart his model. This so-called scrolling line, for example, which shepherds Mario forward and subsumes everything in its path: it's too easily confused with time, I say. And besides, if the grid of POV isn't homogenous enough, a limit that razes everything at once is homogenous to a fault. It's not our experience of the epidemic that a wall of it barrels down. It actually spreads in pockets, in these widely dispersed,

_____

[1] In later, more sophisticatedly animated video games, the principle of the scrolling level actually would be embodied by some elemental threat pursuing the character—like a barreling inferno, or an avalanche, or, yes, a tidal wave—rather than just the leftmost line of the screen. I'm surprised that Matt doesn't use one of these other games as his example, rather than just blurting out 'Mario,' who seems like a sore or touchy figure for Matt to make himself consider (after all, Mario is a plumber like Mr. Mazoch, with warp tunnels to the underworld no less). But I suppose that the association remains latent for Matt.

concentrated bursts. Here Matt holds up a finger. For his third and final model for visualizing the epidemic *is* as 'pockets' of blackness, a graphic that he's borrowed from isometric strategy games like *Command and Conquer*. At the beginning of every level, he describes, a player's units are deployed on a map that is shrouded over with black cloud cover, a dense mist that gets referred to, in the game's instruction manual, as the 'fog of war.' This enveloping fog represents at any given moment the epistemological situation of your army: each inch of terrain that hasn't yet been explored will remain obscured by it, whereas those areas that *have* been explored will have their share of it burned away, disclosing the pixilated landscape underneath (soils, rocks, trees, rivers, and, eventually, the enemy base). The only way to burn off the fog of war is to send units into the thick of it, their reconnaissance serving to clear a path through its bosky dark. When a player scatters a handful of units radially, out from his base to the edges of the map, each infantryman, jeep, and tank will just bore through the fog, clearing it away in narrow runnels of revealed terrain, which gradually come to vermiculate the larger darkness (on tundra levels these runnels are white, since the pixilated landscape that gets disclosed is snow: as white tendrils branch across the blackness of the map, a vision seems to spill like milk). You could imagine, Mazoch tells me, an inverse epistemological situation, one in which the terrain is already revealed but in which all of the units exude contrails of fog of war: inky clouds that stream backward from jeeps and tanks, obnubilating everything, as if they were cuttlefish propelling themselves across the screen. In this model, the units would represent the undead, and the infection as a whole could be measured by how woven over with blindness the world was. Where they had spread, phenomenological darkness; and in the recesses they hadn't reached yet, living vision. 'Can you see it?' he asks.

I shake my head. This is easily Matt's most unnerving example yet. 'The undead don't spread their infection merely by moving,' I remind him, 'by walking across a map as *Command and Conquer*'s units do.' They do so by biting other humans. And whereas the enemy AI in videogames really are mindlessly violent—programmed to attack anything within their radius of awareness—the undead are less predictable. An infected might stagger for hundreds of miles without biting another human, without snuffing out a single mortal POV, and so without exhausting one speck of fog of war. And how is his model supposed to account for that? Do I have a better one, he asks? I consider bringing up *Bubble Bobble*, then shake my head again. Perhaps it would be best to avoid videogames altogether: the more abstractly Matt thinks about the pandemic, I realize, the less capable he is of individuating the undead. They just become blind tiles on a monolith of mini-screens, or an all-obliterating boundary line, or—as with *Command and Conquer*—a literal army of darkness. Points on a chart to be wiped out.

How could he look them in the eye as often as he does, zoomed in through the binocular lenses like that, and not wonder what might be going on inside them? How could he conclude that they are experiencing *nothing*, that there is nothing it is like to be them? 'They just don't *seem* blind,' I say. 'Have you ever seen one in person? Without binoculars, I mean?'

'No,' he admits, shrugging. I lean over the chessboard to get his attention: 'Well, I have,' I tell him. I try to describe my only encounter with an undead: how I was out for a walk one night when I spotted it; how it exuded this eerie awareness, palpable even from two blocks away. 'I couldn't tell whether it saw me,' I say. 'But it definitely knew I was there. It was quote unquote looking directly at me.'

Matt raises an eyebrow, unfazed, then raises his knight from the board. 'It's your move,' he says, setting the knight down between my pawns. I advance the farther of the two—as I have been planning—and place it in the strike zone of one of his. If he captures the remaining fork-pawn with his knight, I'll be able to capture his pawn with my own, moving it that much closer to the eighth rank.

The advance of a pawn to the eighth rank! Now *here* is a model for transformation into undeath. Whenever a pawn reaches the end of the chessboard, it is finally able to metamorphose into a queen. A new system of moves opens up to it. What used to be impossible, even to conceive, has been unlocked inside it, and suddenly the entire board is in play. There has bloomed in its chest, where once a pulsion moved it only forward and only one square at a time, a compass rose, given to limitless extension in every direction.

What if *that* is what it is like to become undead? Not like being blinded, but just the opposite: like being promoted into a new modality of seeing, one that would seem infinitely advanced and incomprehensible to mortals. For all Matt knows, the undead could have communal vision, routed by a hive mind, such that what any undead sees the entire species sees.[1] If that were the case, then whenever a random undead looked at Matt, it would be a way for Mr. Mazoch to look at Matt. Any gesture Matt wanted to convey to his father could simply be conveyed to that undead, as to a courier: one relay in a network of seeing. I try to imagine what it must have been like for him, those first few seconds after reanimation. Mr. Mazoch must have felt whatever it is that the promoted pawn feels, right inside his eyeball: now a vision moves laterally, now backward, with the white ease of

---

[1] If there were a video game model for this kind of communal vision, it would have to be—not the POV of a *character* in *Goldeneye*, restricted to a single quadrant—but the higher-order POV of the human player, who, looking at the TV screen, is able to take in all four quadrants at once. This player can see, not just what lies in his character's line of sight, but what lies in *any* line of sight. His visual knowledge is quadrupled by the reconnaissance of the three other players. He sees, in a word, *everything that is seen*.

the white queen, and so different are these rules that it feels as if there are no rules. Why can't Matt imagine that that is what happened to his father?

'Versmallen, go.' Ah. He has captured my pawn with his, keeping it from ever reaching the eighth rank. I move forward a knight of my own, and a breeze stirs the grass around us. The whole world seems to sway. 'It's getting hot,' I say, mopping sweat from my forehead. Matt nods. He places his finger on the tip of his king and wobbles the piece back and forth a little, as if to topple it in forfeit. But a moment after letting it droop, he cups the base of its skull with his fingertip, then lifts the piece to a standing position. I watch the king as it rises (or seems to rise, uncannily, by itself), gliding from back to feet with this Nosferatu stiffness.

THE NIGHT THAT I FIRST SAW AN INFECTED WAS A few weeks into the epidemic, a transitional period, when conditions were stabilizing but when I was nevertheless still afraid to leave our apartment. LCDC had lifted its curfew; the BRPD had issued a public statement declaring streets 'under control'; and quarantines were by then up and running. Almost no one believed—as initially everyone had, when after The Broadcast[1] all we knew was that the dead were rising, biting, proliferating virally—that societal collapse and its concomitant anarchy were only one breached stronghold away. The grocery stores were actually selling supplies again, rather than being raided for them, and newscasters recited 'findings' from scientific studies on the undead, rather than breathless exhortations to protect our loved ones. In short, much of the chaos of the early days had dissipated, the way a nightmare's logic will midway through the morning's piss, or a morning's mist will mid-afternoon.

Nevertheless, I remained afraid to leave our apartment. It wasn't that long ago, after all, that Rachel and I had been told by panicked newscasters to board up our windows and hoard up on canned goods. During those first seventy-two hours, all of Baton Rouge was barricaded. The only people who dared step outdoors were soldiers in riot gear and virologists in canary-yellow biohazard suits. Then one morning Rachel and I turned on the TV, and LCDC was holding a press conference. A spokeswoman at a podium told us all how safe it was to go outside. The worst had already passed, we were told. The virus

---

[1] 'Every dead body that is not exterminated becomes one of them. It gets up and kills! The people it kills get up and kill!'

was not airborne, we were told. Knowing what we knew now about the infection, an outbreak could never spread that fast again. The LCDC had been working around the clock to print and distribute copies of *FIGHT THE BITE*, which condensed all available knowledge about the epidemic. Copies had been mailed to census addresses, and were available in bulk at relief shelters. So long as we studied these survival manuals carefully, and exercised the proper precautions, it should be safe to leave our homes.

Rachel, heartened by the news, was eager to explore the city. We hadn't seen daylight in days, and our diet had been reduced to microwave-heated green beans and oatmeal. Now that the curfew had been eased, Rachel wanted to take a walk to the LSU Lakes and see sun sparkling on water. She wanted to see what new foods they had for us to eat at the relief tents on the campus fairgrounds. She wanted to drive to the grocery store and buy *real* food. And eventually she wanted to visit her father's grave. She wanted me to come with her.

Only, I didn't share Rachel or the public's faith in LCDC's reassurances. *Pace* the spokeswoman at the podium, it struck me that in fact nothing would be simpler than for a single stray infected to spark another citywide outbreak. Or for a security breach in a quarantine to unleash hundreds of infected at once. Or for the so-called 'virus'—which no scientist had actually identified beneath a microscope, even as they assured us it was not airborne—to simply mutate overnight, as real viruses are wont to do, and *make* itself airborne. Then Baton Rouge would again devolve into a Hieronymus Bosch pit, as we had all watched it do only days beforehand: telephones down, emergency teams unavailable, escape routes jammed with traffic, neighborhoods flooded as at Mardi Gras with bacchantes. Who could guarantee that this stability was anything more than a lull? No, the sensible thing, it seemed to me, was to just batten[1] down the hatches and wait. A week, two weeks, until we were absolutely sure that conditions would remain stable outside. Even if that meant locking and bolting our apartment door and swallowing the proverbial key.

Rachel thought that I was overreacting. Soon she began volunteering at one of the relief centers, and every morning that she left—five days a week—we had to repeat this argument in our living room. I would be sitting on the sofa, and Rachel would be standing in the threshold of our opened front door, framed in sunlight and fresh air. 'You can't stay inside all the time,' she would tell me. 'It'll make you crazy. Why don't you come out for a walk with me? Not even far—just to the relief center. There will be plenty of people there.' Here I would shake my head and chuckle in disbelief. Did she not understand, as I did, that 'plenty of people' was precisely the problem? That there was a plague on out there, and that we were well beyond the stage at which we could take leisurely afternoon strolls together?[2] Had

---

[1] 'Batten' was a word that I was thinking a good deal about at that time. In Greek tragedies like *The Bacchae* or *Oedipus Rex*, the chorus always describes a plague as having 'battened' on Thebes, which I tend to interpret parasitically, as if Euripides's bacchae, those frenzied women who disembowel and cannibalize the Theban citizens (and who, it has occurred to me more than once, may well be the distant ancestresses of our own undead), were in fact fattening like mosquitoes on the city's blood. So throughout the outbreak my mind was worrying this word, 'batten,' like a tongue scouring a peach pit, such that the word would come unbidden to me, even as I was thinking of other things. If I was watching the news, and mentally composing a list of last-minute escape routes, I would suddenly be able to distinguish, buoying up over my interior monologue from I didn't know where, the discrete thought, 'They're battening on Baton Rouge' or 'This plague has battened on Baton Rouge,' which would then submerge again and be forgotten just as quickly.

[2] On this subject, Mazoch likes to appose Robert Hass's version of the famous Issa haiku ('In this world/we walk on the roof of hell/gazing

she not paid sufficient attention to the Youtube video that I had plunked her down in front of (a thirty-second clip of a mass outbreak in a shopping mall), and therefore failed to internalize the agoraphobic lesson that that footage was meant to convey?[1] She didn't, she hadn't, and she had.

---

at flowers') to something that we heard a preacher say on talk radio one morning ('When there's no more room in hell, the dead will walk the earth'): the dead and the living are sharing roofspace now, and it's nothing like so simple as it once was to take a walk.

[1] The clip is security footage from an overhead camera, low quality and grainy but in color. People are crowded in what looks like the food court of a mall, surrounding a woman who has fallen. The people jostle each other, some trying to get to the fallen woman and some trying to give her space, but most just standing there staring on. One man is kneeling beside the woman, holding her hand in his hand. He checks her pulse, then looks up at the crowd and shakes his head. But at just this moment someone points to the woman, who has opened her eyes again, and when the man turns back to her she pulls him down by his shirt collar, biting—battening on—his throat. At this point things become hectic: the screaming crowd tries to flee all at once, and many people end up crushed underfoot; the infected woman crawls on all fours to a trampled boy and bites into him; meanwhile the man, bleeding terribly and evidently having already reanimated, also begins biting people, who are trapped on the ground beneath fallen bodies; consumers from the food court rush into frame, trying to pull the man and the woman off of their victims, only to be bitten in turn by those victims; et cetera, et cetera. It all happens fast (the clip is, as I said, only thirty or forty seconds), and the crowd onscreen is infected so quickly and so uniformly that their conversion has the appearance of an optical illusion. One moment they're alive, the next all undead, the way that a Necker cube inverts itself on the eye:

The way that the eye can pinch that one point—where the lefthand sides of the cube meet in a Y at the bottom—and pull it perspectively forward, such that the cube telescopes out, or else press it back, such that

My behavior put predictable strains on the relationship. As soon as Rachel crossed the threshold, I would rush to detain her, pleading with her not to leave: 'It's a buffet out there—you go, you're going to get bitten. You think the streets are safe. You think, "I'll just avoid the bad neighborhoods," the seedy neighborhoods. But that's not what's at issue anymore. These aren't crackheads who want your purse, who will stalk you only on Plank Road and only at midnight. They don't care that you live in the Chateau Dijon apartment complex, or that it's broad daylight—it means nothing to them to attack you on a tree-lined street at noon, surrounded by respectable people. They *are* respectable people, or they used to be, and they'll roam

---

the cube collapses, and how easy to toggle back and forth between the two cubes. This was how it felt when I watched the whole crowd convert: alive, undead. As if (to adopt Wittgenstein's expression) I was merely 'seeing them as' undead. As if I was merely focusing on whatever point of the crowd drew forth their undead aspect, and as if—simply by blinking my eyes or scanning over the image—I might 'see them as' alive again, their undeath disappearing into their mortal aspect as surely as the Necker cube withdraws back into its sunkenness. Wittgenstein describes playing a similar game himself one day, when he attempted to see human beings as automata: '[C]an't I imagine,' he writes, 'that the people around me are automata, lack consciousness…? …"The children over there are mere automata; all their liveliness is mere automatism."… [It] will produce… some kind of uncanny feeling… Seeing a living human being as an automaton is analogous to seeing one figure as a limiting case or variant of another; the cross-piece of a window as a swastika, for example.' Just so was I trying, as I watched the video, to see the automata there as living people. But they were utterly lost to their undead aspect, no amount of crossing my eyes would draw their liveliness out of them. The only way to simulate the double-aspectual toggling of 'alive, undead, alive, undead' was to rewind and fast-forward the video, dragging the Youtube player's gray progress bar back and forth, so that the crowd onscreen would jerkily revert from corpses to human beings and back again. 'That's awful,' Rachel said, when I showed it to her, and I said, 'Who watches such a thing and wants to go for a walk?'

anywhere. Even the good neighborhoods. Even the Whole Foods! There's nowhere you can go that isn't dangerous. All it would take is for one person to reanimate, for all hell to break loose.' If she stopped to dignify this with a response, it was to tell me that I was being ridiculous. I was out of touch with reality. *Everyone* was going outside now. People were even allowed to visit some of the quarantines, to see and say goodbye to undead relatives there. Public places were well protected, she said, and so was the relief center. If I wanted to lock myself away, fine, but I couldn't bury her alive with me. She needed to do what she could to help. She was going out, and that was that.

Before she left, as despite my protests she almost always did, she would kiss me on the cheek, promising me that she would be prudent. Prudent! In those khaki shorts and that sleeveless tank top, every inch of exposed skin practically begging to be bitten! The whole time she was gone I would sit in my spot on the living room sofa, watching the news in the dark and nursing dark thoughts about Rachel. The news, which showed people being bitten in the streets, the very streets Rachel was now wandering. Every minute that I waited for her someone new on the news was being bitten—some fresh victim. Then, to compound my anxiety during commercials, I would reread FIGHT THE BITE, skimming the chapter on domestic infections, with its thorough list of precautions (such as wearing mouthguards to bed, in the event of nighttime reanimation; or conducting full-body searches; or practicing 'defamiliarization'[1] techniques). When after a few hours of this Rachel did come home, walking

---

[1] This is the chapter's term for the various coping mechanisms required when confronting undead loved ones. Part of the reason that the house is such a treacherous environment, according to the pamphlet, is that people fall prey to fatal misrecognitions there: husbands hug undead wives; mothers dandle undead children. When you see your spouse standing before the refrigerator, or see your child stumbling out of the bathroom at night, you are primed by the context to see them as alive. And so, to prepare

through the door and exclaiming 'It's so *beautiful* outside!', how coolly and paranoiacally I felt obliged to receive her. On bad days I would even make her bare her forearms and ankles, her calves, so that I could inspect them for bite wounds, as if she would ever try to conceal such a thing from me (what was more likely, of course, was that she would have unknowingly ingested infected food, but however much I worried about that I had no way of testing her for it, so it was the ankles that these afternoons I examined). 'What kind of monster do you think I am,' Rachel would cry, as I lifted her pants leg and palpated the unbroken skin of her thigh, 'that I would let my own lover be infected?' Or, if she caught me eyeballing her calf from across the room: 'If you don't stop looking at me like that, I'm going to freak out. Really, I'm starting to freak out.' Then, so that she didn't 'freak out' and begin weeping, I would have to embrace her trembling body, hold her close to me and rub her back, when for all I knew there was some plum-colored ring of teethmarks still hidden, like a hickey, beneath the rim of her sock… which finally one day felt to me so much like hugging a rabid dog (like rubbing a rabid dog's back and telling this rabid dog in an earnest voice that I trusted it) that I grew nauseated with resentment, of her and of myself for yielding to her, and pushed her away from me. To be bitten at the throat mid-sentence, even while I was telling her that I loved and trusted her! To die the death of some dumb Romeo, kissing poisoned lips to prove his love! 'Look,' I said, waving a copy of *FIGHT THE BITE* in my hand, 'we need to observe the proper precautions. We're behaving like idiots.' 'What's idiotic is that if we go on like this we'll kill each other.'

She was alluding to a recent news story, in which a man, returning home drunk, startled his wife and was shot dead by

---

you for these kinds of encounters, the chapter includes a series of mental exercises and thought experiments that you can practice, all involving a process called 'defamiliarization.'

her, who in her keyed-up state had mistaken him for infected. But that premonition—'We'll kill each other'—disquieted me at a much more personal level. It was almost as if Rachel were tweaking my conscience. For at night I would imagine it, killing her, as I lay in bed unable to sleep. 'What would I have to do,' I would ask myself, 'if this creature, asleep on my chest, woke and was monstrous?' There was never really any question: I would have to throw the comforter, verdant and spring-patterned, over her head, not only to keep her from biting me but also to keep me from seeing her face; then I would have to beat her to death with the baseball bat that we stow under the bed. The trick, I thought, was to be beating on a mound beneath the covers. To be beating some soft writhing green thing, rather than Rachel, nude and recognizable. And to drag her body, still bundled in blankets, out to the street without ever once actually looking at her face, which would have to be as forbidden to me as Eurydice's, or Medusa's. I didn't like to think about it.

'That's absurd,' I told her, 'we're not going to *kill each other*.' But I was noticeably shaken by what she'd said, and she probably could have guessed what I was thinking. First, that it was emotionally corrosive to fantasize so much about murdering my lover, to hold her in such distrust, and second, that yes, perhaps it was possible, one night I might make a mistake and strike at her warm flesh.

It was around this time that Rachel wrote me the email reminding me of Tunica Hills, recalling the Bethlehem stars there and insisting on how vital to the relationship our taking quiet walks and watching afternoon light together was. How long could I remain holed up in this gloomy apartment, as if in a nuclear bunker, she wanted to know? And how long did I realistically expect her to stay here with me? If I didn't learn to leave the apartment, *she* would have to leave, even if it meant moving back in with her mom. Eventually, she wrote, I would have to come to terms with what was happening, because in all likelihood it would go on happening for months, maybe years. And if others had come to terms with it, why couldn't I? That there were periodic flare-ups in shopping malls didn't seem to derail people's lives any more than that, in Tel Aviv, there were periodic suicide bombings in cafés and public buses, she wrote. People drove to the grocery store ('Even Whole Foods!') as they always had, and if on the way there they spotted an infected in the road, very well, they might pull over to look at it (the way that when a black bear, a cub, wanders out onto the shoulder of a rural highway, people always pull over to photograph it), or else they might just drive past it altogether indifferently. And when a street *was* overrun with infected, police were quick to block it off with barriers and road flares, warning traffic away, until all the infected could be detained. Was I aware that more people were attacked in their homes than in public spaces? (I wasn't.) Or that, in general, it was safer to walk outdoors, where assiduous police officers combed the streets all hours, than to stay alone inside? (Again, no.) The infected weren't monsters, she wrote, or killing machines. They wouldn't chase you down relentlessly to bite you. They were just diseased, brain-damaged people, and they were only as dangerous as you allowed them to be. If you didn't put yourself in a position to be bitten, you wouldn't be. Any able-bodied person could outrun them. Everyone else had realized this by now. The only reason that I hadn't—Rachel wrote—was that I refused to go outside. Once I saw for myself how calm things had become, the shock would wear off. She concluded her email with a caricature of the redneck-ascetic existence that I risked slipping into: living in paranoid withdrawal in a fallout shelter, feeding on canned goods, polishing my rifles, prophesying dissolution for a society that was as homeostatic and heedless of me as ever. Swearing at a government I didn't trust to protect me. 'Let's not live that way. Love, Rachel.'

So later that same night, at around three a.m., while Rachel was sleeping and while I couldn't seem to, I decided to go for a walk. As if I were both the hands and the child thrown into the deep end by the hands. Heading out from our apartment, I made my way through residential neighborhoods toward the LSU Lakes. It was a typically humid Louisiana mid-morning, and for the most part, through many of the blocks that I passed, things were as Rachel said. While there were no police 'assiduously' patrolling our neighborhood, there were no roving infected either. Only wide streets empty with midnight and orange with the brume of the streetlamps. I kept to the sidewalk, alongside wide-lawned townhouses that seemed—except for their boarded windows—perfectly peaceful. Live oaks lined each street, holding out their heavy branches like armfuls of scooped leaves, and they cast erratic shadows through the foggy light. When overhead a warm wind blew, swaying the trees' branches, the branch shadows would sway too, sweeping darkly over the sidewalk concrete and over my feet. The shadows swept back and forth, like a massive phantasmal broom. In the humid air all around me, the streetlamps' orange brume; and on the ground just beneath me, the oak trees' black broom. What a nice and tranquil evening! Was Rachel right? Were flashmobs of undead an anomaly? Was it actually possible to walk alone unmolested, as if the epidemic—the riots, the fires, the cannibal feeding frenzies—were just a nightmare the nightly news was having? Was it really over, as easily staunched as any other modern outbreak: no more apocalyptic, in the end, than AIDS, the West Nile virus, or bird flu?

She was right. Undeath felt as far from our beautiful neighborhood, from this warm morning, as those bombs in Tel Aviv. Soon I even felt safe, at ease, and after a while I was able to put thoughts of the undead out of my mind entirely. The sky was unusually clear and bright, and all I had on my mind was the full moon. On a nighttime walk before the epidemic, under a similarly clear sky, Rachel had once marveled to me over how many poems had been written about the moon, how many metaphors and similes people had devised, in the history of figurative speech, to describe it. What if the moon was encrusted over with these metaphors, Rachel asked? What if it had built up these centuries of metaphors around itself, like a mollusk secreting its shell? And when everyone dies, she went on, when the human race blinks out and all of its poems are forgotten, what will the moon then look like, having crawled out of that shell?

A day before my three-a.m. stroll, even an hour before it, I would have answered her that we would find out soon enough: that the human race was finally perishing, being extinguished by this plague of undeath, and that as soon as every person (including us) had been infected, she and I could turn our cloudy, white eyes to the night sky and see, uncomprehending, what shape a naked moon took. But while actually *on* my stroll, walking through those peaceful streets, where I could see by the light of that moon that there were no infected, I answered her (i.e., mentally) who knows! It might be millennia yet before we humans die off, and there are still so many more metaphors with which to calcify the moon.

That was when I saw the infected, the first I'd ever seen. He was a middle-aged man in running clothes, standing in the road a couple of blocks away, and even if there hadn't been a blood-stain soaked through his T-shirt (the stain looked more like a great black bib, at that distance, than anything else), I would have been able to tell by his stillness, utter and inhuman, as well as by the posture of his forward slouch, that he was undead, that that white marmoreal figure in the road was not to be called out to. When I spotted him I froze, just (as Rachel had said!) as if I'd seen a black bear. Something wild, dangerous, my own death. He was facing in my direction, his body angled toward me as if he were looking directly at me. But did he notice me? Should I back away slowly? If he did notice me, would he moan and alert others, or would he follow me silently back to the apartment, dogging me like Nemesis? And what was he doing anyway? He only stood there, as if thinking. A minute passed like this, and in that minute my adrenaline receded. I remembered—it occurred to me—that he had been a man once. He would have been a jogger, I decided. Bitten while jogging, on his left shoulder. He would have staggered home for help, where tragically he died, reanimated, and bit into his wife (whose blood it was soaked through his shirt). When he was seventeen he would have run cross-country with Baton Rouge High School's track team, would have been one among that shoal of shirtless boys whom I used to see jogging listlessly, glistening, through the Garden District on humid afternoons. And now that he was undead—a creature of habit now, compelled to return to those sites whose pellets were most prominent in the chaff cloud of his memory—he would have wandered out here to the Garden District, as if reporting for another session of track practice. That was what he was doing tonight, I decided: waiting outside for the track team, for them to come meet him. And maybe they would, one day: maybe other varsity runners from the class of 'XX would be bitten and reanimated, and maybe, like this man, they would be compelled toward the neighborhood where they had trained. They would all find each other here one night, a dozen undead reunited, to begin shambling through these streets as a team.

These and like thoughts are what I found myself thinking. 'So that's the kind of man he was,' I reveried, even as I stared at that revenant—that killing machine!—just two blocks away. That it had had a track team, a wife, a whole life, when what I should have been keeping strenuously in mind was that it had nothing, nothing but this nothing that it was infected with and that it had to give, if I was stupid and slow enough to let it. Of course, when it finally seemed to move—when I saw or imagined that I saw it shuffle one foot out in front of the other—I tensed my entire body. The second it shuffled its foot I remembered clearly all that it was sick with and all that the spit in its mouth meant, how everything breaks with the skin that breaks beneath that bite. Had it seen me? Was it hungry? But they were never not hungry: they fed until they burst. I knew that, just as I knew, if it were to let out its throaty gurgle, exactly what I wasn't supposed to do. Panic, start running, or scream for help, for instance. Instead I was supposed to back away without attracting any more of its attention, or else it would moan still louder, and there would be others. The track team! How could I have forgotten? Twenty spindly undead in short shorts would come trotting out into the street, as promptly as at a coach's whistle, the minute it started moaning! Together they would run me down and feast on my body, I was sure of it. Tearing open my stomach to sift through my intestines, turning me inside out like a Necker cube. My death—my gory death, my careless, ass's, idiot's death—more than my life flashed before my eyes.

And not only my own death. For once I reanimated, I realized, I would return automatically to our apartment, as much a danger to Rachel as the jogger had been to its wife. My hand would bloody the front door, slap after insistent slap, until Rachel, waking alone in bed, would rush worriedly to the peephole to see—me, vindicated by the grisliness of my own end! Victim of the streets she'd insisted on the statistical safety of! She would fling open the door to me, I imagined, unable to do what needed to be done, and hug me, too, as I'd always feared hugging her. And then I would do what I was programmed to: with inexorable reflexivity my mouth would clamp down on her throat, my uncontrollable, remote-controlled mouth, while, entranced, my face and eyes would remain expressionless. Biting into my lover as I'd gnaw a pillow in my sleep. Rachel! Measureless were the remorseful transports that this image of myself reduced me to, as I waited for the jogger to sound its unearthly moan.[1]

---

[1] I often describe their moan as unearthly, but what I really mean is that it is 'earthly' in the most exact sense of the word. When an undead opens

But he never did moan. For a while, in fact, he didn't do anything. He swayed there, and I stood and watched him sway. Above me a breeze passed through the oak trees' leaves, and I watched as a current of rustle traveled up the block, live oak by live oak, in a line of thrashing branches. Eventually they reached the infected's far white figure, overtaking him. As the branches between us swayed, their shadows swished atop the intervening concrete, and I could see that all of the street leading up to the infected was shaded: the pavement roiled with movement— with black turmoil—as if being buckled by an earthquake of shadows. Down at my feet some of its tremors swished over my shoes. And raising my eyes from my feet, moving my eyes slowly along the length of the street, one patch of thrashing shadow at a time, I could almost believe that I was following just a single tremor in motion, one black seism traveling up the block. This shockwave, beginning at my shoes, seemed to ripple outward, breaking over itself in crests and troughs until it broke over the feet of the infected. His white shape stayed in place, being lapped at by the blackness. I lifted my arm at him, as if in a wave, then actually waved both arms. He didn't respond, and I let my arms drop to my sides. The tree shadows continued cascading toward him, in flurries of movement that threw his motionlessness into relief. Why didn't he move? Even as he stood there, he seemed to exist on another plane. His stillness— his total unresponsiveness to everything around him: the wind, the shadows, me—seemed ghostly, as though he occupied some sublime interstice between life and death, and nothing in this world could touch him. Could he perceive *any* of this? There

---

its mouth and produces that low, guttural sound, as dark and compact as garden dirt, what the moan sounds like is an alarm of the earth. As if, by trespassing aboveground when they should be buried beneath six feet of earth, the undead have triggered some tocsin of the earth, and the reediness of their lowing is its own siren.

was a great vacancy in his staring. He was present, but only as the manifestation of an absence. Neither here, nor not here. Neither a brain-damaged human, nor a murderous corpse. Nor even, quite, some indeterminate mixture between the two. It seemed in that moment as if I could go on accreting neithers like this all night—as if I could stand here, all night, frozen in apophatic paralysis—and still be no nearer an understanding of what he was. Of what it would be like to be like him.[1]

I remember wishing I could see his eyes. The way he was staring, he seemed to be gazing into the sublime, or at the face of Death. And so too did sublimity and Death—gazing out into our world through those eyes—seem to be seeing me. I felt something like the awe that the visitant must feel, in the presence of the archangel, or the alien, and I knew then that I would do anything to understand.

I stood opposite him for I don't know how long, watching. And when finally he turned his back to me and departed, I watched him wander, somnolently, into someone's front yard, where he glanced left and right in seeming disorientation before disappearing in the alleyway between two houses. Just like that. There was even this hush lingering in the air behind him.

For how many minutes did I remain there, waiting to see

---

[1] Even today, I cannot conceive of undeath except in terms of these neithers: to the degree that I understand it at all, it is still as that which resists understanding. A limit condition, irreducible to the usual dichotomies. For this reason the designation 'living dead'—in its oxymoronic self-negation—seems to sum up best the fundamental in-between-ness of the creatures. In any given dichotomy, they will constitute neither the positive nor the negative pole—neither living nor dead, neither psychopath nor psychopomp—but everything that circulates between them. That is why any 'neither _____ nor _____' construction, yoking together any two oppositional terms, will approximate the essence of undeath for me: the creatures coincide with the very structure of the correlative conjunction. They are like walking 'neither _____ nor _____'s, Janus-faced with blanks.

him again or another one? Ten, at most. Then I phoned the police and walked home. I woke Rachel coming in, and told her, when she asked where I'd been, that I wasn't afraid of outside anymore. She was right, I said: I did need to get out of the apartment.

It wasn't long after this that Mazoch emailed about the search.

TUESDAY

THIS MORNING RACHEL WAKES EARLY, AN HOUR or two before she usually leaves for the shelter, and waits with me in the kitchen while I wait for Mazoch.

Last night I told her about the traces he had found (the broken window, the plaid cloth), and also about his conviction that we were 'closing in.' She pursed her lips and repeated, 'Closing in.' That was all she said on the subject, and her tone was hard to read. But I sensed there was something she wanted to say, so I was not surprised this morning when she woke with my alarm. Now, while I stand beside the toaster, I'm waiting for her to speak.

She's been brooding at the kitchen table, her face still pale from sleep, her blond hair frazzled into an aureole. When I turn my back to her I can still feel her watching me, and so—to have something to do with my hands—I prematurely pop the toaster. I busy myself with the butter knife, frowning down at the soft slices, barely warm. When I glance back up, she is indeed still watching me. Even her *pajamas* are watching me: the polka-dot pants; the white tank top, semé with cartoon owls. They ocellate her body, multiplying her watching a hundredfold. Finally she clears her throat: 'What—' she begins. 'What if you *do* find Mr. Mazoch?'

Ah. So that is what she woke so early to ask. I should have guessed. It's not a question that I have posed, in so many words, to Matt. But it's the very first question that Rachel posed to me, back when I initially broached the search with her. 'He doesn't want to *kill* him, does he?' she asked. When I didn't respond right away, she brought her hands to her cheeks: 'Oh my God. He wants to kill him.'

At the time, I told her that I had no idea what Matt's plans were. We hadn't discussed them, I said, and anyway, the search was more emotionally complicated than that, for Matt. He himself probably didn't know deep down what he was doing. Nor was it something I felt comfortable putting him on the spot about. She was making it sound as if I were knowingly abetting Matt's Ahabism, manning the oars while he sharpened the harpoons, in some monomaniacal manhunt. When in fact the situation was much grayer, I told her.

This was all strictly speaking true. I really didn't know what Matt was planning. We really hadn't discussed it. And because we haven't discussed it since, I've been able to continue the search in good faith. Rachel's been able to condone it as well, so long as we both operate under the tacit assumption that it is a rescue mission: that Matt intends to commit Mr. Mazoch to a quarantine. On most days of the search, this interpretation seems viable. But then there are days—such as yesterday, at Highland Road Park—when I harbor my suspicions. Although I've never admitted as much to Rachel, it does seem at times as if Matt might entertain the prospect of euthanasia: that he might be driven to put Mr. Mazoch out of his misery. While I personally would advocate strongly against this (it's illegal, for one thing; and for another, we can't be sure that what the undead are experiencing is misery),[1] I also recognize that I can go only so far in dissuading Matt. It's ultimately his decision to make.

I have never admitted this to Rachel. Thankfully, over the past few weeks, I haven't had to. As it began to seem less and

---

[1] It seems clear, at any rate, that the undead don't feel pain. Matt assumes that they don't feel anything at all. For my part, I have always assumed that being undead would feel the same way that a sleeping foot feels, when you sit on it for too long and try to flex your toes: there is numbness initially, then a cold prickling sensation, following fast behind that first rush of blood. Wherever an infected bites you, I imagine, the bite wound must form a nidus of numb tingling, which spreads steadily outward: starting

less likely to her that we would ever actually find Mr. Mazoch, Matt's motives ceased to be an issue. With Mr. Mazoch out of mind, Rachel has been free to conceive of the search as a purely ritual activity. When she imagines Matt and me driving around the city, it is as if we are circling an empty center, like two monks raking sand. The search is aimless, autotelic, without object. It serves its own purposes. For Matt, she imagines, it must be a ritual of mourning and memorial: he is visiting the sites of his father, so that he can reflect on the man and remember. Whereas for me, it must be a ritual of routine: it is a structured excuse for me to get out of the apartment each day, as well as a safe way of encountering the undead (to conquer my fear of them, on the one hand; and to come to understand them, on the other). We will simply perform these rituals until Friday, she imagines, and then we will be finished.

She's not half-wrong. The search really is each of those things, for each of us. Except it is also, in its own way, a search. Rachel was able to forget this only when the search was returning no results. But now that Mazoch is actually discovering 'traces,' she evidently feels a burning need to know his plans.

Looking at her there, with her arms crossed over her owls, I can tell that equivocation will not cut it this morning. I won't get far by reminding her that these so-called traces are so many false hopes and red herrings, or by pointing out to her where their true danger lies: not that they might lead us to Mr. Mazoch, but that they might lead Matt—as I am beginning to worry—right off the deep end, into a bottomless obsession, where every minor coincidence is imbued with meaning and grief. I can already tell that this is not the response that Rachel will need to hear: putting the traces aside, she will still want to know—hypothetically—what

---

from the arm and climbing up the shoulder, across the chest, over the stomach, until your whole body feels asleep. That is what it would feel like to be undead, I often think.

Matt's motives are. What he would do *if.* The words 'closing in' are clearly still fresh in her mind, and in the bedroom this morning, when I grabbed my baseball bat, she blanched.

Here is where Rachel is coming from. Her own father was diagnosed with lung cancer when she was in seventh grade, and survived—or, really, 'was sustained'—in a moribund state from then until she was seventeen. She has explained the medical details to me before. Soon after his diagnosis, it was recommended that he have his dominant lung removed, a procedure so risky—Rachel's family was to find out only later—that most doctors refuse to perform it. The surgery itself went well, except not without attendant post-operative complications,[1] which were to prove disastrous. His remaining lung began to fill with fluid, and he had to be attached to a ventilator. Too weak to be weaned off the vent, he instead became dependent on it, such that he was left susceptible to a succession (Rachel: 'a domino effect'; the hospital staff: 'a train wreck') of medical crises. If he fell into an unsupervised sleep, he risked suffocation, but, because his blood was highly ammoniated, he was beset with a lethargy that made keeping awake even for fifteen minutes a trial. Unable to move, and likely deprived of oxygen in what unsupervised sleeps he did fall into, he suffered limb atrophy; he suffered short-term memory loss; he suffered, regularly, organ failure. One crisis precipitated another in the body of this man whom the hospital—Rachel informed me with unbelievable bitterlessness—had actually come to *nickname* 'The Train Wreck.' How many times, during the year and a half that he was hospitalized, did Rachel believe, in the panic in her heart, that her father was dying? How many mornings was she woken briskly and told, with no explanation, that she had to accompany

[1] From what I can gather her father, exposed to all manner of diseases and antibiotic-resistant microbes circulating through the hospital, eventually developed something like staph infection.

her mother to the hospital, that it was an emergency? In how many garish conference rooms did her mother explain to her that her father was not going to last through the day, and how many times was Rachel made to stand by her father's (The Train Wreck's!) bedside to tell him goodbye? Each time, she said, she turned her head to hide from him the tears in her eyes.

Of course, each proved in turn to be a false alarm, and it eventually became evident that, while he wasn't going to die in the hospital, neither was his condition going to improve there. So his bed and ventilator were moved to a room in Rachel's house, where her mother assumed the responsibility of operating and maintaining the equipment that was sustaining her husband's life. Rachel recalls specifically a pump, a suctioning device designed to clear blockages from the ventilator's air passage. Whenever her father's oxygen intake dropped, sounding the vent's alarm, her mother would have to be on hand to feed a small hose through his tracheotomy tube, snaking it deep into the interior of his chest; then, once the vacuum had been activated, the strawlike hose could be slowly withdrawn, until it had deposited in a plastic bag dangling beneath the ventilator whatever mucous had been obstructing the man's breathing.[1] It was often the case that nothing was the matter, he had just woken alone in the night and, afraid, purposefully held his breath, setting off the vent's alarm so that Rachel's mother would come to his bedside and talk to him. That this woman—who worked from home as a graphic designer to support herself and Rachel and to pay her husband's increasingly steep medical bills; and who exercised such vigilance in her caretaking that she left the

---

[1] For the first few weeks, the mucous comprised black chunks of tar, which were discharged darkly into the fluid in the dangling bag. When Rachel first described this, I imagined ashy particles weightlessly afloat, stirred up then sinking, like tealeaves in the wake of a press pot's plunger. She said that that's more or less right, except that after a while the discharge tended to be 'more phlegmatic.'

house only twice a week, to shop for groceries (when a nurse's assistant relieved her), and carried a baby monitor with her even into the backyard, listening even there for the vent's alarm; and who had to tend to her husband as to a quadriplegic (so atrophied had his limbs become), brushing his teeth, cutting his hair, trimming his fingernails, shaving him, daily removing the gauze from his pus-filled, cavitary bedsores in order to disinfect and re-dress them, bathing him too and cleaning up after every bowel movement (which movements, because he needed to be fed directly through a tube in his stomach and because this led to several digestive issues, were always a subject of concern [not least the concern of constipation, in which event Rachel's mother apparently had to 'reach inside and loosen things up'])—that this woman was a pillar of selflessness is beyond doubt. And though Rachel, I suspect out of modesty, has gone into considerably less detail regarding her own responsibilities, she has mentioned before that she began helping out her mom more in high school, when she assumed the task of maneuvering her father out of bed and into his wheelchair, and I know that for his birthday she sewed him sheets and hospital gowns, printed with moons, stars.

When Rachel turned seventeen, there was a discussion in the family, and a decision was reached (in spite of Rachel's protests) not to treat any of her father's future medical problems. Comatose now, he had at some point stopped urinating, and his doctor diagnosed kidney failure. If untreated, the doctor said, he would drift off painlessly in his sleep and simply never wake up. Which is just what he did, two days after diagnosis. The sight of his corpse laid out in bed, gaunt and gowned and as if estranged from itself, didn't move Rachel half so much as the sight of it in the mahogany coffin: buried in his old LSU sweater, and enjoying, in the mortician's makeup on his face, a veneer of rude red health, her father resembled for the first time in many years her father, and she wept as she hadn't even on the day she'd found him dead. To mourn him, she has explained, meant mourning two men, or at least two sets of memories: those of the young, vigorous father who raised her, as well as those of the debilitated, dependent, infantilized man-child whom in sickness he became. And it really wasn't until the day of the funeral, when she saw again that sweater, that face, that that first set of memories was heartrendingly returned to her.

Even before The Broadcast and the advent of undeath, Rachel described to me a recurring dream she had, in which her father, a revenant, would visit and speak with her from beyond the grave. Sometimes he appeared as the healthy father, others as the bedridden father, but more often than not he appeared as the corpse that in reality he was: his clothes tattered, his body in advanced stages of decay. Because the extent of his decomposition was directly proportionate to the amount of time that he had spent in the ground, his dream image grew increasingly gruesome as the years drew on. Though never so gruesome as to disrupt the grand feeling of benevolence that as a parent he gave off. Even with black sores eaten into the flesh of his cheeks, even with bone showing in his hand, he visited her dreams as a father, not a fiend, and she apprised him as she would a mortal father of all that had transpired in her life between his last appearance and this one. Rachel, who does not believe in ghosts, nevertheless describes her gratefulness for these dreams in hauntological terms, as if she were being afforded the opportunity to do with the spirit of the man what with his living self she could not: 'It's just nice to spend time with him—for so much of my adolescence he wasn't really present,' or, 'It was good to talk to him again last night. It had been a while,' or, 'At least it's some sort of contact.' Always in the same comforted tone of voice, as uncomplicatedly glad to dream him as she was to breathe in the smell of his smoke from her car seats (and in fact: on the comfort that she derives from looking at her parents' photo albums, or from asking her father's friends and relatives to share with her their memories of him, Rachel once remarked, 'When you lose your dad as early as I did you take him where you can get him'—even [especially] from strangers' smoke on the car seats).

Now imagine Rachel's relief at the first reports of the dead coming back to life. And imagine how much she staked, everything, on the afternoon that we drove out to the cemetery where her father was buried. This was before LCDC had determined that, wherever the undead were coming from (whether from morgues and hospitals or from their deathbeds, whether from one irradiated neighborhood or from all over the city), they were decidedly not returning from their graves. For Rachel it was still reasonable to assume that her father would be among the dead whom the public then believed to be reanimating in their coffins.[1] That her father, buried years before, wouldn't have reanimated, Rachel could not know. One morning she woke from a dream in which her father's corpse visited her in a pitiful state: unable to lift his left arm, unable to move the left side of his face, having returned from the grave only to find his wife married to another man and therefore forced to rent out a squalid tenement room by the railroad tracks. Describing the dream while lying beside me in bed that morning, she said that she was sure it was a sign. She simply sensed that he was suffering. She had to go see him.

'He's regained consciousness in his grave,' she said. 'He's cramped in this dark box, barely bigger than his body. Just whimpering and waiting for someone to unearth him.' 'And you're the one to do that?' I asked. She hesitated, so I pressed on: 'You're going to drive out to the cemetery, dig down to his casket, and

---

[1] It wasn't until a week later that LCDC—in part to quiet the public's Judgment Day-flavored anxieties—conducted two experiments: first, they excavated a control group of corpses, all of them buried before the first reported case of infection and none of them reanimated; second, to be certain, they injected syringes of infected blood into their bodies (with no results). Which is to say, it wasn't until a week later that people realized that only the freshly dead and mortally infected were reanimating.

pry it open like a ghoul?' 'You say that as if it's incredible—'
'It is incredible!' '—but I know you would do the same. What
if it were me lying underground somewhere, buried alive and
waiting for you in my coffin?' 'More likely he's doing in his coffin what for several years now you've taken him to be doing:
reposing and decomposing. There's no reason to think that now,
this morning and after all this time, he's reanimated.' 'It's just a
feeling I have.' 'You're convinced of this? "A daughter knows"?'
'I have to see for myself.' '"See for yourself"! I'll tell you what
you'll see. It won't be the serene face you saw buried, I can guarantee you that, embalmed and all made up for the prom: it will
be unspeakable putrefaction and decay. You open that coffin lid
and what you'll see is two creepy eyeballs staring back at you,
no eyelids, just bulbous whites lolling around in his head, like
the ones animatronic dolls have. And that shit-eating skeleton
grin! That lipless rictus of exposed jawbone! That's what you'll
see! Have you ever even seen maggots? Do you have any idea
how revolting they are to see? Do you know what garbage men
call them, when they find them writhing in the trash? "Disco
Rice." Well, your father's face will have contracted a full Saturday
Night Fever of disco rice, it will be alive and white with disco
rice, I can guarantee you that, when you open that coffin lid.'
'Jesus, Michael, you think I haven't thought of all this already?'
'Honestly, I don't think you have. If you had thought this all the
way through, if you'd really considered the emotional damage
you're going to sustain when you see your father in that condition—and not in a dream this time, Rachel: in real life, in full
Technicolor 3-D!—you wouldn't still be asking me where we
keep the shovel.' 'You're right. I may regret it, he may not have
reanimated, I may be better off forgetting about it. But I can't
just forget about it. He's my father, and I have to see for myself.
I couldn't live with myself if I didn't.' 'You may not live long
with yourself if you do. Because what if he has reanimated? We
bring him here and tie him to a chair in the kitchen? Strap down

his arms and legs, like Wolfman, so that he doesn't bite us in our sleep?' 'You're my boyfriend—I need you to support me in this.' 'That's exactly what you don't need me to do. You need no more support in this than you did in caring for him. You know, or you think you know, that this is the right and daughterly thing, and what you need right now is for me to tell you that it's insensible, a bad idea.' 'Is that what I needed when I was caring for him? For you to be there telling me that helping him into his wheelchair was "insensible," "a bad idea"?' 'If he had been undead, yes, absolutely, that's precisely what you would have needed: a friend to tell you that it's insensible for anyone but a government agent, in a Hazmat suit, to help an undead man into his wheelchair. No one is in more awe of your dedication to your father than I am, but even I can see that grave-robbing is above and beyond the call of daughterly duty.' 'You would have me leave him in his coffin.' '"You would have me leave him in his jail cell." "You would have me leave him in his hospital bed."' 'Stop it, I hate it when you do my voice.' 'The dead belong in their coffins. You wouldn't spring your father from prison, just as you didn't help him abscond from ICU. That's not your duty to him. In all the time we've lived together—' 'A year?' 'In all that time I haven't once heard you say, "My father is in a coffin, how uncomfortable, I have to dig him up." You've made peace with your father's death. Every time we talk about it you seem at peace and announce how at peace you are. Even when it happened you were at peace, not only with his death but with his burial. You've told me this before: how hard his relatives lobbied for his cremation and the scattering of his ashes and how it was you, not your mother, who defended his desire for a traditional burial. Now who is it who wants to drive out to his grave with a shovel and dig him up? Not his widow or any of his relatives but you. Have you even spoken with your mother about this yet?' 'She doesn't believe that the buried are reanimating. She thinks only the recently deceased are.' 'A sensible woman. There's no proof, not conclusive proof anyway, that any of the undead are coming from cemeteries, and in fact that seems more and more unlikely. Are any of them wearing suits and dresses? No, they're all wearing pajamas and hospital gowns, if they're wearing anything at all.' 'But that's my point: what if he's stuck in his coffin and is too weak to free himself? Even if the undead that you see on the streets aren't from the cemeteries, that doesn't mean that there aren't buried corpses reanimating too.' 'So, what? We dig him up and bring him here? You watch the same news I do—his skin flakes off into my glass of milk and I'm dead, dead, then undead and on my way to contaminating you. Even if we take all precautions, we're still bringing a rotting body into our apartment, to generate filth and disease, to make us and all of our neighbors sick. And the neighbors! As if we could keep him here without their noticing! They'll hear him moaning the first day, and it won't be LCDC they call, it'll be the police. Because what you're proposing is a crime, Rachel—' 'You only ever say my name when you're mad at me.' 'I'm not mad at you, I'm just trying to talk sense. Your father belongs first of all in his coffin and secondly in a quarantine, and if we house him here instead, we're in violation of the law. This isn't the Underground Railroad, it's the Chateau Dijon apartment complex. And if in fact your father has reanimated, he is decidedly not a runaway slave. He is—*in your own words*, Rachel—a diseased and brain-damaged man, a dangerous man.' 'I don't know where you got the idea that I want to bring him here. I never said that. I just need to see for myself that he hasn't revived in that horrible box, and, if he has, I need to let him out of it. Then I'll call LCDC myself and be the first to commit him to a quarantine.' I sighed. 'A quarantine,' I said, 'someplace safe. And that would be all? Check the cemetery, call LCDC?' 'It's not as if there aren't visitation rights. There would be no need to bring him to the apartment. If I wanted to see him I could just visit the quarantine. Actually *see* him, instead of relying on these dreams.'

It was noon when we arrived at the cemetery.[1] Still abandoned after the outbreak, it was unsupervised by any guard or caretaker, and we were the only visitors—the only graverobbers—there. Alone among the green hills and the orderly rows of headstones, I stood by with the shovel while Rachel, kneeling beside her father's grave, pressed her ear to the plot of grass above him, as if auscultating the ground for his heartbeat. She was probably listening for a faint and muffled moaning, or for clawing sounds at the coffin lid. She knelt like that for many minutes, then many minutes more, and the whole cemetery seemed deathly quiet indeed as I loomed uselessly above her, the shovel propped against my right shoulder. Whether she heard anything there she didn't say. What I heard was her breathing and my own. I was thinking, then, about how Rachel would react to the sight of her undead father. The sight of his white eyes. If he actually had reanimated, I wondered, and if she actually did

---

[1] Here's what I remember about the drive there: that Rachel stared gloomily out of the passenger-side window and said nothing for the duration, and that I felt too self-conscious about the momentousness of the trip to try to say anything myself. What might have been said? The rural road that led to the cemetery was lined with tall, fresh pines, and in the spare ten-a.m. light only their tips were lit. Sunlight slanted across the uppermost branches, leaving everything below cold with shadow, and the sight of it reminded me of the sensation of doing dishes in the sink: that moment when the drain has been plugged and the basin filled with frigid water, and the hands are plunged, wrist-deep, into the cold to scrub the dishes, leaving everything from the forearm up dry. Something might have been said about that. But the more calmed I became by this comparison—as I watched the sunstruck treetops lean and all the pine needles waver a little in a wind that I couldn't feel, and as I recalled the glovelike encompassing frigidness of reaching my hands down into dishwater—the more frivolous I felt it to be, as a thing to say, given the circumstances. So I didn't share this comparison with Rachel, who generally likes it when I point out effects of light. Instead I placed my hand on her thigh, and, letting out a surprised grateful noise like 'Mm,' she covered it with her own.

end up hearing something; if she actually did insist on digging down and if she actually opened that coffin lid—would we see the same thing? Would Rachel see, with me, the awesome otherworldliness in those eyes? While she knelt there with her ear to the grass, I braced myself for anything, including the shock of a pale hand bursting out of the soil. Though what eventually ended up happening was just that Rachel stood up and stretched and suggested that we leave. She seemed disappointed, but then, she didn't cry, and on the ride home she was even able to announce—as if weighing the other side of the thing—that by this point he was probably merely a skeleton anyway.

So that is where Rachel is coming from. That is where she is coming from when in the kitchen this morning she asks me what Matt plans to do once he finds Mr. Mazoch. *That* is where she is coming from when she asks me (not explicitly, but with the injured expression on her face, and with the expression, too, of all the wide-eyed owls on her tank top and all the eyelike polka-dots on her pants, which together stare me down like the members of a jury box) whether Mazoch plans to beat his father's brains in with a baseball bat.

And how can I go about answering this question? Even if I knew for certain that Matt's plan was to dispatch Mr. Mazoch, I could never explain this to Rachel, who helped care for her father in ways Matt probably never dreamed of caring for his, and who objected out of principle to her family's decision to euthanize him, and who visits him regularly on an oneiric plane, and who worried about his comfort and wellbeing even into (un)death. How could I explain to her that a son might prefer a dead father to an undead father, that an undead father might weigh like a burden on a son's conscience? How to convey the sense of filial duty that might be motivating Mazoch to put down, not his father, but the shell of his father, the corpse of a man who had been ready to die and who in all probability did not wish to return from death? To do so I would have to persuade her of the logic of 'Mr. Mazoch is not Mr. Mazoch,' 'My father is not my father,' this sense in which a hungry creature that has inherited only the body, the remembered itinerary, and the gait of a man (or, if you rather, a man from whom everything but his body, muscle memory, and gait have been pared away, and to whom a hunger has been added) is not the man himself. No need to invoke the Ship of Theseus here! Such an argument would mean nothing, or next to nothing, to Rachel, who will take her father where she can get him. Mr. Mazoch is barely there, consciousness-wise? He responds as an automaton to only the most basic stimuli? No matter. Her own father, laid out in his sickbed as a baby in its crib, could acknowledge only by the glaze in his eyes all the distractions that his family had set up in the room for him: Christmas lights, shiny garlands, balloons, flowers, a television set and a radio, countless other mobile-like devices intended to ward off his boredom. Mr. Mazoch is rotting as he moves? His entrails hang in strands from his stomach, and his eyeball dangles from its socket by an optic nerve? Trifles. Her own father appears in her dreams as a Frankenstein's monster, patched imperfectly together from bloated corpses, with only half of his amassed body parts working properly at any given moment, and still she takes him where she can get him. Mr. Mazoch is capable only of inchoate moaning? So be it. For years the only phrases that her father was able to form through the pain of his tracheotomy tube were 'You're beautiful,' 'It hurts,' and 'I love you,' and even in her dreams he's occasionally afflicted with undead Tourette's, involuntarily shouting obscenities in response to all of her questions about the afterlife. Did she not have to hide her tears as she was delivering one-sided goodbyes to her bedridden father, is she not now grateful for any dreams of a verbally incontinent father? On the contrary, she takes him where she can get him. Even Matt's strongest justification for disgust—the fact that Mr. Mazoch feeds compulsively on the living—would cut no ice with Rachel. In the span of her adolescence her father went from eating spoonfuls of peanut butter straight from the jar (with such gusto that a whiff of Jif on my breath still reminds her, powerfully, of him) to folding all foods directly into his stomach, with the indifference of a mussel. 'Cannibalism?' Rachel would say. 'Pah! A father's diet is not his child's concern.' No, Rachel would take her father where she could get him, even a rotting aphasic anthropophagous father, and she would be aggrieved and confused to hear that Mazoch feels any differently.[1]

Would be aggrieved and confused, for that matter, if I were to defend Mazoch, to devil's-advocate for him, or especially if I were to continue to accompany him each morning in full knowledge of his 'plan.'

This would all be easier for me if, like Rachel, I could simply condemn patricide outright. If I were not even tempted to defend it as an option. But the fact is that the ethics of undeath are murky to me. The questions that Matt and Rachel have been made to face, in the wake of the epidemic, are not questions that it has made me face. This choice between the grave and the quarantine, the shovel and the baseball bat… I have trouble, truthfully, even imagining myself in their shoes. Because my own parents both died (car crash) and were cremated years before the

---

[1] Could anything rankle Rachel more than what must seem like Mazoch's breezy disregard, his flagrant ingratitude, for the luck of a recrudescent father? Her own father taken first by disease, then by death, then by an undeath that did not bear him forth on its tide… and here is a son whose apparent new lifegoal is to find and eliminate, once and for all, the father who is always so reliably returned to him. Returned from divorce (for Mr. Mazoch did stick around to help raise Matt), returned from a near-fatal heart attack (which Mr. Mazoch survived), returned even from death: gliding back like some obedient fatherly boomerang from every distance into which life heaves him from Matt, who, as if mistaking him for skeet, steels himself now to pull the trigger. Unthinkable and unfair, it must seem to Rachel, probably.

epidemic, they have always been ineligible for undeath. I scattered their ashes myself. I never had to worry about their reanimating, or ask myself what I would do. What my duties would be. Unlike Rachel and Matt, I've never had to think of them in terms of undeath. I've had to think only of myself in terms of undeath. So whenever I try to align myself with Rachel, and work up some primordial disgust at the thought of patricide, I find that I cannot do it. Who knows how I would react, if I were Matt? It's his decision.

This, like so much else, is not something I can explain to Rachel this morning. So I do not try to. Having finished buttering our barely toasted toast, I bring the plate to the table and sit beside her. 'I still don't know,' I say to her. 'I don't know what he wants to do. But I'll ask.'

'Michael,' she says, reaching over to put her hand on my hand. 'Mm,' I say. 'Just promise me you won't let him use that bat.' And here I exhale, immensely relieved, for at last she has given me something that I can truthfully tell her: 'Rachel. Honey. You know we never use the bats.'

LATER THIS MORNING, I WATCH FROM THE passenger seat as Matt uses his bat to break into a building. We're staking out the antiques mall in Denham where Mr. Mazoch used to rent a booth. It's a squat stucco box isolated on an empty stretch of road, and it's been locked up for as long as we've been coming here: the glass double-doors in front are both expertly boarded from inside, with a length of chain wound around the push bar and a heavy padlock dangling dull and scrotal from the links. Since Mr. Mazoch couldn't have broken in, we've never tried to. Normally Matt just cases the place and we sit in the parking lot to wait.

But today Matt pauses at the double doors, and I watch from the car as he scrutinizes the windows. He taps at the glass, as if experimentally, with the bat handle's beveled knob. Then, before I understand what is about to happen, he plants his feet apart, cocking the bat at his shoulder, and swings a tremendous arc into one of the windows, which must be shatterproof, for it wobbles indomitably and the bat recoils. Even from across the parking lot I can hear the hollow *pdunk* of it. Undeterred, Matt simply rides the recoil of the bat and heaves his hips into a second swing, which recoils again, and then into a third swing, and so on.

After the fourth or fifth swing, I realize what Matt must be thinking. It is the same thing he was thinking at Mr. Mazoch's earlier this morning, when he insisted on inspecting the house for a second time: he is determined to find another trace today. A trail of muddy bootprints. Another scrap of blue plaid cloth. He's going to find *something*, if not at his father's house then here, and he'll beat down those double doors to do it. Never mind that the mall—likely boarded since the outbreak—cannot be home to any recent traces. And never mind the incredible risks he's courting. For instance, any infected in the vicinity, whom Matt might be summoning with each resounding drumbeat of the bat. Or else the police coasting down the road, who might catch him in the act of trespassing. Or else—it finally occurs to me—whatever is *inside* the antiques mall, which was probably padlocked for a reason. I roll down my window in haste and shout across the parking lot: 'Hey, Bambino! Barry Bonds! Cool it!'

Once Matt returns to the driver's seat, we have very little to say to one another. I don't ask him what he thought he'd find inside, and he doesn't tell me. We just stare out the windshield at the antiques mall in silence. As usual, there is nothing to see: sunlight radiates off the gravel and onto the storefront's stucco, which looks buttered with noon light.[1] The only shade comes from a drooping birch tree, planted at the edge of the lot, where it casts sprays of shadow onto the façade. Eventually

---

[1] This is an effect that Rachel and I have often admired together in Chateau Dijon's courtyard. What is it about white stucco that makes it so absorptive of sunlight? At noon especially, a wall of it will glow with weird, back-lit intensity, sort of throbbing with light, whereas other surfaces (such as cement sidewalks) are merely sheeny. Why is it that stucco, uniquely stucco, can be slathered over with these rich gold glazes? Is it its pebbly texture? I have in mind, by way of 'slather,' the example of toast, how much easier toast is to butter than the downy smoothness of fresh bread. As I confirmed for myself at breakfast with Rachel this morning, you can never 'spread' butter over fresh bread, only nudge it ineffectually across the surface, the knife's edge like a push broom guiding its little garbage of butter (pressing down on the knife, or applying any kind of force at all, will just make matters worse, since the delicate bread punctures easily and is twice as hard to butter torn). With toast, though, the crisp bristles where the bread burns provide a pleasantly resistive force, abrading the butter as it's being dragged over them, firmly withstanding the knife's scraping, even helping to trap the melted butter's runoff. Is stucco architecture's toast?

Matt reaches into his backpack and withdraws an apple. Over the next several minutes the silence in the car is punctuated by the log-splitting sound of his bites. I glance now and then from the windshield to watch him, waiting for him to finish so that we can leave. But he is eating the fruit with ruminative slowness, staring intently out the window as he chews, and he lets long moments pass between each bite.[1]

Can sunlight be slathered over it more easily, does light deliquesce better on its rough, raised pebbles, is this why it glistens with sopped goldenness like the photo-toast in Denny's menus? It certainly seems that way.

[1] The apple is a red delicious, which, I've noticed, tend to oxidize faster than other varieties, their exposed cores embrowning almost instantly. Matt's is no exception. Each time I turn back to him, some crater that his bite marks made—initially a white, kind of whittled color—has already started tarnishing, turning the same shade of brown as every aged thing. Because the aerated patches of apple meat 'age' in a matter of seconds, it's like watching in timelapse lace fading in an attic: something snow-white fogging over with brownness. And it has occurred to me, as I've been watching him, that this 'brown fog of decay' is not unlike Matt's black fog of war: namely, that it too could serve as an apt representation for the epidemic. For what is the infection if not a breath of decay that is blowing over the world? There is a sense in which the infection is accelerating our aging, not only at the level of the body (instantly cadaverizing it, fast-forwarding the corpse's decomposition), but at the level of civilization (turning buildings into premature ruins, tainting them with ancientness). Whenever I stare out the windshield at the boarded-up antiques mall, I can't help imagining that that is what is happening inside: that it is a ruin now, suffused with brown fog; that the trapped air in there has become polluted by particles of infection, filling the building—over the course of its abandonment—with sepia tones as with floodwater. I picture clouds of it drifting brownly down the aisles, over the furniture and the clothing racks, fading whatever they touch and aging it on contact. In this way, I imagine, the boarded-up antiques mall would function as a hothouse of aging, a microwave of aging, such that if you placed a lace nightgown inside, you could watch the cloth grow foxed like an oxidizing apple core, and such that if you placed your own hand inside, it'd instantly blanche

At last, to break the silence, I ask him what he's looking at. He explains: he has also been admiring the storefront's stucco, he says, watching as the nearby birch's shadow ivies up the building. Its branches cast a fine, fernlike pattern against the emblazed plaster: 'Like veins,' he says. And indeed the flattened shadows, branching slenderly into twigs and thin tendrils on the surface of the wall, look veiny in ways that the three-dimensional shoots do not. Before I can say anything about this, Mazoch asks, rhetorically, whether I know what the birch's shadow reminds him of: 'Other than veins I mean.' 'I don't know,' I say, 'I give up.' 'My father.' '…Yeah?' 'It reminds me of my dad's heart attack, actually.'

He proceeds to tell me that when he visited the hospital, a cardiologist showed him Mr. Mazoch's coronary angiogram, an X-ray in which only the heart's blood vessels, not the organ itself, were visible. The branching veins—flushed for this purpose with radiopaque dyes—showed up ash-gray on the monitor, a network of dark tendrils swaying in an undyed mist of X-rayed whiteness, and there they looked so much like the shadow of a tree (or else just a tree at night, its silhouette outlined by the ghostly fog that Mr. Mazoch's translucent heart appeared as) that to this day, years later he says, he still reads the tracery of trees' shadows angiogrammatically, as the calligraphy of his father's heart. 'It looked just like that,' he remarks, pointing again to the capillary shadow on the brilliant storefront. 'The angiogram did.'

This is only the second time that Matt has ventured more than

---

and embrown (turning the dead-leaf color of hands in monochromatic old photographs) before shriveling off altogether. It is curiously satisfying to consider that *this* is what Matt would have found inside today, if he'd succeeded in breaking open the double doors: that a stream of pressurized brown gas would have come whistling out from the cracks, like steam from a burst pipe, and scalded his face with age. Wrinkling him, graying his hair, melting the flesh from his skull. Turning him into a cadaver no less quickly than undeath would.

a passing reference to Mr. Mazoch's heart attack. The first was one morning while we were driving, during which he gave tactful but evasive answers to my questions until, once it'd become clear he didn't really want to talk about it, I stopped asking them. All I learned then was this: over six feet tall and three hundred pounds, and for that matter over sixty years old, Mr. Mazoch worked full time as a plumber (which, according to Matt, was more backbreaking and labor-intensive than one would think [it often involved carrying claw-footed bathtubs up the steep staircases of un-air-conditioned houses, for instance]); at work he sustained himself on Snickers bars, eating on his half-hour lunch break every day only these turd-dark sticks of saturated fat, and elsewhere as here his diet consisted of whatever was worst for him, his dinners spent at fried-chicken chains and his breakfasts, if he bothered to eat breakfast at all, at McDonald's. Oh, and he smoked too, about a pack a day. So one night after handling a jackhammer all afternoon Mr. Mazoch suffered that seized-up pain in his sternum and vomited gray spume into the shower. Matt, in college and living on campus at that point, wasn't there when it happened. It was only much later in the night that he received a call from the hospital, where Mr. Mazoch had managed (while undergoing myocardial infarction! while his great heart fibrillated!) to drive himself.

His father had had a heart attack, Matt was told, and was being operated on as they spoke. A quadruple bypass. Could he come to the hospital? He could. I know now what he saw on arrival—the treetop angiogram of Mr. Mazoch's X-rayed veins—but at the time all he mentioned of his visit to the hospital was what the cardiologist had told him: (1) that it had been 'this close'—accompanied by a hair's breadth of air between two demonstrating fingers—that if Mr. Mazoch had arrived 'even ten minutes later' he'd be dead; and (2) that when asked for his son's cell number Mr. Mazoch had instructed them to tell the boy, not that he'd be okay or that there was no need to worry, but that he loved him, last-words words, just that he loved him and nothing else. Matt's tone spiked when he related these two things, in his voice a little anger flashed like mica.[1] And it was here that I backed off from what struck me as a sore subject. Today, when he remarks the birch's resemblance to the angiogram, I can hear the slightest echo of that anger, and so I refrain—for the time being—from asking him what Rachel asked me to. I wonder how long he has been brooding over this association: whether the shadow could have reminded even earlier of the heart attack (of all the excesses that led up to it: the obesity and the greed and the sheer ignorant gourmandism), and whether it was out of anger that Matt attacked the double doors. At this thought I imagine him battering the façade itself (swinging that bat like an ax into the shadow, as if chopping into the trunk of the tree of the veins of his father's heart), and at this thought I imagine him battering Mr. Mazoch, beating on his undead body, just as Rachel fears.

---

[1] I didn't ask, but I assumed that that anger was at Mr. Mazoch: (1) for recklessly neglecting to dial an ambulance and to that extra degree imperiling himself, for stopping at stoplights on his drive to the hospital even as his cardiologist's fingers, unbeknownst to him, were pinching that much more of the air between them, squashing like a bug the ghost of a chance that his heart had; and (2) for being willing and resigned to die, for issuing at the critical moment last, rather than fighting words, the message 'Tell him that I love him' really bearing the double meaning 'I give up,' as in, 'I'm ready now for death, so please send my love to the son whom I won't fight hard enough to live to see.' Or this was the best explanation I could come up with, anyway, for the anger in Matt's voice: namely, that Matt felt that Mr. Mazoch was shirking his duty to his son to survive. It's possible that I'm wrong. Matt might have just been angry with the doctor: (1) for fetishizing the nearness of death ('*This* close,' 'Only *ten minutes*'), tormenting a son with details he ought to have kept to himself; and (2) for failing to deliver on the phone the message that Mr. Mazoch had asked him to, namely, by informing Matt that Mr. Mazoch was in the operating theater but not that he sent his love.

Mazoch is finished with his apple. He has eaten the entirety of the core with grim efficiency, and I watch as he spits the dark seeds out of the driver-side window, where they patter onto the gravel of the parking lot. How far from the tree the fruit falls, it occurs to me! The father ashes a cigarette onto the gravel, the son spits out apple seeds. Is this what the heart attack meant to Matt, in the end? A memento mori, spurring him to eat an apple a day? Was Mr. Mazoch's incised chest, bloated and vulnerable on the operating table, Matt's own archaic torso of Apollo, exhorting him to change his life? Probably not. Matt, with his wrestler's build and workout regimen, has likely been eating an apple a day for ages, and he definitely didn't need his father's brush with death to scare him off Snickers bars and greasy hamburgers. If anything, Mr. Mazoch's heart attack would have only confirmed Matt in his habits. But I'd still be willing to bet that those habits—the bookishness no less than the bodybuilding—were formed in direct contradistinction to Mr. Mazoch. That is, I'd be willing to bet that Matt styled himself consciously as his father's opposite.

It can't be an accident that the fruit has fallen as far off as it has. Indeed, it's as if Matt's entire life has been engaged in this one Sisyphean task: to roll the fruit as far uphill from the tree as possible. That Mr. Mazoch was a college dropout and plumber, Matt should graduate summa from LSU's English department; that Mr. Mazoch preoccupied himself with the most quotidian artifacts from the past (lamps and church hats and farm tools, interesting only secondarily, for the dust of history they were coated with), Matt should devote himself to books, the past's loftiest artifacts; that Mr. Mazoch held his gut in his hands before the mirror every decade, his expanding gut, and appraised the deep concavity of his belly button (like a prostate it had enlarged! Big as a grape now, so unbelievably extended from the tight punctum it had made in his washboard stomach when at twenty he was slim as Matt!), and that Mr. Mazoch, staring each decade at his widening, worsening reflection, had the naivety to ask (his wife, Matt, the reflection itself), 'Why do I keep putting on weight? Plumbing is such physical labor. I'm out there sweating every day, working with my hands, but I can't seem to keep the pounds off!', that as his wastebasket brimmed with Snickers wrappers he had the naivety to ask why he couldn't keep the pounds off… Matt should do weighted pull-ups from the bar suspended in his doorframe,[1] and each morning complete a set of one hundred elevated pushups (his feet propped on the cushion of an office chair), and hold his body horizontal to the ground for quivering, minute-long sessions of core-strengthening planks, and not only that, but should also mind his diet, eating organic apples whole for lunch, and spitting the seeds out hard, the way cartoon characters spit bullets, as if each ballistic spat black apple seed were itself the force that was keeping the doctor away.

What an antonymic existence Mazoch's led! The wage laborer inverted as the scholar; the car cluttered with bronze lamps and landscape paintings inverted as the car cluttered with OEDs and usage guides (or, to put it another way, junk in the trunk

---

[1] And really, what other purpose could the working out serve? It is so impractical and even dangerous an activity, under the given circumstances: it's not as if the crowded undead will be intimidated by Mazoch's bench max, or deterred by the body blows that he rains on their insensate bodies. By focusing so much athletic attention on bulk strength, rather than on cardiovascular stamina or speed, Mazoch is not only failing to train the survival skills he might actually need (sprinting, cross-country endurance, stamina) but training skills directly impedimental to them (weightlifting power that will only slow him down, literal 'dead weight'). The working out seems designed solely to correct Mr. Mazoch's physical indifference, his obesity and ill health, at the level of the son's body, which by brute determination and for no other reason Matt has transformed into the opposite of his father's body. Flexing shirtless before the bathroom mirror, basking in his own oppositeness, heaving that fruit farther and farther from his father: this is the only purpose that the working out has served.

inverted as Strunk in the trunk); the three hundred pounds of the quadruple bypass inverted as the three hundred pounds of the all-time bench max.

It has been a noble effort on Matt's part, but, of course, no son can succeed in such an antonymic project. No matter how differentiated the son thinks he's become, in actuality he has never left, never escaped out from under, the law of patrimonial synonymy that this whole time has been mastering him. The father's habits, gestures, and ways of being end up predetermining him, such that even as he 'differs' from his father, he's nonetheless bound to the man by some common denominator.[1] Matt crouching in a dank aisle, browsing the spines of second-hand novels; Mr. Mazoch crouching in a dank aisle, browsing a Depression-era child's doll set. Matt unable to say no to a bargain, even if it means pushing his apartment to capacity, stacking long-dead authors' books in teetering hoodoos on the bedroom floor; Mr. Mazoch unable to say no to a bargain, even if it means pushing his dilapidated house to capacity, ranging a long-dead child's dolls across the seat of his living room couch. Matt living by himself, in lonely, disorganized reclusion, consoled only by his library; Mr. Mazoch living by himself, in lonely, disorganized reclusion, consoled only by his antiques. Two collectors, two hoarders, casting a wide net over the past tense and trawling its goods into their rats' nests. No, so far from being antonyms, there could be nothing more identical than Matt the scholar of dusty sentences and Mr. Mazoch the scholar of dusty whatever else. Even the bodybuilding, so ostensibly oppositional to

---

[1] Undeath, too, is just such a system of synonymy. By biting its victims, an undead passes on to them, as if genetically, all the physical characteristics of the infection (necrosis, moaning, whited eyeballs), thereby rendering them synonyms of itself. That's why all undead, though returning to idiosyncratic haunts and observing distinct behavioral patterns, seem driven by the same motor, so to speak. The surest way for Matt to become his father would be for him to be bitten by his father.

everything Mr. Mazoch's dietetics represented, is just one long way around the barn among others. For once Matt is his father's age (once his slowed metabolism renders weighted pull-ups and pushups insufficient exercise, and once he aches too much or is too tired or weak to do even them as regularly as he'd need to, and once his lifelong disregard for cardiovascular exercise starts catching up with him), all this otiose muscle that he's spent his youth building up will gradually atrophy and sag, deteriorating into so much fatherly fat. Then the symmetrization will be finished. Surely Matt is aware of this! At least subconsciously, he must appreciate the fact that this final symmetry between him and his father is preparing itself even now in his body, latently stored there like the heart disease that he's probably inherited as well. He must understand that if I were to submerge him in the antiques store's stale miasma, aging him, he'd come out in minutes resembling Mr. Mazoch.

This, too—just the fact that he's here right now, in the antiques store's parking lot, whether he's spitting apple seeds onto its gravel or gristly beef—bespeaks a synonymy with his father. For it's clear that the crowning similarity, the point of pure identity where he and Mr. Mazoch converge, is this itinerary that Matt's acceded to. In shadowing Mr. Mazoch (in staking out his haunts), Matt follows literally in his father's footsteps. He begins each morning in Denham just as Mr. Mazoch did; visits the same gas stations and grocery stores and, today, the same roadside antiques mall; sits in his car in the parking lots of these places, haunting another man's haunts. He's picked up precisely where Mr. Mazoch left off. At least before, prior to this search, Matt (however synonymous with his father he may otherwise have been) had unique routines to distinguish him. The map of his activities throughout Baton Rouge—were he to mark in thick ink the streets that he traveled—would have diverged notice- ably from his father's, his own red route coursing from LSU to the gym to the library. But now that route, briefly diverted, has returned like a tributary to the river that Mr. Mazoch's synonymy is. Now Matt, who forswore a life of manual labor and fast food, reports every morning to the plumbing warehouse and the McDonald's, slavishly reiterating the dailiness of his father's existence. Their two maps are congruent now—the symmetrization is finished!—to the last cartographic detail.

Perhaps that more than anything is at the root of Matt's anger: that he has become his father, or else is doomed to become him. I glance at him again, at his strong square jaw and blunt nose and cleft chin, and try to match him up in my mind with Mr. Mazoch (a man I've never met, or even seen a photo of). Imagining the tendrils of brown fog from the antiques mall, I try to visualize how Matt's features might change if they were aged in timelapse to Mr. Mazoch's age. If his face decayed as fast as that apple he's finished eating.

Matt lets loose a sigh and drums the steering wheel impatiently, then honks the horn three times. Nothing, anywhere, stirs. Even the birch, whose shadow we've been gawking at like Platonic troglodytes, is unruffled by breeze: its leaves are all still, and green as the Real.

'Do you want to get out of here?' I ask. 'Are you hungry?' 'I guess so,' he says. 'I guess I do.' But after starting the engine he just sits for a minute before moving the gearshift into reverse.

TYPICALLY FOR LUNCH WE EAT PACKED sandwiches in the parking lot of Louie's Café, but today Matt decides to order a meal inside. I sit opposite him in a red vinyl booth, watching him tear into a grill-striped breast of chicken. I still haven't asked him what he wants to do when he finds his father, but all throughout lunch I've been working up the nerve to.

'If you ever *did* find him,' I begin… but almost immediately I lose my resolve. Instead of asking what he wants to do, I decide to ask—in a roundabout way—where he'd want to do it. That is, I ask *where* he'd most prefer to find the man. 'If you could find him anywhere,' I continue, 'where would you want it to be?' 'Out of all the sites?' Matt asks. 'Let me think about it.' He picks up his silverware and resumes eating, as if to defer the question, and I watch as he keeps shoveling in bites, shredding white threads of chicken through the fork tines, chewing with his mouth open. Each time his teeth part, flashing a clump of meat, I wince a little.[1]

Matt sees me staring: 'You're looking at me like a starving person. Why don't you order something?' 'Do you know how nervous it makes me just to watch *you* eat? I'm not going to order

---

[1] What the sight reminds me of is the cover illustration of *FIGHT THE BITE*, a starkly outlined drawing of cartoon jaws. Opened in a wide ellipse, the jaws form a wreath of teeth around the pamphlet's title, I guess as if about to bite down on it (this is probably what the graphic designer intended), but actually resembling, to an even greater degree, the mouth that a willful boy makes when he wants to display chewed food at the dinner table: a 'say "Ahh"' mouth, gaping rudely, as if exposing to a grossed-out sibling all the mashed-up bits of title inside.

a dish of infected food for myself. With a side of infection. And who knows what in the water, which probably it's not even bottled, just straight from the tap.' 'Not even the tap: squeezed fresh from an infected's lesions.' I cringe. I'm remembering the footage of this one Youtube video, in which the wounds and pustules along an infected's skin dehisce from sunburn—there is a runny yellowness like yolk. Mazoch regards me skeptically: 'Not even dessert?' 'Confections?' I say, allowing for a beat: 'More like *in*fections.' 'Very good, Vermaelen.' 'I mean, I'm exaggerating, but what a dumb risk.' 'Yeah, I'm a real daredevil. It's like, I'm such an Evel Knievel, of eating chicken breast and rice, I'm not even wearing a condom right now.'

I, who engage daily in sessions of unprotected sex with Rachel, appreciate that my armchair mysophobia is at some level an overreaction. The chicken meat would, after all, have been well cooked, and the infection itself (of which basically nothing has been empirically verified: not whether it can be transmitted across species, or even whether animals, which are universally asymptomatic, can in fact serve as carriers at all) could probably still be assumed to sizzle and be sterilized in a frying pan. Even the bit about the tap water was merely rhetorical. While *FIGHT THE BITE* strongly discourages drinking anything other than bottled or boiled water, and while FEMA has supplied citizens with aluminum cans boldly and majuscularly labeled **FILTERED DRINKING WATER**, there have been no reports, so far as I know, of the contamination of wells by infected effluent. Yet it would be as meaningless as an aggregate of spit on the surface of his ice water, or as meaningless as blood let from a minor wound into food handled by an ungloved hand, for a kind of absence to uncoil in Mazoch by the end of the week. Even assuming that he could trust a line cook or a server not to intentionally infect his meal,[1] there's no accounting for ignorance, or carelessness. Mazoch knows all of this. I don't understand what's gotten into him. Eating chicken now, after a month of packed lunches? It reeks of 'He had a week left till retirement,' a kind of fate-baiting self-endangerment and heedless hamartia. It's like he's daring the infection to infect him.

But by far the dumber risk is that we're even inside right now. Although the diner is empty of other customers, there's still the staff on hand: our waitress; a police officer stationed as security; some cooks. Paradoxically, the presence of the officer has the effect of making me feel *less* safe. He's just one more body to reanimate. Any person in this room—if not all of them—could drop to the floor at any moment, and begin to reanimate. Then it would be like that food-court footage all over again, in which a single person manages to spark a mass outbreak. And if it were Mazoch who reanimated today—going limp in his booth, twitching in revivification—there would be only three feet of the formica of the tabletop separating him from me. As he sprawled across it, clutching at me with his thewy hands, I would have to fend him off, fend off his huge strength, for as long as I could, until the officer a few booths over rushed here to restrain

---

[1] *FIGHT THE BITE* refers to this phenomenon as 'spite bites': namely, when people who are nonfatally contaminated (e.g., by a scratch, or a bite on the ankle: any manner of infection that—instead of killing them instantly—leaves them with a week of fever and dread before they become undead) decide to spend their last days alive contaminating as many other victims as they can. They mete out to others the dumb luck and injustice of it, either by having unprotected sex, or splitting meals and drinking after people, or sharing needles, or even, fantastically, biting strangers in the street, in a kind of rehearsal for undeath. For this reason, *FIGHT THE BITE* warns readers to exercise caution even around living, asymptomatic humans. It also lists the 1-800 numbers of several 24-hour hotlines, so that—in the event that you are nonfatally infected—psychiatrists and counselors can talk you down from spite biting anyone yourself, before you get to a quarantine.

him. Assuming, that is, that the officer himself hadn't already reanimated. I look over Matt's broad shoulder toward the officer's booth, trying to make out whether the man has ordered or eaten anything since he's been here, but all I can see is the back of the seat opposite him.

When the waitress returns to take Mazoch's plate, she offers him a laminated dessert menu, and he props it on the table so that I can see its centerfold photographs of brownies. Such a menu as the devil might have shown Jesus in the desert, each brownie stage-lit and provocatively angled, glinting in places throughout its morsel moisture and the deep obscene brownness of its glaze. Mazoch must be able to tell by my expression that I'm little tempted: 'You know we're talking a thousandth decimal place? What are the chances,' he asks, emphasizing the word 'chances,' 'that one brownie or one piece of chicken, from this diner, this afternoon, is going to infect either of us?' 'In my case, no chance,' I answer, 'because I refuse to order anything.' 'Suit yourself,' he says.

I remind him that he still hasn't answered my question, about where he'd want to find his father, and he folds the dessert menu down on the table. 'I know where I *wouldn't* want to find him,' he says. 'I do too,' I say. 'Feeding, right?' When we first discussed this, toward the beginning of the search, I asked Matt whether he was ever *afraid* of finding Mr. Mazoch. And he confided in me that there were certain scenarios that kept him up at night. He would never want to find Mr. Mazoch feeding, he said: to see him crouched over his victim, hands rooting inside an opened stomach, the ribs pried and the long guts unspooled, and to hear the sloppy wetness of his chewing; for his father to turn back, looking over his shoulder, and for the man to be unrecognizable by the cloudiness of his eyes, so vacant, wide, and white, and by the blood, too, smeared carelessly across his mouth, as by a child's finger-painting hand. Even worse than finding his father feeding, he said, would be to find him at the moment when, having fed too much, his undigesting stomach burst: to see him lying helpless in a ditch, his legs and arms rotating futilely, like an upturned beetle's, around the scene of his unseamed belly, the gore steaming in the grass where it spilled, and his mouth giving terribly of froth, a white flow down either side, as if vomiting moonlight. These and like places, these and like positions, Mazoch would prefer not to find his father in, he told me. They belong only to the undead, are images that the undead have introduced.[1] Better to see his father shrouded in some illusion of humanity—better to find him brushing, out of habit, his teeth, or standing peacefully above his bed—than to see him utterly transformed by undeath, feeding as only they feed, dismembered and atwitch as only they can be. Or at least these were Mazoch's sentiments the last time that we discussed this.[2]

---

[1] How often, before this epidemic, would Mazoch or I have witnessed an image of cannibalism, or of a disemboweled man still walking? Maybe once a year, when we watched a horror movie or some samurai seppuku scene? Now these and similar sights are broadcast semi-nightly and are indissociable from the undead. We recognize the undead by the posture of their feeding (the way that packs of them will hunch over the torn-open stomach of a corpse, sifting its intestines through their fingers), as well as by their cadaverous imperviousness to dismemberment: the way that one, cut in half at the waist, will drag itself forward by dogged fistfuls of grass. In images like these we recognize the undeath in them. Compare *that* recognition with the kind we feel when we see them performing echopractic rituals of motor instinct—when, watching them sit in their cars or drag razors across their rotting cheeks, we might halfway mistake them for human—and it's no wonder that Mazoch's preference lies with the latter.

[2] He even referred me to a relevant passage of Wordsworth: '[We] grieved/ To have a soulless image on the eye/That had usurped a living thought/That never more could be' (*The Prelude*). In context Wordsworth is describing the anticlimactic Alps, but it really would be grievous for Mazoch to have the soulless image of his undead father branded irreversibly on the eye, to have some trademark gesture of undeath—his father's teeth tearing into warm flesh—usurp the living memory of the man. (Mazoch's

So I'm surprised today to hear him give a different answer: 'Where I wouldn't want to find him,' he says, 'is at his elementary school, or high school, or another childhood place. Places that predate me and his fatherhood.' Not out of vanity or some need to be remembered, he explains, as if he should be the figure who looms largest in his father's memory, and whose apartment it is that the man should return to in undeath. But even to find him at the antiques mall, or his house in Denham, would be better than finding him in more ancient neighborhoods. At least then he'd be returning to portions of his life that Matt understood of him: he'd still be making sense of himself, in some way, as a father (as related to Matt), rather than as a son, returning to his own father's home but otherwise… unattached. 'Does that make sense?' he asks. It does, and I tell him so. In fact, I am momentarily relieved to hear him say it. Because if Matt prefers to think of his father's corpse as a father, to find it in a fatherly space, then he can't possibly be intending to kill it. Could he? He must want—as Rachel did with her own father—nothing more than to rescue Mr. Mazoch. See him safely to a quarantine. Hence the strong emotional incentives Matt has for believing (or for making himself believe) that it is 'his father' he is saving. If his plan really were to put Mr. Mazoch down, then all the emotional incentives would have to be running in the opposite

bibliomantic ability to flip through old poems and find auguries of undeath has never failed to impress me, so one day I tried flipping through his copy of *The Prelude* myself. Within minutes—and as if guided—I stumbled upon the following passage, unmarked by Mazoch: 'And, on the shape of that unmoving man,/His steadfast face and sightless eyes, I gazed,/As if admonished from another world.' Reading it, I caught my breath. It really did seem unmistakable as a description, not just of any encounter with any undead, but of my own with the jogger. In context, of course, Wordsworth is simply describing his encounter with a blind beggar, and the passage's applicability to undeath can be only an artifact of hindsight bias: an open-and-shut case of poetic postdiction.)

direction. Wouldn't they? Assuming that he seriously intended to one day swing a bat into his father's body, Matt would almost certainly prefer to dissociate that body from the idea of his father, to reject any recognition of Mr. Mazoch there. Baseball bat in hand, Matt would need to think himself to the point at which his father was *not* his father. In which case a 'childhood site' or an 'ancient neighborhood'—a place devoid of paternal associations—would be exactly where Matt would want to find him. Somewhere that he could regard him as a stranger.

'So these are the places?' I ask. 'The antiques mall, or in Denham?' Alternately massaging each bicep with the opposite hand, Matt reconsiders: 'No. Maybe just in a neutral space. Standing in a field off the interstate, maybe, neither like himself or not.' During those first weeks, whenever we drove down the interstate, we would often pass fields such as this, peopled by their white shapes. Stray infected that had wandered off, like cattle, into a cool place to stand before noon. Lit up by our headlights in the morning fog, they would stand out so lustrous and ghostly that, yes, 'neither like themselves nor not' is right: it was as if they occupied some intervening space between the living and the undead, not speaking and not breathing, but not cannibalizing anyone either. Just standing purposeless and still. And the mist was so thick in the fields that it was easy to imagine that dew had settled on their bodies, dampening their night-gowns, and to imagine that the dew on their bodies would catch the light, when the light came, in a vivid glistening. Easy, too, to sympathize with Matt on this point, to imagine him wanting to find his father there. For who wouldn't want to find a father like this, undead or otherwise, standing in a misty field at dawn and slanted upon by a shaft of rising sun, which would give every droplet to flash momentarily on his skin, flaring out whitely, as if he were sprinkled, not with moisture, but with roscid light? I can imagine with perfect clarity and ease Mazoch swinging a bat on such a father.

The waitress returns, and when Mazoch hands her the menu, she asks whether we won't be having any dessert. 'No,' he says, 'I'll be having this gentleman here for dessert. In about an hour.' 'That's not funny,' I say. 'I think it's funny.' 'Well, it's not.' How graceful of this waitress, Elizabeth, to laugh before leaving, as if she did think it was funny, or even understood.

WHEN I GET HOME THIS AFTERNOON, THE FIRST thing Rachel asks me is whether I've asked Matt about his plans. I have to confess that I haven't. 'But I didn't even need to ask,' I tell her. Recounting what Matt said in the diner, I reassure her that I have no doubts about the search (this is not true, of course. But it would be impossible to confess my doubts without worrying her even more [and even more needlessly] than I have already). Rachel seems satisfied with my answer. At any rate, she doesn't ask any follow-up questions, and before she can, I suggest that we try an exercise together. Inspired by my conversation with Matt, I ask whether she thinks *we* ought to be making lists: whether we ought to compile some of our personal rendezvous points, the respective and mutual haunts that we expect ourselves to return to. That way, if one of us ever goes missing, the other will know approximately where to look. Rachel agrees that this is a good idea, and we each grab a pen and notepad, and a beer, and step out onto our apartment complex's concrete walkway. Sitting single file, we set to work, writing in steady silence. Now the sun is low, but the day is still warm, our beers cold, and the sky brilliant above us.[1]

---

[1] At this late date in the epidemic, it still strikes me as strange that I can enjoy such simple pleasures—the warmth of sunlight on my arms, the freeing bitterness of this beer—when chances are that someone is being bitten and infected not very far from here. This seems to be a special talent of Louisianans: how citizens' sensibilities can remain unsynchronized with their city's. When a hurricane heads for New Orleans, the city shuts down: schools close, work is canceled, news stations broadcast storm warnings. But all that the people do to prepare is stockpile alcohol. They celebrate as on any other holiday: they drink drinks called Hurricanes! One can detect

Cross-legged, with my back to our apartment door, I watch Rachel ahead of me. She appears to have stopped writing for the moment. Her journal is pressed against her knees, which she's drawn up to her chest, and she leans forward a little, hugging her shins, her long bare limbs beautiful in the sunlight. I take in the sight of her blond head, the arc of her back. Sensing that she's being watched, she turns her head over her shoulder to face me now, smiling, and I understand that she's having a truly pleasant time with this. This exercise delights her. She's treating it as an opportunity to turn certain memories over in her mind, to meditate on the moments in her life when she's been most present. 'Where would my reanimated body return to?' she asks herself, and it is a happy question. As in: where would my body be happiest to go? Where would it want its afterlife to take place? Which locations did I love enough to want to make a heaven of?[1]

---

in Louisianans' reactions to disasters like this a reckless kind of hysteresis, as if—even after sociocultural institutions have acknowledged an apocalypse, and even after larger fields and forces of normalcy have withdrawn—there remains this ferromagnetic lag in the people themselves, who behave as if nothing has changed, who persist, charged with quotidian energies in an apocalyptic system. Who drink Hurricanes and barbeque brisket beneath skies blackened with ominousness. It is this same native trait, no doubt, that enabled Mazoch to enjoy his chicken breast at Louie's this afternoon, chewing mouthful after insouciant mouthful.

[1] Rachel, to clarify, doesn't actually think that her undead self would *experience* happiness at these sites, only that past happiness would be a motivation for return. She doesn't believe that the infected are capable of appreciating their reasons for returning, or of taking joy in mortal spaces. In fact, she finds this aspect of undeath almost unbearably sad, and she even remarked, earlier this afternoon, as we were beginning our lists, 'What's sad is that I'll be going to all these places without ever even really *seeing* them.' Like Matt, Rachel associates undeath with blindness, though not clinical or even phenomenological blindness so much as, maybe, existential. She means by this those times in your life when you're your worst

Needless to say, the question is proving more complicated than that for me. In fact I find this exercise perplexing, and in between each rendezvous point that I've been able to come up with (Tunica Hills, our apartment, a campus lawn that she and I once picnicked on), I've allowed countless minutes to pass. My problem, I know, is indecisiveness. I lack any confidence in myself or the list, in my predictive capacities or the predictability of my undead body. For what do I *really* know—aside from a popular-science version of the process—about the undead's supposed homing instinct? In undeath, a reanimated body can somehow navigate around the streets of its past, returning to sites that have been memorialized as loci in its unconscious. In interviews and newspaper articles, neurologists have even coined a word for this process: mnemocartography. As if the undead could simply read their memories like roadmaps, to keep from getting lost in their labyrinths.[1] But what does this really

---

self, soulless and unobservant, reverting to a kind of robotic autopilot, in which you move through the world in a daze, without noticing any of the details that you usually take so much pleasure in noticing. That's what she expects being undead to be like. And what's sad, she says, about the idea of being stuck like this in undeath, is that the sites you'll be returning to will be places from the exact *opposite* times in your life. Places like Tunica, where you were *most* awake and *most* attentive, most in love with the world and filled with joy for phenomena, where you were so alive and alert to detail that the scenery has been seared—eidetically, nostalgically—into your unconscious. The sad irony of undeath, for Rachel, is that your worst self is the one seeking out your best self's sites. You get to return to the regions of presence, the places in your life where you were most present, but you have to haunt them as a vassal of absence.

[1] That is yet another way that I sometimes imagine undeath: like being lost in a labyrinth, in the maze of the underworld. Staggering down infinite hallways of smoky shade. What first inspired this comparison, I suspect, was simply the morpheme 'maze' in Mazoch's name. It was probably a free-associative, onomastic accident that I began thinking about labyrinths at all. But it makes a certain kind of sense, when I stop to consider it.

explain? How accurate are these maps? Do only happy sites get maps? Sad sites, shameful sites, traumatic sites? Sites of repression or repetition or rage? How must a memory be affectively inflected for the body to make a note of its postal address? With what authority could I guarantee Rachel that she could find me at that campus lawn?

It was a perfectly ordinary campus lawn. Just an average stretch of grass that we brought blankets and a gin handle to a single dusk last October (a 'liquor picnic,' she'd called it), lying alone on our spot in the quad to drink and admire the sunset. What I remember especially is the sweater Rachel was wearing, white cashmere, the kind whose threads fray upward in a fuzz of invisible cilia. She was careful to lie across the red plaid blanket that we'd laid out on the grass, so that she wouldn't get dirt stains or chlorophyll on the cashmere. Nevertheless, a rogue dead leaf that had found its way onto the blanket somehow got enmeshed in her sweater. It was caught in her right sleeve's field of fuzz, floating half a centimeter above the sleeve itself on the tips of all those fine white threads. From a certain angle, this gave the brittle leaf the appearance of hovering in the air, and when I pointed out the illusion to Rachel, she laughed with delight. Beaming down at the levitating leaf, she said it looked as if it were bodysurfing on a crowd of ghosts. And by God it did: that dead leaf, brown and crispate, seemed to be borne aloft

---

Classically speaking, labyrinths are places where fathers deposit their monstrous sons: mazes where they bring their sons to get lost, dungeons to disinherit their minotaurs in. And now it's Matt who's in search of his monstrous father, the minotaur Mr. Mazoch, who is himself banished to a kind of maze, the Cretan corridors that he accretes around himself as he wanders across Baton Rouge. While Matt pursues him, I ride along as his guide, leading him deep into the labyrinth and back again, my folder of Mapquest directions like some Ariadne's thread. Meanwhile Mr. Mazoch, if the neurologists are to be believed, has maps of his own to follow: he isn't lost at all.

by a thousand invisible, white hands. And she had noticed it and said so! I was so overcome with love for her then that the entire afternoon seemed to be corroborating the joy in my chest: how crisp the dusk was; how warm I felt from gin; how, even in the early darkness, low as a storm's shadow, the fall hues around us were still so vibrant and lush, almost to a threatening degree;[1] and then that creaky song of geese overhead, two-toned and pendular, like the swaying of an unoiled porch swing—how, if you closed your eyes, you actually felt as if you were lying in a field of unoiled porch swings.

A fine memory. If a couples counselor asked me to adduce memorable moments from our courtship, this memory, surely, would make the cut. But if I were asked, as in fact I have been asked, to adduce memorable moments from my *entire life* (to survey all of my private Bethlehem stars, drawing up the mnemonic astrolabe that my undead body might be navigating by), who's to say that this memory—one pinprick of light in my life among many—wouldn't be lost in the glare of another? Aren't there strong reasons for doubting that my phantom-footed shape would bother returning there? The lawn is a comparatively limited site, given that I visited it only once and associate only one happiness with it. So it could feasibly be superseded by some older site, a place that has afforded me heterogeneous joys on multiple occasions. If I were being completely honest with myself, wouldn't I cross the lawn off my list, and replace it, say, with my elementary-school playground? It was on this very playground that I enjoyed—for fifty minutes a day, five days a week, eight years of my childhood—*recess*, a period of unfettered,

---

[1] The trees had turned a vespine yellow, as if trying to terrify what would eat them. This was Rachel's suggestion, anyway, her explanation for the world's lushness: that it had to color-code itself like a bug. What an autumn afternoon needed most, she said, was to flare bold in the eye of its predator, the encroaching winter. The hues of the sky and the trees would deepen accordingly, in keeping with the aposematism of the season.

enthusiastic play. Wouldn't the steady, daily, decade-long accumulation of this enthusiasm all but guarantee the playground a first-magnitude memory, more alluring by far (to my undead self at least) than the campus lawn would be?

When I first started brainstorming for this exercise, I thought that it would be a rapid-fire, first-thought-best-thought process. I thought that I would just jot down the most obvious sites that occurred to me, on the assumption that they would be the ones to occur to my undead body. That's exactly what Matt and I did on behalf of Mr. Mazoch: we stuck to the surface of Matt's memories of his father, picking out all the prominent spaces from the final years of his life.

But look where that has gotten Matt. Look at how arbitrary and unscientific that selection process is, and how much inefficiency has been introduced into Matt's search algorithm as a result. Every day he has to check his father's house, the antiques mall, Louie's Café (what are all, after all, only best guesses), visiting a dozen such sites with equal vigilance, even though Mr. Mazoch is likely to return, at most, to only a few of them. Matt's forced to spread his time indiscriminately, among both likely and unlikely sites, simply because he has no way of distinguishing them. He can never be sure, when staking out the house in Denham, that his father isn't at Louie's, or vice versa.[1] That's

---

[1] Or even somewhere else altogether. In addition to the sites Matt doesn't *want* to visit (the high school, the childhood home), you also have to factor in the unknown quantities, any places Matt hasn't thought of yet, plus the ones he has no way of even knowing about. There are bound to be certain epistemological blocks and search biases that have been acting as blinders from the outset, preventing him from conceiving of every potentiality. And this is a serious obstacle. If every Thursday Mr. Mazoch frequented a gentleman's club, it's doubtful that Matt would know about it: not only because Mr. Mazoch never would have told him, but also because Matt, just as a matter of epistemological blockage, would be biased away from imagining it, from even entertaining it as a possibility.

why these traces must be so crazy-making for Mazoch: if only he had been in Denham an hour later, he must be telling himself, instead of at Louie's. Then he could have *seen* his father shattering that window.

This scenario is what my own list is supposed to be preventing for Rachel. I should be presenting her with a conscientiously compiled, manageable handful of places that I'm 100% sure of my visiting. That's the degree of certainty I should have—100%!—about my sites and myself. I owe it to her to give my selection process that kind of deliberation and thought, because otherwise she'll be putting herself as fruitlessly at risk—frustrating the work of her mourning just as much—as Mazoch is whenever he patrols by trial and error the full miscellany of his father's haunts. I can't bear the thought of Rachel waiting alone in the rain, jilted by me in undeath, due to the carelessness with which I've compiled my list. What if she's waylaid by undead at a site she never would have gone to if I hadn't thoughtlessly assured her I could be found there? I imagine her calling out my name on the campus lawn, dangerously calling attention to herself, all while I'm standing beneath the monkey bars on the playground of my old elementary school, a place that she's never heard me speak about and so has no reason to associate me with. Does Rachel even know where I went to grade school?

'Done?' she asks. Looking up I see that she's set her journal on the concrete and twisted around to study me. Her legs are still propped in front of her, dangling between the balusters of the safety railing. I nod distractedly, then ask, 'Do you know where I went to grade school?' 'St. Aloysius. You've told me that.' 'You attended Sacred Heart?' 'Kay through eight,' she says, 'St. Joseph's for high school. But they're not on the list.' Her face scrunches in sudden concern: 'Should they be on the list?' 'That's a matter for you and your conscience.' 'But did you put Aloysius?' 'The playground,' I lie (though I now have every intention of adding it). 'Oh, the playground!' she sighs. I can tell by her voice, a whimsy of transported joy, that it's been years since she's remembered recess, and that the very word 'playground'—like the ringing of the recess bell—has sent a crowd of childhood reveries stampeding forth from the recesses of her memory. She writes something down on her list. 'What about the lawn where we went on that picnic?' I ask. 'Do you remember?' 'Of course I do,' she says, 'the little leaf! I have it down already. But thank you for reminding me.' She has it down already! Oh, what a jolt of confidence—in that memory, in the list, in myself—it is to hear her say that! Why did I ever doubt the campus lawn? I imagine the other sites that would lie above and below it on her list (her father's grave, surely, plus the wing of the hospital where he'd been kept; her mother's house; Tunica probably; and, now that I've reminded her of it, the playground at Sacred Heart), and I gratify myself with the illusion that we know everything about one another, are transparent to each other, that our memories share everything.

'So are you ready?' Rachel asks. 'To read them?' I glance over at her open journal, in which her tight, clean script has filled an entire page, and I note that her list is already much longer than I had been expecting. Maybe five times as long as mine. The amount of ink alone outstrips the half dozen sites I've attributed to her so far, and I estimate that after her father's grave, the playground, and the campus lawn, after Tunica, the hospital, and her mother's house, there will be room enough still for ten more sites on the lines she's filled.

Yet which ten sites? When I try to fathom them, I feel an abyss opening within me. I recall what Matt said today, about needing to find Mr. Mazoch in a fatherly space. Almost despite myself, I find that this is what I'm hoping now—desperately— with regard to Rachel. I'm actually anxious to hear the results of her list, which I would prefer to comprise solely *our* spots. I want those extra ten lines to hold no surprises, only sites I recognize.

For every site that has nothing to do with me, or even with her in relation to me, I will feel strangely rejected.

I don't just mean places that precede[1] me, sites from before we met. There are plenty of moments from Rachel's past that she has shared with me, and I think of these as memories that she has put in relation to me by relating them to me. Take the story of her father's death. When she narrates this to me in bed at night, what she's doing is putting it into play in our relationship. All the locations that this memory colligates (the hospital, her father's grave, the bedroom that he died in) become *our* sites, even though she acquired them before we met. The reason she's even sharing that memory to begin with is that she wants me, as her lover, to know that about her. It's a biographical experience she considers so fundamental to her sense of self that I couldn't properly love her—couldn't know her as my beloved—without first having incorporated it into my own personal sense of who she is. The subtext of any memory that a lover shares is, 'I want you, my lover, to know this about me, because this is the facet of myself I want you to love. When you say, "I love you," mean by "you" the subject of this memory.' That's why those initial late-night self-disclosures are so important. In developing a coherent narrative of her life, the beloved ends up constructing a self for the lover to love. So I'm keenly mindful of the fact that Rachel related her father memories to me for a reason. She wants me to know and love her as the daughter she used to be: that's one self she self-identifies as when she self-identifies as my lover. Rachel-qua-daughter and Rachel-qua-lover are contiguous—if not altogether overlapping—selves in her. As a result, any sites

---

[1] 'Predate' was the word Matt used in the diner, but it strikes me as uncomfortably loaded, and I prefer 'precede.' After the outbreak, it's impossible to ignore the double meaning of 'predate,' its twinned temporal and carnivorous connotations. For what predates undeath in you (the past that becomes activated, your prior self's muscle memories and habits and haunts) is what predates in undeath (preys, hunts, feeds, and so on upon).

deriving from the daughterly period of her life might still qualify as *our* sites. That's why I wouldn't feel rejected by the presence of the hospital on her list.

Whereas if she lists other sites, from memories she's *never* shared with me, I'm not sure how I'd feel. There must be millions of moments in Rachel's past that have yet to come up in conversation, entire years of biographical material and life experience that have gone unmentioned, not because she's forgotten about them, or because she's hiding them from me, but simply because there's never been a real occasion to bring them up. Yet some of these incidental memories might nevertheless be fondly nostalgic, qualifying as destinations for her in undeath. These are the kinds of sites that could be lurking on her list right now. As soon as Rachel reveals them to me, I'll be duty-bound (should she ever reanimate) to go searching for her there. Like Matt, I find this prospect slightly disquieting. This idea that the version of the person I'll be looking for won't be the version I've personally known... that I'll have to search for Rachel in buildings and neighborhoods unfamiliar to me, concealed from me, hidden on the dark side of her memory's moon.

If she were just returning to a tree house or childhood idyll that she'd never thought to tell me about, or a gymnasium where, a decade ago, she practiced some sport I didn't know she played, I might not mind so much having to find her there. But what if the site she returns to is the bedroom of a high-school sweetheart, a guy she dated even longer than she's been dating me, and whose memory—despite her having never mentioned it—she's apparently been cherishing the entire time we've been living together? Imagine if he were the secret love of her life, whose loss she's never recovered from. What if she self-identifies more deeply as this other guy's lover than as mine?[1]

---

[1] I'll bet Joyce could write a good short story about this titled 'The Undead,' in which an oblivious and self-satisfied husband goes in search

What if his bedroom is on her list right now, one of the ten extra entries from her promiscuous memory? What if he is her paramour from the past tense, cuckolding me from her unconscious, such that her body will break up with me in undeath, leaving our apartment for *him*? Am I supposed to just stand vigil outside his bedroom, waiting for my moonstruck undead lover to shuffle back? But it wouldn't even be 'my' lover who was shuffling there! The Rachel *I'm* dating, the 'you' I mean when I tell her 'I love you,' the self she's constructed as a backdrop for me to project my love on, has never so much as mentioned this adolescent passion. Its memory isn't included in the version of her I love. His name has never even come up in conversation between us. Where I'm concerned, she never dated the guy. So if Rachel returns to him when reanimated, it means that undeath has set her clock back: not *my* Rachel, but some decade-ago Rachel, a high-school Rachel, a beta Rachel[1] who is *this* guy's lover and (more to the point) this guy's responsibility. If, in undeath, it's Michael Furey whom her unconscious is oriented toward, then let Michael Furey go looking for her, is what I'm tempted to say, when I think about it.

But before I can say anything, Rachel clears her throat, preparing to read from her list. And in the moment before she begins, I realize how dangerous I've allowed my anxiety to become. I'm investing entirely too much emotion into these sites. For if I

---

of his reanimated wife, visiting all the landmarks of their courtship in Dublin... only to suffer a rude surprise when he finds her ghoulish body back in Galway, standing on the street where decades ago a young suitor, Michael Furey, had serenaded her.

[1] The way that a crashed Word document will restore, not the state of its data the moment it crashed, but the state of its data from whenever it last auto-recovered, a minute or an hour or a day ago. The reanimated Rachel would then be like a first-draft Rachel, auto-recovered from way back, preserving none of the sentences leading up to the crash. All the words I've left in her would be lost.

would be heartbroken to find Rachel at Michael Furey's, how might I feel to find her on the campus lawn? To see her kneeling in the grass, as if in search of the little leaf? Surely I would be overcome with love for her all over again. And in that case, who knows what I would do? I might even make the fatal mistake of hugging her. Nor is there any doubt that Rachel—if she were to find *me* there—would be doomed: that joyous context would prime her to see me as alive. Clearly neither of us is prepared to encounter the other in undeath, not psychologically, not emotionally. Soon, I decide. It will have to be soon. We'll have to do the defamiliarization exercises.

Rachel looks up at me now, with a conspiratorial grin. As she starts to read from her list, I lean over and see that she's beginning from the top, with the very first site she wrote down today: 'The campus lawn,' she says.

WEDNESDAY

WHEN MATT AND I ARRIVE AT MR. MAZOCH'S THIS morning, the front of the house is damaged. There's a beige dent of chipped wood in the door, and two of the windows have been shattered. It appears as if someone tried—and failed—to get inside. Looking at the gaping holes in the windowpanes, the jutting stalagmites of jagged glass, I'm too shocked at first to know how to react. Matt's reaction is unequivocal. 'Shit,' he whistles. 'Do you believe that?' When he turns to me, his face is expressionless. 'He came back.'

As a matter of fact, I do not believe it. Matt is already unbuckling his seatbelt to go inside. But before he can leave I ask him who he thinks 'he' is, exactly. 'I don't know,' he admits. 'I don't want to jump to conclusions. But why *couldn't* it have been him?' I bite my tongue. 'You're not going into the house again?' I ask him. 'For the third day in a row?' 'Mike,' he says. I study the windows, still unsure what to make of them. They don't seem low enough for an infected to crawl through. And they're too haphazardly shattered—their panes still too intact—to have admitted a human body. Matt shakes his head. 'The house has been vandalized,' he says.

Though I do not go so far as to accuse Mazoch of break-ing those windows himself (of coming here last night, bat in hand, and swinging into them as he did at the antiques mall, then denting the door for good measure), the possibility has not escaped my notice. Even if Mr. Mazoch would ever dam-age his own property like this, his sense of timing really does strain credulity. After I've dismissed the other 'traces'?[1] Two days

---

[1] Suddenly it occurs to me—*I'm certain of it*—that Matt planted the other

before the deadline? I do not say this to Matt's face, of course. I simply ask him to walk me through his logic. 'Tell me why,' I tell him. 'Why the systematic destruction of property? Why march up and down the front of the house, punching holes in windowpanes, instead of just breaking in through a single entrance? That's not how they behave.'

This is actually a question I've devoted a considerable amount of thought to, even before this morning. If we were to ever find Mr. Mazoch here—I have often asked myself—what might he be doing? How would he be behaving? I have pictured him in countless scenarios: fumbling with the knob of his locked front door; dragging a rake behind him in the driveway; standing in the yard with a plunger, pumping dumbly at the grass. But never punching his own windows. And in fact, the more that I try to imagine it, the more difficult it is. He would *remember* that this was his house. Before he could shatter his window, some memory in the hand would stay his hand. The recognition would be as much a matter of muscle memory as of reasoning, engrained as deeply in his hand as in his head. Only if he saw fresh meat beyond the windowpane, some victim on the other side, would his instinct to feed override his hand.

That is one of the few aspects of undeath that I feel certain about. In addition to their homing instinct, it is clear to me that they have something like equipment memory, a residue of know-how in their hands. Every night I watch them on the news, operating tools from their mortal lives: pushing a shopping cart down a grocery-store aisle, lamely striking at a tree with a hammer. Their faces are vacant, and it's evident that they don't quite

---

traces as well. If he's willing to shatter these windows, then why not the rear door's fanlight? And why not hike into Highland Road Park last weekend, leaving a scrap of plaid for us to find? But then—just as suddenly and certainly—I reject the idea.

know what they're doing. But the hand knows: it is seeking a handle, gripping at instruments from its former life. The hand remembers what the head does not.[1] Whenever I see an infected swinging a hammer, I am convinced that some memory of carpentry is compelling it to: the feel of polished wood, a familiar heft in the palm, a range of motion—at least this (and who can say what else?) persists in the hand.[2] Even if an infected cannot

---

[1] Taken to its limit—I have often reflected—this kind of muscle memory would persist even in Frankenstein's monster, whose undead body comprises not just one memory system, but dozens. After all, Dr. Frankenstein quilted the monster together from the segments of various corpses, and there is no reason to believe that these disembodied appendages (sewn onto the monster and there reanimated) would behave any differently from our own undead. The muscle memory of his right hand, harvested from one German peasant (a carpenter), would differ from the muscle memory of his left one, harvested from another (a farmer): whereas the one hand might reach for a hammer, the other might reach for a pitchfork. As with the undead, this equipmental knowledge would remain unconscious for the monster, who literally 'lets not his right hand know what his left hand doeth.' In this way, the borders of his know-how would be strictly delineated by stitchwork, making his body a map of gerrymandered memories: the left hand would be zoned off, county of the know-how of baling hay; and the right hand zoned off, county of the know-how of swinging the hammer; the right foot zoned off, county of the know-how of punting; and so on.

[2] Here my model is Martin Heidegger, a philosopher who located both epistemology and ontology in the hands. In his account, the know-how of a hand handling its equipment, the 'ready-to-hand' knowledge of a hand, is the most immediate way that man (what Heidegger calls 'Dasein,' literally 'Being There') has of understanding objects. The more that a hand uses a hammer, the more that it unveils the true 'hammer-being' of the hammer. And granting that this epistemology of the hand doubles as an ontology of the hand—that is, an account of how hands go about being in the world or otherwise constituting the Being of that world—such ready-to-hand knowledge is naturally fraught with existential significance. Whenever Dasein uses the hammer, he relates not just to the hammer but

see, or is seeing into some other world, its body still goes about its business in *this* world. The hand maneuvers the shopping cart around obstacles, it hits its target with the hammer. It is operating purely by memory.[1]

---

to everything: the nails in his desk drawer, the desk, the chair at the desk, the room itself, with its walls and windows and doors, the hallway outside and the house, continually spiraling outward, ad infinitum, until the hammer has formed a total world. Being-in-the-world means being caught up in just such a network of equipmental relations, which Dasein is enmeshed in anytime he grabs a tool. For Heidegger, to hold something is both to know and to be. In the case of our undead, the ramifications of this chiral ontology are clear. If an infected breaks into its old bedroom, and its hand roots under the bed for the hammer that it 'knows' is there, then doesn't the infected also 'know' the equipmental totality of the mattress, bed, room, and house, that is, the entire Being-in-the-World of its quondam Dasein, which is to say, couldn't the infected be, in some qualified way, precisely *the same* Dasein? And in the case of Frankenstein's monster, these ontological ramifications multiply mind-bogglingly across all of his limbs. Because each hand wants to root for a different tool from a different life, and because each foot wants to walk toward a different home—because the monster has to coordinate all of his limbs independently, just to stumble forward and turn a doorknob—it's as if his entire body were a gangline of Daseins, pulling the musher of his madman's brain.

[1] Here my model is, not Heidegger, but Viktor Shklovsky, the Russian critic who writes about habituated memory in his essay 'Art as Device.' He refers to the phenomenon as 'automatized perception.' Humans can perform one task so often, he writes, so unconsciously, that we gradually cease to see what we're doing: 'The object fades away... We know it's there but we do not see it.' Shklovsky compares this state of unawareness to death, and quotes from the diaries of Leo Tolstoy, who reports having been habit-blinded one afternoon while dusting his room: when he came to his sofa, Tolstoy writes, he couldn't remember ('for the life' of him) whether he had already dusted it or not, so unconsciously had he been sleepwalking throughout the space. It was exactly like being dead. After quoting this passage, Shklovsky delivers his famous motto, which does not fail to raise the hackles on my arms whenever I remember it now: '[L]ife fades into nothingness,' he writes. 'Automatization eats away at things, at

That is one of the questions I have to ask myself, when I ask myself what it would be like to be undead. Not only what and whether I would see; not only which sites my body would return to… but also what my hands would do. How they would behave. Coursing through them—filling them to the tips of their fingers, like the faucet water that engorges a latex glove—must be all the habits and motions that they serve as the phenomenological repositories of. They could never really cease being *my* hands. I try to picture them on my undead body, compelling it to perform some echt gesture from my mortal life: cradling Rachel's face; massaging my eyeballs; buttering toast. They would do whatever I'd done with them—whatever I'd taught them to—beforehand. They would *be* before-hands. And so they would never adopt new habits, in undeath. They would not try to play the piano, for instance, or to casually vandalize my apartment. Even if they did things that I never did with them (like tear into another person's flesh), they would do them somewhat in my *manner*: ripping into the meat in the same way that, at barbeques, they used to rip into ribs.

It's one of the few aspects of undeath I'm certain of.

I do not say all of this to Matt. I tell him, in short, that Mr. Mazoch could not be responsible for these windows: that this was not the handiwork of his hand.

But Matt has theories of his own. He shakes his head throughout my speech, and once I'm finished, he asks: 'Why *wouldn't* an infected break some windows? That's all you see them doing on the news. Beating on windows, punching through walls. They hate the inside.'

Matt has expatiated before on the exteriority of the undead, their compulsive nomadism and aversion to shelter. Unlike

---

clothes, at furniture, at our wives.' For yes, that is exactly how it is with our undead: they do not see us, but they know we're here. They push their shopping carts, pick up dusters, eat our wives.

ghosts, he has often observed, the undead do not linger in a single space. They're too itinerant for that, wandering restlessly between a whole chain of spaces. That is usually what he means by 'They hate the inside': that they are exterior creatures, the opposite of ghosts.[1] But today is the first time that he's ever

---

[1] Matt is actually quite insistent on this point. I learned this for myself one morning several weeks ago, when we drove past a field and I made the mistake of referring to the stray infected there (five distant silhouettes, standing perfectly still in the morning fog, pale and spectral in what must have been white nightgowns) as 'ghostly.' 'No,' Matt corrected me, with a vehemence I found surprising, 'they're not like ghosts at all.' He spent the rest of the morning in lecture mode, elucidating all of the irreducible differences between the undead and specters. For one thing, he said, you would never see ghosts just standing out in a field like that, beneath a bare sky in broad daylight. They are fundamentally interior creatures. Once a spirit returns to haunt a house, there's this sense in which it's bound to the premises, almost by a spatial loyalty, a sedentary fidelity to place. It's the undead who are free (or rather, compelled) to roam about. That's the difference. You can tell the infected apart from ghosts not by the corporeality of one, or the insubstantiality of the other, but by their relation to space, he claimed. At the time, Matt's spatial distinction reminded me strongly of Mr. Mazoch. For his life, too, had had two distinct relations to space: before his heart attack, he had been a veritable man about town, driving from job to job and moving from house to house; whereas afterward, he mostly stayed inside, becoming an eremite in retirement, the final years of which he spent (by Matt's account) with the agoraphobic unimaginativeness of a ghost. Ever since then I've wondered whether this is the true subtext of Matt's ghost/ghoul dichotomy, the reason he was so vehement about maintaining it: that if the undead aren't ghosts, then neither is his father. In undeath, Mr. Mazoch can be the opposite of a ghost, and, to the degree that he had led a ghostly life, he can be the opposite of himself. Freed from the physical restraints that had anchored him so long in Denham, Mr. Mazoch (or his body) would be at liberty to wander wherever it wanted, shuffling for indefatigable miles all over Baton Rouge. Quickened, at last, after five years of ghostlike motionlessness. (According to this view of things, Mr. Mazoch must have just split the difference when he died: he must have divided up his kingdom of infinite space, with

adduced this so-called spatial hatred as an explanation for their destructiveness. When he says this I look again at Mr. Mazoch's house, trying to see the thing from Matt's point of view. Is this what he thinks 'hating the inside' would entail? That it wouldn't be enough for Mr. Mazoch to simply be outside all the time, wandering from site to site? That he would also have to destroy his house, shattering his own windows? 'You can't really believe that,' I tell him. But Matt refuses to back down. Not only does he believe it, he says, but, 'I have always believed it.' He has *always* noticed this about the undead hand: how it has a wrecking ball's abhorrence of interiority. How anytime it encounters a wall, a door, it just pounds automatically, beating without rest to bestow openness. Whenever he watches the nightly news, he says, and sees an undead hand bursting through a boarded-up window, grasping at air, he imagines that it hates the inside: that what it is grasping for is more boards, another layer to destroy.[1]

---

his undead corpse taking the outside [banished to Mr. Mazoch's mortal paths], and his ghost taking the inside [unable to exit its house in Denham, where even now it might be trapped, pacing translucently from room to room]. This is assuming, of course, that Mr. Mazoch would get both, both a reanimated corpse *and* a ghost. You'd have to say that he was cleaved in twain, leaving both a spiritual remainder and a bodily remainder, and that these opposite supernatural energies, diverging from his death, went haunting in different directions: the one inside, the other out. It makes rigorous, dualist sense. [I can't help wondering, though, what would happen if the undead corpse and the specter of Mr. Mazoch ever met each other. I imagine the mutual shock, the dropped monocles: 'My good sir, *I* am Mr. Mazoch.' 'But I'm afraid that's quite impossible—for you see, *I* am Mr. Mazoch.'])

[1] I have seen these images on the nightly news as nightly as he has. But it has never occurred to me to associate them with demolition, structural destructiveness, an anti-interiority or spatial hatred. I've always associated them instead with parturition: my mind juxtaposes the image of the undead hand, grasping through the broken window, with that of the obstetrician's hand, groping in the womb for a baby's ankle. Never in so

And whenever he sees, on the nightly news, a group of undead hunched around their victim's stomach (prying open the rib cage to pick through the intestines, not even feeding, just as if for the joy of it), he imagines that they are destroying the architecture of the body: the abdominal wall, the posterior, anterior, lateral walls. 'Something there is that doesn't love a wall,' he quotes for me now, as if citing Frost as an authority. 'That wants it down.'

'All right,' I say. It doesn't matter, at this point, whether Matt even believes what he's saying: he's hell-bent on inspecting the house. 'I get it. You need to go inside.' 'I'll just be a minute,' he says, climbing out of the car. Before he can leave for good, I call after him. He bends back down in the open doorway, resting his hands on the roof to look in at me. 'Promise me this at least,' I say. 'Today's the last time. Tomorrow and Friday—we play it safe.' He nods ambiguously, then rises and swings the car door shut. After I watch him disappear into the house, I wait for what seems like much more than a minute—five minutes, ten—before I finally stop counting.

While he's been inside, I've had ample time to think over everything he said. And no matter how I look at it, it leaves me feeling queasy and suspicious. For one thing, I find it worrisome that he keeps defining undeath in opposition to his father: unlike the mortal Mr. Mazoch, who remained indoors like a ghost, the undead are driven to roam about; and unlike the plumber Mr. Mazoch, who helped construct buildings for a living, the undead are supposedly destructive. He seems determined to disambiguate his father's reanimated body from his father: it is not only not his father, but the *opposite* of his father. And why would Matt

_____

many words do I complete this analogy, never consciously, but as a matter of tone and mood, connotation and texture, as a kind of nightmare inversion or necrotic mirror, what the hand always seems subliminally to be doing is birthing people. Reaching into the house as into a womb, to drag out the inhabitants feet-first: not into life, but into undeath.

need to believe that, unless he was planning to kill it? Unless he was planning to put it—if not out of its misery—then at least out of its antonymy?

I have been trying to push these thoughts out of my mind. I would like to give Matt the benefit of the doubt. I would like to believe what he wants me to believe about the windows: that he did not break them; that he truly believes Mr. Mazoch broke them; and that he might be right. To believe this, I have to believe that Mr. Mazoch punched those panes, either out of muscle memory (my own reading), or 'spatial hatred' (as Mazoch says), or for some other reason altogether.[1] But the more I try to imagine it, the more difficult it becomes, and what I end up

---

[1] One possibility I have been considering is the numb tingling of undeath, that asleep-limb feeling that I assume all reanimated bodies experience. If that is what it is like to be undead, then this might provide one explanation for why they thrash around so compulsively. Because imagine how fidgety it would have to make you: to feel smothered in this way—your whole body—as claustral and cramped as being buried alive. The moment you reanimated, your skin would be washed in that haptic static, compacted by it: surrounded by itching as by earth. And no matter where you wandered, you would still feel suffocated and underground, even when standing in an open field (even those peaceful corpses I saw in the pasture, in their white nightgowns, might have been feeling this way: they might have just been carrying their caskets with them, a virtual box around their bodies, like an aura, or a snail shell). Maybe it is only by punching in windows or beating down doors, only by clawing at barricades or tearing through stomachs— only by ceaselessly reenacting the breaching of the coffin lid—that they can achieve any kind of peace. Maybe bursting through surfaces is just a form of burrowing therapy, a way of digging their way up out of the buried-alive feeling. As if to be undead is to be coated in this restive, meta-physical taphephobia, an unyielding feeling of being crushed by space. And so maybe *that* is a reason that Mr. Mazoch might have walked from window to window last night, punching the panes. He could have been rooting his hand into interiorities for the relief. Groping for moments of rupture, of puncture, the way that a sleeper's hand will keep seeking out new cool parts beneath a pillow. It certainly seems unlikely, though.

imagining instead is Matt: planting his feet apart at each window, cocking the bat at his shoulder, swinging his tremendous arcs. Anything to convince me that 'he' came back. To keep the search going.

A month ago, when we first established the deadline, Matt made me promise him that I would enforce it. 'Don't let me get desperate,' he told me. 'Don't let me go a day beyond the deadline.' If he ever suggests an extension, we agreed, I am supposed to remind him why we settled on one month in the first place: not only because hurricane season will be beginning in earnest in August, but also because four weeks is the maximum amount of time we thought that anyone could spend looking for his— for a missing person. If all else fails, Matt told me, I'm simply supposed to abandon ship. To inform him that my month is up, and that while he doesn't have to quit, he'll be carrying on alone.

At this thought, the car doors' locks thump upward, on signal from Matt's remote key fob, and I look through the windshield with a jolt. He is standing in the front doorway, holding up some kind of trace for me to see. A red piece of paper, like a crimson color swatch. It looks like a Netflix envelope, at this distance.

MATT AND I ARE STANDING ON THE ROOFTOP OF Citiplace Cinemas, surveying the empty parking lots below us. The only thing down there is Matt's car, parked parallel to the boarded-up tickets window. The theater itself has long been abandoned, as have all the other businesses in the shopping center: the Barnes and Noble shut down and the Marble Slab shut down, the baby boutique, the deli, the Federal Express shut down. These buildings are gathered across the parking lot, arrayed side by side to form a village of beige plaster, and the theater looms over them like a kind of castle. When we first got here, I narrowly talked Matt out of breaking into the multiplex, in order to inspect its eleven empty screening rooms. As a compromise, he talked me into climbing up the safety ladder out back. From the roof, he said, we would be able to see for hundreds of yards in every direction. For hundreds of yards there is nothing to see.

Matt stands on the opposite edge from me, commanding a lateral view of the Barnes and Noble. I'm supposed to be keeping an eye on the plaza's entrance, which I watched through the binoculars awhile. The traffic lights there were still blinking green, then amber, then red, even though the plaza's intersections have all been barren for weeks.[1] Now I'm training the

---

[1] What I was watching were the pedestrian signals, those boxes attached halfway up the traffic poles. I was especially transfixed by the 'Walk' signal, a bright-white profile of a man mid-stride. To the naked eye, the man is just an anthropomorphic white smear. But when magnified by binoculars, he's revealed to be composed of numerous miniature lightbulbs, a dozen or so individual pearls of whiteness. Seen up close, these lend the silhouette a bumpy, knobbly texture, which makes it seem, not like a man, but

binoculars on Matt. I study the back of his head as he studies the parking lot, waiting for him to turn around and call it quits. He hasn't so much as stretched his neck. He is keeping a stiff and steadfast vigil for Mr. Mazoch.

On the drive over from Denham, he explained the significance of Citiplace to him and his father. It was the Netflix envelope, he said—for indeed it was a Netflix envelope, spotted in a trash pile on the carpet—that finally reminded him of the site. He was an idiot not to have thought of it before, he confessed: we should have been staking it out every day. He spoke for the duration of the ride, breathlessly briefing me on his history with the building. He and his father had always bonded here before the heart attack. They caught a film more or less monthly once Matt went off to college, when Mr. Mazoch fell into the habit, if he hadn't seen his son in a few weeks, of calling him on a Sunday and asking (this was the code they'd developed) whether there were any good movies playing. There rarely were. But the movies were only a pretext, Matt said, and he didn't mind opening the listings and picking a title at random. Superhero films, the stateside remakes of Japanese ghost movies, heist flicks. They always arrived in the early afternoon, sat always in the back row, and were almost always the only audience members there, alone in the bargain darkness of the matinee theater. Mr.

---

like a berry of light: his head especially (an aggregate of glowing bulbs, all syncarpous and starlit, a perfect oval of refulgent drupelets) looks like the kind of berry that would grow in outer space, on a star bush or something. At first I found this mesmerizing. But the longer I stared at him, the more each bulb just reminded me of an undead eye. It was as if his entire body were ocellated with white eyeballs, the way Rachel's body had been by the owls. As if every inch of his skin could see me. I almost had to turn away. But soon enough the 'Walk' man faded, and the signal box went black. Then there rose in his absence the rusty 'Yield' hand, flat and orange and still, like the bloody palm prints that the infected leave, slapping at the door to get inside. That was what *did* make me turn away.

Mazoch paid. He liked to pay in cash, Matt said, and a memory he didn't expect to have of his father—but which he says has persisted in him with startling vividness—is of the man standing outside the theater's ticket booth at noon: squinting in the harsh, concrete-refracted sunlight, wedging a meaty hand down into his jeans pocket for a wad of wrinkled twenty-dollar bills. After the movie let out Mr. Mazoch typically suggested that they go to the Barnes and Noble across the plaza, where he would entertain himself among the thick antiques guidebooks shelved on the second floor,[1] while Matt, over in the literature section,

---

[1] Fat, flimsy paperbacks, Matt described these guidebooks as, almost like telephone directories, except filled with low-quality, black-and-white photos of esoteric objects, complete with detailed descriptions of their provenance and up-to-date price listings. Mr. Mazoch had to consult these whenever he bought something at a garage sale without knowing exactly what it was, and so without knowing what price to put on it in his booth at the antiques mall. I asked Matt for an example. A buff-colored stuffed lion with a Steiff logo on its paw, for example, which Mr. Mazoch paid twenty dollars for at an auction and didn't look up in a guidebook until later, where it was listed at several hundred. Or the strange vehicle he found at an old farm's estate sale, a rusted-over, steel-frame cage on wheels, with a rotted leather seat and two pump-action wooden handles, which looked like something out of *Mad Max*, but which turned out to be a 19th-century hand-and-foot recumbent tricycle, for women in gowns to get around in, and which Mr. Mazoch paid seventy-five dollars for and later sold for several hundred. (The profits of these items aren't incidental to their narratives. It has emerged in Matt's stories about his father that Mr. Mazoch really did see himself as a swashbuckling arbitrageur of antiques. The thrill of the game was to root out potential diamonds in the rough, paying twenty-five cents for a porcelain bowl in one market [the flea market] and trying to sell it for twenty-five dollars in another [the antiques mall]. So as interested as he was in the strange histories of his collection, and as engaging as he found researching odd facts about them [e.g., that Steiff was the company that invented the teddy bear, and hence the progenitor of innumerable stuffed collectibles], the invariable punch line of any antiques anecdote he told Matt was just what he paid for an item and for

skimmed through a novel or collected poems or volume of criticism (which Mr. Mazoch, if he saw Matt holding on to it when they were getting ready to leave, would gently grab from him like a restaurant check, and pay for at the register himself). To conclude the afternoon Mr. Mazoch treated Matt to coffee and bagels in the bookstore's café, which is where most of the actual 'bonding' took place: Matt asking his father whether he'd come across any good finds at garage sales lately, Mr. Mazoch asking his son how his schoolwork, weightlifting, and love life were going. The coffee, the caffeinated conversation, was the real point of their day together. But when Mr. Mazoch called on the weekends, he never asked, 'Wanna grab some coffee?' He always asked, 'Any good movies playing?'

This changed after the heart attack. It's not that they stopped going to films altogether, but that the ritualistic dimension of the afternoons, the self-consciousness of the bonding, grew to be morbid, and oppressive, and distracting for Matt. He was no longer just spending an afternoon with his father at the movies. Privately, in back of his thoughts, he was always spending *what might be their last afternoon together at the movies.* So if they were to watch *The Ring* together one Sunday, and if Mr. Mazoch were to suffer a fatal second heart attack the following week, *The Ring* would go down forever in Matt's memory as the last movie he saw with his father. Their last conversation together would have been about the haunted videotape in *The Ring.* One of Matt's last images of his father's face would have been of its being bathed in the projector light of *The Ring*: Ring light gleaming in his father's eyes, Ring light tinting the gray threads of his shaggy

---

just how much he sold it. The way that a fisherman ends any story with the size of the fish. 'Bought that lion for twenty dollahs,' he'd always conclude, Matt said. 'Sold it for *three hundred.*' [Whenever Matt is impersonating or doing dialogue for his father, he unconsciously pronounces 'dollah' the Louisiana way, presumably Mr. Mazoch's way. Matt himself pronounces it 'dollar.'])

hair. These were the thoughts that Matt was having, these were the things that he was thinking, in that delicate time, he told me. He had no way of knowing then that Mr. Mazoch would live several healthy years beyond the anniversary of his bypass, nor that what would eventually do him in would be, not another heart attack, but—*literally* no way of knowing this—the walking dead. For the first year after the operation, Matt couldn't take it for granted from week to week that his father was still alive. In the shower he wondered, *Even now, is my father dying?* And if at an odd hour he felt his cell phone vibrating against his thigh, that nightmarish ice-water feeling would immediately flood his chest, for he was convinced he was being notified of his father's death.

They did try going to the movies. They went to *The Ring*, in fact. But instead of watching the film with his father, Matt watched himself watching the film with his father, trying to carefully stage and frame the mise en scéne of this memory, in case it was his last. He described this watching-himself-watching sensation almost as an out-of-body experience: as if his imagination, detached and astrally projected toward the ceiling of the theater, were looking down on him and his father in their theater seats, filming the memory from an external vantage point. Even as he was 'in' the moment with his father, Matt was seeing how he would one day remember the moment with his father. So in a sense he wasn't in the present moment at all, but already far in the future, viewing the edited-together memory of that moment. It was as if he had managed to transport himself, by an act of self-conscious prolepsis, years ahead of time, skipping beyond his father's actual death, to the point decades hence when, reminiscing, he would be able to look back fondly on the afternoon that he was even then looking forward from. He could not help seeing his father—who was sitting and breathing right there next to him—through the filter of the future tense, seeing him the way that he would remember him once he was dead. It reminded him, he said, of the experience of visiting a landmark that's been scheduled to be destroyed, or of touring a monument in a city you know you'll never revisit: the logic of your self-consciousness petrifies those buildings as already-vanished, already-ruins, already-lost, even as you're inside them, such that you can never really *see* them in any present-tense kind of way. Your experience of them becomes mediated by the memory of them that you're anticipating. This was how his experience of Mr. Mazoch felt mediated, those last afternoons at Citiplace, Matt said. He felt like a tourist to his father's presence, a sightseer of the monument of his mortality. Which just wasn't a way he wanted to relate to his father at all.

So they stopped going to Citiplace. At this point I had to interrupt Matt to ask: *did* he remember the last movie they saw together? *Solaris*, he said, the Hollywood remake of Tarkovsky's classic, directed by Baton Rouge's own Steven Soderbergh.

After *Solaris*, Matt declared a tacit moratorium on going to the movies. It was simply too charged an activity. The solution that most pleased him was this: since getting coffee together had less baggage as a tradition (since Matt wouldn't ask himself at a café, 'Is this the last time I'm going to have coffee with my father?', or, 'What if my last memory of my father's face is of him stuffing it with a poppyseed bagel?'), Mr. Mazoch started inviting Matt, not to the movies, but to grab a coffee, which monthly they would catch up with each other over a couple mugs of, not at the old Barnes and Noble in-store Starbucks by Citiplace, but at Louie's, a considerably less cathected café. And since Matt still wanted to be able to talk about films with his father, and to have movies (if not movie theaters) continue to play some part in their relationship, he gave Mr. Mazoch, that first Christmas after his operation, a subscription to Netflix. So if they stopped *seeing* movies together, still they didn't stop discussing them. Over coffee Matt would ask Mr. Mazoch about the films he'd rented recently, and Mr. Mazoch would ask Matt which films he should rent next. Matt would recommend the movies that meant the most to him (the three-hour Swedish chamber dramas and the whimsical Italian metafictions, the jagged-shadowed German silents and the melancholic French heist films), and for their subsequent meeting Mr. Mazoch would come prepared with capsule reviews: what thrilled him, what bored him, what he felt he didn't understand. What shot or image or line of dialogue he hadn't been able to get out of his head all week. 'What was his favorite?' I interrupted a second time to ask. *Solaris*, Matt said again. 'Really?' I said. '*Solaris*?'[1] Matt nodded, not taking his eyes off the road. He said that Mr. Mazoch had rented Tarkovsky's

---

[1] The incredulity in my voice had nothing to do with *Solaris* itself, which I think is a fine candidate for a favorite movie. But I was struck by the uncanny symmetry: that their relationship should be bookended by the same movie, and that it should be *this* movie, essentially an allegory for undeath. In it, a group of cosmonauts on a space station orbit the titular planet, to study its odd telepathic properties. Solaris, which can somehow materialize their memories, has begun incarnating doubles or doppelgangers of people from their pasts. Appearing aboard the space station out of thin air, these 'visitors'—as the cosmonauts call them—haunt them just like ghosts. But they behave in a way creepily prescient of our own undead. For one thing, they reanimate: if a visitor dies, its prone body will eventually undergo a resurrection on the floor, twitching grotesquely back to life. For another thing, the visitors are creatures of memory and habit, mimicking their models back on Earth. Yet as Matt was describing his history with *Solaris* to me, I couldn't tell whether he was alert to these parallels himself. Nor was it clear to me whether *he* had seen Tarkovsky's version, which I was reluctant to actually ask him about. For the original *Solaris* ends with the protagonist's decision not to return to Earth (where in reality his father has died) but instead to descend to Solaris, where he can submerge himself in the memories that it generates: when last we see him, he is entering the simulacral projection of his childhood home, reunited with the Solaric incarnation of his (un)dead father. It would seem that Matt—whether he has seen this movie or not; whether he remembers this ending or not—is subconsciously reenacting its ending every morning, when he breaks into his dad's house in Denham. Hence my reluctance to discuss it with him. (Soderbergh's version has a different ending, but

version out of curiosity, because he recognized the title and remembered having seen the remake with Matt. And he evidently loved the film enough that he kept on renting it, having Netflix mail him the DVD once every few months, so that he could rewatch it whenever the mood struck. In fact, that was the DVD that Matt found this morning: a copy of *Solaris* had been slipped inside its red Netflix envelope and discarded on the carpet. It was likely the last movie Mr. Mazoch had watched in mortal life. He had probably been intending to mail it back the very day he got bitten. So the movie that would have been foremost in his mind after reanimating, Matt said, was *Solaris*.

He said this just as we were arriving at Citiplace, and there could have been no more staggering an anticlimax to Matt's narrative (after that final detail about the *Solaris* DVD, whose red envelope at the scene of Mr. Mazoch's death was meant to seal Matt's entire argument) than pulling into the whitish salt flats of these vast and vacant parking lots, where you could see, almost at a glance, that the place was utterly deserted. If Mr. Mazoch had been anywhere on the premises—a dark figure marring any inch of that white field—he would have stood out as stark and alien as a man in an Antonioni landscape. But it was clear he wasn't here. No one was. And as Matt circled the theater in the car, then began insisting that we break inside, it became clear to me that Matt felt betrayed by his absence.

I don't think Matt was deluding himself about the theater, necessarily. I can see how a site like Citiplace, attended ritually enough over enough weekends, might function for this father and this son the way that a baseball stadium or campground would for others, and I can even see a case being made for Mr. Mazoch's reanimated corpse returning to it, out of habit if

---

the film is no less prescient about undeath. Assuming that Soderbergh has survived the epidemic, I wonder what he makes of his hometown now, haunted as it is by these visitors.)

nothing else, and for Matt's prudence in including it in our itinerary. But after watching Matt grow excited as we approached I-10's off-ramp, and seeing his disappointment now that we've arrived, I find it hard not to think of him as a man grasping at straws. He didn't just believe that Mr. Mazoch might have returned here: he needed to believe that we'd find him *today*, on our very first visit. None of the other sites are working out, so Matt is struggling to come up with new ones. After three and a half weeks with no trace of his father (unless you count the traces in Denham, which I am becoming more and more convinced—as I observe him from across the roof—that Matt himself manufactured), he must be starting to ask himself whether he has miscalculated. 'How well do I really know him?' he must be asking himself. 'Do I really know him at all?' Now that his sense of his father, of where he would return to, is faltering, Matt must be subjecting it to revision. If not Highland Road Park, then Citiplace. And if not Citiplace, then where?

The mistake Matt is making is the same one I made yesterday, when I grew anxious over Rachel's list (which did not, thankfully, include any Michael Fureys). Namely, Matt is treating the theater as a place that Mr. Mazoch would think of. If the theater meant something to both of them, Matt must be reasoning, and if it meant as much to Mr. Mazoch as it did to him, then Mr. Mazoch would 'think to come here.' That is why Matt grew so excited at the sight of the Netflix envelope, and why he kicked himself for not having thought to come here before. That's also why he must feel such anger and disappointment now, as though Mr. Mazoch had somehow let him down by letting Citiplace slip his mind. By forgetting—out of self-centeredness or indifference or neglect—this place that meant so much to his son.

But the problem with this reasoning is that Mr. Mazoch *couldn't* 'think to come here.' Matt hasn't miscalculated his father by failing to find him here, and Mr. Mazoch hasn't betrayed his son by failing to come. For it isn't Mr. Mazoch's mind that

Matt has to try to imagine his way into, or Mr. Mazoch's mind whose memories, impulses, and destinations Matt has to try to anticipate. It isn't even Mr. Mazoch, anymore, whom Matt is really looking for: it's Mr. Mazoch's undead body. That is the paradox: Matt has to think his way into the mind of a creature that may not have one. A creature of unknowable impulses, of ineffable instinct. Given that that's the case, it's no wonder that Matt's emotions are so confused. Because on the one hand, the undead behave *as if* they are consciously retrospective beings, returning to sites that 'meant something' to them in their mortal lives. Yet on the other hand, it is *as if* they are blank automata, shuffling to these landmarks absently, merely carrying out a program, like robots of remembering. On the one hand, they are creatures of pure memory: they return only to sites from their past, and can find their way back to neighborhoods buried far in their childhoods. But on yet another hand (and this is turning out to be a real Shiva of dialectical reasoning), they are creatures of pure forgetfulness: the sites they return to, so potent with mortal nostalgia, mean nothing to them, and they navigate them unconsciously, are as sleepwalkers there. What they are propelled by is a blind drive. They know they want to return to certain spaces, but they don't know why. They know the spaces are there, but they do not see them. In this way, they inhabit a radical in-between-ness: between total recall and total amnesia, total nostalgia and total obliviousness, between all remembering and all forgetting. And not only in between, but both at once, somehow. It is as if they recall the space (as a destination) at the exact same time as they forget it (as conscious content, as memory). So it is as if the undead are constantly being fed mnemonic madeleines, except that the tea the madeleines are steeped in is actually Lethe water: the crumbs of each memory come soggy with their own forgottenness, they are simultaneously remembering the place (qua destination) and forgetting it (qua memory) while they chew. Even as the site is recalled it dissolves, and what is left, in the undead, is something like an aftertaste of memory, a sudden and inexplicable craving for place. They know they want to go there—the house, the movie theater, the campus lawn—but they don't know why.

Staring at the back of Matt's head through the binoculars, I know that he knows all of this. Still, knowing it does not help, and I can only imagine what he is feeling right now. Something like the rejection I felt yesterday, when imagining Rachel's list; or else the rejection that I *would* feel (exponentially bitterer) if I failed to find her at the campus lawn. Whatever the scale of Matt's disappointment, I do know that he can't go on feeling this way. One month seems like enough for a lifetime. As if he can sense me staring at him, he turns around now, and I lower the binoculars. He has finally given up on the site, it looks like. His distant silhouette waves at me, and I wave back, and with that we begin to trudge across the rooftop toward one another.

We meet halfway, by the safety ladder, where Matt nods once in greeting before bending to grip the handlebars. 'Hey,' I say, and he pauses. 'Why don't we come back here tomorrow?' I ask. 'Or Friday?' His back straightens when I say this. Letting go of the ladder, he stands to face me, and in the moment before he speaks, I dread what he is about to say. 'About tomorrow,' he says. 'I think I need a break. Maybe decompress, do some reading. What if we take the day off?' I nod quickly in relief. 'Sure,' I say, 'no problem. We can always come back Friday.'

'About Friday,' he says, and I feel the dread return. 'I know we settled on that deadline. But we hadn't foreseen—' He looks away, searching for words. 'These are extenuating circumstances,' he continues. 'Someone's prowling my dad's property. What if they come back? I can't just abandon the place now. I need you there with me.' Why not give it one more week, he asks? What do I say?

'Matt,' I say. He doesn't respond, or even look at me. He has no doubt been preparing this speech the whole time we've been standing here, and now he is bracing himself for the speech that we both know I am supposed to have been preparing as well. How he's getting desperate. How we set the deadline for a reason. How I'll quit if he doesn't.

But I find that I cannot say this, any of it. At least not here, not yet. Not after all the disappointments of today, not with Matt meekly avoiding my eye, and not mere moments before he has to make his descent, braving the katabasis of the safety ladder, to climb down into that hellish, heartbreaking parking lot, where once again his deadbeat undead dad has jilted him. So instead I say, while shaking my head, 'Let me run it by Rachel.' Hopefully he will recognize this for the stalling tactic that it is, and will call it quits on his own. For now he nods, then turns without a word to clamber over the top rung. He keeps his head bent on the climb down, watching his feet and the emptiness of the parking lot beneath him, until he disappears beneath the rooftop's ledge. I give him a lead of five or six rungs before following him.

TONIGHT, AFTER MUCH STURM UND DRANG, I finally talk Rachel into practicing defamiliarization with me. Presently we're trying it out in the living room, sitting in meditative silence and locking eyes across the coffee table. Because the room is dim and the atmosphere one of intense concentration (and also because both pairs of our hands have come to rest pronated on the tabletop), anyone seeing this might mistake it for a séance. Which wouldn't be altogether inaccurate: we are indeed invoking a kind of dead. Each of us is invoking undeath in the face of the other.

'It's a hateful thing to do,' Rachel protested, when I first proposed the exercise to her. This was shortly after I got home. We had just finished discussing how my day went, and I had chosen—in the end—not to run the extension by her. In fact, I didn't run anything by her: neither the broken windows, nor Matt's suspicion that someone has been 'prowling' his father's property. I added these to my mental checklist of things to confess to her one day—when they will be too far past to worry her—as I summarized our trip to Citiplace. When I announced our surprise hiatus tomorrow, she smiled and clapped her hands: 'A holiday!' She would take the day off too, she said, from the shelter. But how should we celebrate tonight? It was here that I suggested—in what I thought was an offhand way—that we try another exercise like yesterday's. I opened our copy of *FIGHT THE BITE* to the defamiliarization chapter and handed it to her. Why not pass the evening practicing estrangement techniques?

Rachel had barely glanced at the first page before refusing, and I knew that it was the diagram that was distressing her. The illustration features a blank-faced man and a blank-faced woman[1] seated in profile, staring into each other's eyes, as if competing in a blinking contest. Between their pupils a single horizontal line extends, and crawling across this wire is a series of wriggles, such as a cartoonist might use to depict heat rising off of a road. But what each wriggle really resembles—in this context—is a graveyard worm, inching from one eye to the other. As the caption explains, the participants are projecting these wriggles to 'estrange' each other's faces. 'At least read the thing,' I said to Rachel. 'Give it that much of a shot.' She made a theatrical sigh and started reading.

Defamiliarization techniques were designed by psychologists

---

[1] Throughout every chapter in *FIGHT THE BITE*, the artists hew to the generic convention (observable in most safety manuals) of not conveying emotion in their subjects' faces. Like the passengers in aircraft manuals, who seem to suffer plane crashes apathetically, reaching for oxygen masks as calmly as for a ceiling light's dangle-chain, the characters in *FIGHT THE BITE* are curiously underwhelmed by the epidemic. By placing a strict taboo on representations of panic (or of any other human feeling), the safety manual effects a kind of iconoclasm of affect, portraying a world in which the imperiled meet death like stolid pod people. So whether characters are boarding up windows, being bitten, or bleeding to death, they each wear the same fixed facial expression: bored, prim-lipped, unblinking. What's fascinating about this generic convention in *FIGHT THE BITE* particularly is that the undead are portrayed with the same glazed faces. The expression is probably meant, in their case, to signify automatism, but it is in fact indistinguishable from the 'calmness' or 'equanimity' of the living. A curious result is that the transition from life to undeath in the pamphlet is artistically understated. Since the undead faces are equally affectless as the living ones, the only aspect that distinguishes them is their empty, white eyeballs; and since all that the reanimation sequences entail is the blanking of a victim's eyes (in three panels a man can be brutally bitten, collapse, then get up again without the expression on his face changing; in each stage identical except that, in the final panel, the artist enucleates his pupils), it is as if whited eyes are the only price to pay for undeath. As if that is the only toll for entry into the underworld: not two pennies on the eyelids, but two clouded contacts in the eyeballs.

early on in the outbreak, to prepare people for the shock of seeing their undead loved ones. The idea is that 'My wife!' is the exact last reaction anyone needs to be having when confronted with his reanimated wife. Better to react, 'My wife is not my wife,' or, 'My wife is undead,' or, best yet, 'That undead is not my wife.' Since reacting in this way requires disabling the parts of you that exclaim, 'My wife!' whenever you see your wife's face, you have to find some way of shutting down momentarily the complex of your facial-recognition software, in a kind of willed prosopagnosia. Only then can you forget the 'wife' in your wife's face. Then you can react to it as merely a stranger's face, as some indifferent 'this woman's' face, which (de-wifed, and thus far deracinated from all the marital and erotic symbolic orders in which it'd been ensconced) means as little to you as a face passed in the street. This is where the pamphlet's exercises come in. People can use them to practice not-recognizing each other while still alive, the better to damp down recognition when they see each other undead. Hence the blinking-contest diagram. If, like the man, you were to stare into your wife's face every night until it went weird, teaching yourself to say, 'My wife is not my wife' while looking at her (and not only that, but if you practiced doing this until you could actually estrange her face at will, as if toggling a defamiliarization filter on and off), then, when your wife *was* undead, and you found yourself being attacked by 'her' face, you could avoid making the fatal mistake of responding familiarly to it. The moment you saw it, you could simply flip on your inner estrangement switch. Then, drained of all recognizability, it would appear merely as some undead's face, as strange and primally frightening to you as one encountered in an alleyway at night, and you could respond to it (reflexively, unthinkingly) in the way that self-preservation demanded you respond to every undead face.[1]

---

[1] The dialectical point that goes unmade in FIGHT THE BITE (and

The chapter laid all of this out quite clearly. But even after Rachel had finished reading it, she still refused. It was a hateful thing to do, she insisted. 'I understand why you would say that,' I said. 'I do. But the thing about this "hateful thing"—the thing to really keep in mind right now—is that you may have to do it eventually. Whether you practice it with me tonight or not, in the future you may have no choice. Because when I come at you like that, and my face is pale and affectless and a bloody mess, the reaction that's going to save your life is, "That's not Michael."' 'That's not Michael,' she repeated. 'That's right. All I'm asking you to do is to look at me and say that's not me. Estrange me once, two times, while I'm still alive—train yourself to not recognize the me in my face—so that you won't be caught off guard when I'm undead.' 'If you're undead.' 'If I'm undead.' 'But you're not undead,' she said, 'not yet. And I don't want to have to pretend that you are, and "estrange" your face. You're my lover, I love your face. You *are* you.' 'Except that someday soon I might not be, Rachel. And there will be precious little difference between this face—' Here I let my face slacken, dropping my jaw and emptying my eyes of all liveliness. '—and the face that you see on that day.' 'Then I'll "estrange" it when the

---

which I myself neglected to make, in my argument with Rachel about it) is that this so-called estranged or defamiliarized way of seeing—in which you reduce familiar faces to indistinct blurs, drained of all memory and affect—is precisely how the undead 'see' by default. They always already see this way: they know we're here, but they do not see us. That is why they can so uniformly ignore *their* loved ones' faces, and why undead husbands can eat their wives. The dialectical point, then, is just this: that you have to briefly make yourself undead to avoid being made undead. Confronted with an undead face, you have to perceive it in the same way that it is perceiving you—to see as it sees and to that degree participate in its vision—in order to escape being bitten. That's one of the secret reasons I'm so fascinated by these exercises: it's as if I'm teaching myself to see as the undead see. As if—by estranging Rachel successfully—I could see her as the jogger was seeing me.

time comes. What do you want me to say?' 'You won't know how when the time comes. You won't have the slightest idea how to estrange my face when the time comes. You won't know because you'll never have practiced. It's no different from anything else. Imagine if this were CPR I wanted to practice, how absurd you'd sound. "But you're my lover, I love your lungs. Your lungs *are* functioning."' 'You're being ridiculous.' 'Tell me about it.' 'You're being ridiculous because there is a difference. Nothing changes if I pump on your chest, breathe into your mouth. And if you asked me to prod you away from me with a foam bat, or to lock the door on you and build a barricade against it as you pounded, I would do that too. Because it's just play. But it's not play for me to look at your face and dehumanize it, to will myself to see you as a stranger or a corpse. It's hateful. Everything changes then, and that's the difference. How could I get in bed with you tonight if all I was thinking was, "That's not Michael"? "Who is this person, this stranger? What is he doing in my bed?"' 'Okay, that's fair—I'll grant you that it's a little creepy. But surely you're exaggerating the aftereffects. How long could the estrangement last? A few seconds? A minute?' 'It doesn't matter. I love your face. I don't want to think of it that way.' 'Tell my corpse you love my face!' 'Michael, please—' 'Tell me how much you'll love my face when you see it gnawing on your arm! With your blood smeared all over its cheeks—my cheeks!—like barbeque sauce!' I was pawing grotesquely at my cheeks. 'I don't understand you,' she said. 'At first you refuse to leave the apartment at all, and now you're gone eight hours a day, looking for infected with Matt. Which is fine. But then, when you do come home, all you want to do is pretend that *we're* infected. Not, let's watch a movie. Not, let's go for a walk. But: Rachel, let's pretend that we're undead. This search is making you morbid, Michael. You'd rather pretend you're undead with me than actually live with me.' 'Come on, you don't believe that. You said it just because it sounds dramatic, but you don't really believe it. Look, you're even smiling.' 'Stop.' 'Rachel, of course I'd rather we didn't have to do this. But it's not about what I'd rather, it's about what's reasonable. It's about what one of us is going to have to do if the other is ever infected.' 'You know that's not going to happen.' 'Oh? It used to happen every other night in this city. Who knows when it might happen again? Or what might happen if a hurricane hits and breaches a quarantine? Your problem is that you're still underestimating how difficult it can be—and I mean both emotionally and psychologically difficult—to reconcile a face's familiarity with an unfamiliar state of being. And there will be no face more familiar to you than mine, and no state of being more unfamiliar than undeath.'[1] 'I'll cross that bridge when I come to it. Okay?' 'You wouldn't know how to cross that bridge if it bit you on the ass! Rachel! Turn on the news right now, pick any channel, and you'll see someone who thought they could just cross the bridge when they came to it. And they'll be bleeding to death most likely, if they're not already dead. You think Mazoch could ever cross that bridge? You think that if we had found his father at Citiplace today, he would have simply trotted across that bridge?' 'Oh my God. Was this Matt's idea, Michael? Don't lie to me. Is he the one who told

---

[1] Here I had to stop myself from bringing up her father's funeral. Hasn't she herself said that she found it impossible to believe, on that day, that the peaceful and composed face in the coffin belonged to a corpse? That she kept expecting him to open his eyes or smile at her? That, no matter how insistently she told herself that he really was gone, his face kept resisting the death that she attributed to it, as if rejecting a graft of ontological tissue? Now imagine if his eyes did open, I wanted to say to her, and if the state of being that you had to attribute to him was, not death—a concept people are pretty well accustomed to and know more or less when to apply—but undeath, this weird thing that no one understands, and that seems so unlikely, and unlikeliest yet when those white eyes are open like that, looking at you. How hard would that be, I wanted to ask her? How difficult? For all the obvious reasons I bit my tongue.

you about this? Is that what he's been planning this whole time? To "defamiliarize" Mr. Mazoch, so that he can kill him? Is that why you want to defamiliarize *me*?'

And so on in that vein, for what felt like an hour. Ultimately Rachel came around, but only after I had assured her that Mazoch was not—to my knowledge—plotting a patricide. The second I said this, I realized that I was effectively forswearing an extension: I couldn't go on hiding my doubts from her for another week. As it was, she could barely wait for Friday. She insisted that we invite Matt over for dinner that night, in part so that we could celebrate our 'last day' (her words), but also so that she could put her mind at ease about his motives. I felt a premonitory chill at this—imagining what Matt might say at such a dinner, if Rachel asked him point-blank about his motives—but I nodded. I'd invite him tomorrow, I said.

Once that was settled, Rachel voted that we begin with the blinking-contest exercise, so we rearranged the couches in the living room and positioned ourselves just like the man and woman in the diagram. It's been fifteen minutes now since we started. Following the pamphlet's instructions, I've been focusing on a specific feature (the asterism of freckles to the right of Rachel's nose) and waiting for its isolated oddness to overflow her entire face. Rachel, apparently, has been focusing on my philtrum. Neither of us knows what to expect, what this estrangement is supposed to feel like. Will we be able to tell when it happens? During the first couple of minutes we joked about how awkward what we were doing was: I said I felt as if I were looking at a Magic Eye poster, staring and staring into this pointillist assemblage of monotonic dots until—seething and rearranging themselves like television static—they begin to rise up and resolve into a three-dimensional image; Rachel said she felt as if she were looking at a Rothko painting, staring and staring into the margin between two color fields until—the marine below and the crimson above intensifying in her peripheral vision—the whole canvas starts to glow. Indeed, when I made this observation, the spandrel of skin between my eyebrows was tingling fuzzily, as happens when I concentrate too hard on Magic Eye posters, and Rachel was looking at me with an expression that I'd only ever seen her look at Rothkos with. But now, a quarter hour later, no three-dimensional defamiliarization effect has risen from her freckled dots, and I doubt whether her patient gaze has kindled any Rothko glow of estrangement in my face.

'This isn't working for me,' I say. 'Is this working for you?' 'No,' she admits, 'but I think something might have been starting to happen.' 'It's the eyes. I can't pretend you're a stranger, much less undead, when your eyes are so distinct and green.' 'You have such dark eyes,' she says softly, and I expect her to compare them to night sky or to coffee. She mentions something to this effect every time that we stare into each other's eyes,[1] in the same

---

[1] For my part, I've only ever compared Rachel's eyes to Hitchcock's *The Birds*, specifically a brief sequence in which seagulls can be seen breasting light against a green hill in the distance of Bodega Bay: their white flecks, hovering over verdure, are what I'm always reminded of when I stare into Rachel's eyes indoors, for typically swimming in her eye water are little glints from the light bulbs overhead, gull-like gleams winging throughout her irises' green. I made this comparison well before the outbreak, but since then I've had to keep mum about Rachel's beautiful Bodega Bay eyes, because *The Birds* has become something of a sore point between us. What happened was that we were rewatching it one night after The Broadcast, and I made the reasonable observation that it could be viewed as a prescient or prophetic undeath film, i.e., that *The Birds* seemed to be 'about' the very epidemic we were now living through. All you had to do was substitute Hitchcock's avian monsters with our own undead: crowds of birds begin inexplicably attacking the human population; the film's characters have to board their windows and barricade their doors against waves of aggressive birds; the birds, having destroyed these barricades, flood into the houses and devour their victims alive; characters announce that it is the end-times, an apocalypse, that there are just too many birds,

tone of voice and with undiminishing tenderness, and I know now that she would be defenseless, utterly, against the beguiling blackness of my undead body's eyes. Except—of course!—that my undead body's eyes *wouldn't* be dark, they'd be glaucomatic and milk-white. Nor would her eyes be at all green, or recognizable in their greenness. 'Why don't we try it with our eyes rolled up?' I say. 'We can take turns. Let me try with your eyes rolled up.' Dutifully she exposes to me the flayed-grape undersides of her eyeballs, fixing her pupils on some point in her skull. But almost immediately what this reminds me of is the face that she makes during orgasms (especially when she is astride me, her head hung back and her eyes emptily white, as if filled with

---

et cetera. At this point in my analysis Rachel let loose an exasperated sigh and complained that we couldn't watch *any* movie anymore, not without my finding some way to connect it up to the epidemic and proclaim it an 'allegory for undeath.' Guilty as charged, I suppose, though I'm still right about *The Birds*. And in fact, much of Hitchcock's corpus seems to prophesy undeath. There's *Psycho*, of course, in which a son keeps the stuffed corpse of his mother in the cellar, dressing up as her so that he can wreak havoc in the guise of her reanimated body. But there is also *Vertigo*, which (as with *Solaris*) Matt seems to be subconsciously reenacting. In this movie, a lover—believing his beloved to be dead—begins to revisit and stake out all of her haunts: the park, the museum, the apartment. Like Mazoch, he is recreating the route of her undead itinerary, for when he knew her she had been caught in a kind of undeath: seemingly possessed by the ghost of her great-grandmother, she would often fall into somnambulistic trances, wandering to all of her ancestress's haunts, visiting the park, the museum, and the apartment on a hypnotic circuit. It is to these spaces that the lover returns, expecting to find his beloved's undead body there. At each site he spots a doppelganger, a look-alike whom he mistakes for his beloved, just as Matt—peering through the binoculars outside of Mr. Mazoch's haunts—sometimes identifies a false positive as his father. I don't know whether Matt has ever seen *Vertigo* (as with *Solaris*, I've been reluctant to bring it up with him). And I suppose it's out of the question to rewatch it with Rachel. But it *is* uncanny. You'd think Hitchcock knew about the infection half a century before the rest of the world did.

the Zen emptiness of her own pleasure), and I am so far from thinking of her as infected that my penis stiffens. 'Okay, that doesn't seem to be helping,' I say. 'Do you want to try it on me?' 'No,' she says, rightening her eyes. 'I'm fine.'

Who knew this would be so difficult? The way the pamphlet described it, I thought defamiliarization would be the kind of thing that one could get the knack of, as if, having mastered it, you could always call upon it as a private parlor trick. As if, while sitting at dinner on Friday, I could amuse myself by estranging Matt and Rachel, crossing my eyes and projecting rays of alienation onto their faces, which, spotlit with oddness, would be as unfamiliar to me then as if caught in the beam of a recherché-light ('Now I know him, now I don't: Matt, stranger, Matt, stranger'). Then it really would be a matter of simply switching it on or off in the presence of the undead. But what good is it as a survival reflex if you have to concentrate on the undead's face for thirty minutes? If you have to fixate on its freckles and be careful not to let your thoughts wander, not to get distracted or glance elsewhere, lest one sudden saccade disrupt the steadiness of your gaze, shattering your concentration and forcing you to refocus on the freckle and start all over? If this is what Rachel would have to do when confronted with my undead body—if this is what would be required of her to build her way up to 'Michael is not Michael'—then God help her if she ever finds me on the campus lawn.

I look at her again, trying to see her as my undead body would. I take in her entire face this time: her green eyes and high cheekbones; the Dutch jut of her nose; her hair, shorn short, jagged and blond as grass in December. I love this face. But to my reanimated eyes, it would just be a stranger's face. And if this *were* a stranger's face, would I still love it? If I were just seeing it in a crowd somewhere, having never met Rachel, not even knowing to call the face by the name of Rachel? No. It would be as inert to me as any other. I know that. I know that there is nothing *intrinsically* beloved in these features. When tonight I say that it, as a face, is lovely, all I mean by this is that I invest it with loveliness, that the parts of me that love rush out to meet the face halfway. The face acts as a vessel for my own emotional responses, my memories and associations, the personal narratives and idiosyncratic reactions that I pour into the face on seeing it. If I could somehow stem the flow of those from inside me, her face really would be drained of all recognizability, as bare and dry as a bowl.[1] So just pretend that you never met her, I tell myself. Imagine your way into the nothing you'd feel if you passed this face as a stranger in the street. Pretend that she's just a stranger in the street, whom you're staring intently at for some reason. A human face, as yet nameless, infinitely other than you. Now (is it happening?) her face does seem to recede into a weird distance. It withdraws, just as occasionally my own face will if I peer too long at my reflection: that unsettling moment, which you can always feel coming on like a sneeze, when your face sinks ten layers deep into the silver of the bathroom mirror, and begins to stare back at you like a stranger. Is this how her face would appear to me in undeath?

'I can't do it,' Rachel says. Her concentration breaks like a wave breaking across her face, which breaks my concentration on her face. She starts blinking rapidly and jawing her cheek

---

[1] Odd that 'draining the face' is a metaphor I've thought of before, only in a diametrically opposite context; that is, the context of vividly committing Rachel's face to memory. The way in which I kiss Rachel when I'm overjoyed by the beauty of her face—this is how I kissed her at Tunica, for instance, beneath the waterfall, when I saw her smiling goofily at me—is to cup my hands on either cheek and tilt her face toward mine, toward my mouth, the way you bring in a cereal bowl to drink the leftover milk. And while I'm 'draining' Rachel's face in this manner, bringing it slowly toward my own as if to sip from it, I'm usually looking at her and thinking something like, 'I'll never forget this face, at this moment,' which is precisely what I'm trying to forget by 'draining' her face tonight.

muscles in a fit of relaxed tension. 'No no no,' I say, 'I was just getting it!' 'Well, I was getting nowhere.' 'You really have to think of it as an absolute estrangement. That's the key, I think. You're not just concentrating on my face, you're uncovering in it a kind of infinite otherness. You're not just forgetting the me in my face, you're restoring to it this mask of radical alterity.' 'You make it sound like an exfoliating cream,' she says. And it's true, I was making it sound that way. When I try to visualize the very thing that I was describing, the image is undeniably ridiculous: me, laid out on a Levinasian spa bed, with white dollops of alterity rubbed into my cheeks, cucumber slices over my eyes. 'You're right,' I say, 'forget the mask. But there are still techniques we haven't tried yet…' And I go on to explain one of the pamphlet's other methods for inducing defamiliarization.

How it works is that both partners, still seated across from one another, close their eyes for five minutes, meditating unbrokenly on some other person's face. They clear their heads of all interfering thoughts and images, then really try to *see* that face. They build up the face painstakingly, detail by accreted detail, starting with just a wire-frame template of a head, then gradually filling in its surface area with skin, a mask of flesh out of which they can then mold a nose, a mouth, a brow, adding only in the final stages of the meditation the colors and shades that will render nostrils, lips, and hair. When this high-resolution face hovers graphically before the mind's eye, close enough to kiss, they're to hold it like this for the whole five minutes (keeping it the sole content of their consciousnesses) so that when the time's up, and they do snap open their eyelids to look at one another (dissolving the dreamlike scrim of the meditated face), the rush of sense data will be overwhelming. They will be staring at the real live face seated opposite them, but their mind, still stamped with the meditated face's afterimage, will lag behind the eyes. The mind will be slow to recognize the partner's face qua partner's face. It will comprehend it only as an assortment of skin-toned shapes, a jumble of geometric flesh, a *strange* face. For a few seconds at least, it should be possible to look at the partner freshly, to see their face as a bare percept, before eventually all the emotional responses and memories and personal narratives percolate through the afterimage filter and obtain to it (i.e., the partner's face) like a name (just as, when you wake suddenly from a powerful dream, it may take up to half a minute for your mind to figure out that what you're looking at is a ceiling fan). Having tricked yourself into seeing your partner estranged in this way, you'll have an important baseline experience from which to practice the more advanced estrangement exercises, which, by refining technique, train you not just to stumble onto but to actively control the defamiliarization effect.

'What do you think?' I say, and Rachel seems game. So I set my cell phone's alarm for five minutes from now and place the phone ceremoniously on the coffee table. Straightening my back, closing my eyes, I ask Rachel whose face she will be imagining. Her father's, she says. I say Mazoch's.

THURSDAY

I CALL MAZOCH AT SEVEN THIS MORNING TO confirm the hiatus, but he doesn't answer. This morning (our penultimate morning) is the first time in three and a half weeks that he's requested a 'personal day' like this. When the voice mail picks up, I leave a message asking whether we'll be resuming the search tomorrow, then invite him over for dinner afterward ('to celebrate,' I say, hoping he'll get the hint). I know that he turns his phone off when reading, so I don't think much of it when I hang up.

But I've been thinking about it ever since. It's seven thirty now, and I'm back in bed with Rachel, who I expect will sleep in later than usual (last night we both tossed and turned, as unnerved by the estrangement exercises as she predicted we would be). While waiting for her to wake, I've been staring into the boarded-up darkness of our bedroom. For a while I tried to fall back asleep in this way,[1] but then I gave that up and started

---

[1] I employed my usual trick, of focusing on the power light of Rachel's computer speakers across the room. In the perspectiveless blackness, this glowing green bead (floating where Rachel's desk should be) always seems suspended in infinite interstellar space. Nothing is visible but it, a pseudo-sidereal point of light, with cavernous darkness between us. To help myself fall asleep, I like to imagine that I am an astronaut adrift on a NASA mattress, at the very edge of space (where there are no more stars, only far chill emptiness), and that the point of light that I'm descrying is actually a rift at the end of the universe, a tear in the black fabric where the cosmos stops. Having reached the point where the expanding universe finally dead-ends, I am glimpsing what lies beyond it: I can see the obverse side of spacetime, shining through this tiny chink. This keyhole into something inconceivable and green. As I said, I frequently play this game with Rachel's speaker bead, but today was the first time that it occurred to me to

to think about Mazoch reading. Specifically, about the likelihood that he is actually reading. Or whether he might be back at Mr. Mazoch's right now: crouching down to the carpet, a muddy boot on each hand; walking a trail of footprints back and forth. Just a little something for us to find tomorrow morning.

How could he be reading, I wonder? How can *anyone* read? Once, at the start of the search, I asked Mazoch what he'd be doing for the weekend, and he said reading. When I asked how he could manage to, he said that it relaxed him, eased his tension, otherwise did him good. There was too much time to think, he said, driving around the city all day. Whereas if he sat at his desk and concentrated on a Milosz poem, it was like lighting a thought-repellant candle in the mind. He didn't specify which thoughts it was that he wanted to repel, which thoughts would be fluttering, mosquito-like, at the edge of his reading, but I could guess: thoughts of his father, of the epidemic, of the apocalypse, of death.

Thoughts like these are what make it impossible for me to read, and in fact they're the reason that I haven't picked up a book, not really, since the start of all this. Occasionally I'll try to read with Rachel in bed, but I always find myself skimming distractedly. How am I supposed to follow a text when I know

---

compare it to undeath. Perhaps *this* is what it is like to be undead, I found myself thinking. You cross infinite darkness, with only a virid dot in the distance, shining like a Bethlehem star. At the far edge of the blackness of your mind, you see this single stab of green: the little gleam of what's left alive in you, visible through a rift in the underworld. And condensed into that dimensionless point would be all the memories that you are trying to get back to, there on the mortal side of your life. In my case, Tunica, the apartment, and the campus lawn would all be compacted together, stellified, pulling at me with their green gravity. And so as I lay there (drifting into half-sleep, feeling myself drift toward this bead, as if caught in its nostalgic tractor beam), I thought, dreamily, 'This is what it is like to be undead.'

that, at any moment, my reading might be interrupted—my life imperiled—by the beating on the door of an undead fist? When page by page I am viscerally aware, in all my nerviness and coiled energy, that I might suddenly be called upon to leap up from the mattress and slide the dresser against the threshold, in an improvised barricade, and that with emergency haste I'll have to alert the authorities, lock myself and Rachel in the bathroom, and wait patiently—alone with the sound of its pounding and moaning—for the creature to be detained? These fantasies are difficult to subdue, so more often than not I just lie still, with Rachel reading next to me and with my own book splayed open on my stomach. I stare indolently into the ceiling. I watch the ventilator grille directly overhead, with its little scrap of paper taped to the end, acting as a kind of telltale: when the air conditioner is off, the scrap hangs inertly vertical there, but the moment that the air conditioner switches on, it wags out in a lateral drift, so as to signal that the grille emits a live breeze. For minutes this little tag of paper will float passively along, like some remora on a shark of wind, and it will be enchanting to watch, will put briefly out of mind what the book on my stomach cannot.

After he said that he'd be reading Milosz, I asked Mazoch—whose apartment is a minor library—what good he thought his reading would do him, when you could almost still *see* an apocalypse, on the horizon, like a storm.[1] The day that I asked him

---

[1] Earlier that same week, during a heavy summer thunderstorm, one of Baton Rouge's processing centers—i.e., the temporary way stations where LCDC vans can unload their undead, until space has been made for them at an actual quarantine—lost power and suffered a security breach. LCDC was equivocal about what happened, but a guard was rumored to have been careless, and was bitten, and certain fail-safes would appear to have failed. The upshot is that a dozen undead managed to escape from the so-called processing center (in fact a high-school gymnasium in a residential neighborhood) and to go on a biting spree, infecting more than twenty nearby civilians, including three small children. The public uproar

this, the sky actually was black and overcast with storm. Darkling clouds banked all the way down I-10 to the western horizon, where alone there was a clearing, a backlit strip of sky, still glowing a little from a sunset we'd missed. Driving in this direction, speeding a little in this direction, toward where the margin of sky had, in the afterglow of the sunset, turned the color of vanilla cream, and where wisps of cloud were so gilt and silvered that they looked like breath on fire, Mazoch evaded my question by adducing examples of readers who had not been deterred by apocalypses, waving one hand then the other off the steering wheel as he described them to me: first, there was Mr. Henry Bemis, the bookish librarian and sole H-bomb survivor in the *Twilight Zone* episode 'Time Enough at Last,' who after a lifetime of postponed reading is finally left alone in a deserted city, with no humans to distract him and with all the food and supplies he might need to survive, and who decides, in the teeth of this apocalypse, to organize for himself a two-year reading syllabus from among the books at the public library (only, famously, to

---

surrounding 'the spill' (as newscasters decorously referred to it) eventually led to the decommissioning of residential processing centers altogether. As a result, unprocessed undead are now being housed on cargo ships and barges on the Mississippi—far from any neighborhoods—while officials weigh all the options for some more permanent solution. Naturally, these 'death ships' (as talk-radio pundits fearmongeringly refer to them) have only escalated debates over hurricane season, which is all that pundits seem to be screaming about, these days. What if New Orleans floods, they scream? Or Slidell? Or New Iberia? Tropical storms have already begun brewing off the coast, and earlier on in the season hurricanes hit Veracruz and Cuba, which came to serve as worldwide object lessons in disaster preparedness: floodwaters freed floods of undead from the quarantines, and both governments—unprepared, underfunded—were powerless to prevent mass outbreaks. As pundits like to point out, the same thing could easily happen here. So FEMA, anxious to avoid any similar swivets stateside, has been urging all of the Gulf Coast towns to evacuate their quarantines, and to ship their undead to safer cities. So far, none have.

have his reading glasses shatter); then there was the Arab from Book V of Wordsworth's *The Prelude*, who, in an apocalyptic dream sequence, rides across the desert bearing a stone (which, in the logic of the dream, is actually a 'book,' Euclid's *Elements*) and a seashell (also a book, one that, when the narrator holds it to his ear, prophesies 'in an unknown tongue... Destruction to the children of the earth/By deluge, now at hand'), and so the Arab rides across the desert to bury these books and preserve his 'twofold charge' from apocalyptic destruction, even with 'the fleet waters of a drowning world/In chase of him' ('[M]ine eyes/Saw, over half the wilderness diffused,/A bed of glittering light: I asked the cause:/ "It is," said he, "the waters of the deep/Gathering upon us"'); and finally there was the character of Borges in Borges's short story 'The Book of Sand,' who buys from a rare-books dealer an 'infinite book' (the titular Book of Sand, which comprises an infinite number of randomly generated pages, such that a reader can never find the same page twice), and who, on realizing that this book is the apocalypse itself ('I considered fire, but I feared that the burning of an infinite book might be similarly infinite, and suffocate the planet in smoke'), does not bury it or cast it into the sea but leaves it instead on a shelf of the Mexican National Library. So why *not* read in an apocalypse, Mazoch seemed to be asking me, via each of these examples. Why not commune solitarily with books, as Mr. Bemis did?; or preserve books from a flood that will leave no humans to read them, as the Arab of the Bedouin tribes did?; or, not only read *in* the apocalypse, but read the apocalypse itself, as the character of Borges did, and as he allowed future readers to do by stocking this apocalypse among the novels and poems of the Mexican National Library? Following these readers' lead, why *shouldn't* Mazoch cram his apartment with books, or spend the weekend reading Milosz, or take this morning off to read? And why shouldn't I try to read today as well?

I have been asking myself these questions as I lie here in

bed, and I keep arriving at the same answer: I cannot read today because my reading has always been (before the outbreak I mean) teleological in nature, and this strikes me as unsustainable in an apocalyptic state. Take undergrad for example. Why, before the dead walked, did I study Kant? I never took a class on Kant, so the usual incentive structures (seminars, papers, grades) were not what motivated me. Why did I read him then? Because scholarly comprehension seemed valuable and because I looked forward to the day when each great thinker, like a grocery item, was scratched off my list; because, in certain circles, quoting or paraphrasing or alluding to the fact of having read Kant carried potent social cachet; because the thick gray spine of the *Critique of Pure Reason* was so conspicuous on my to-read shelf, so baldly visible a monument to my ignorance (not like the niggardly maroon spine of Descartes' *Meditations*, which it was easy for a cursory glance to pass over, and so which I could comfortably leave on the to-read shelf, even though my not having read it was in some ways even more embarrassing and scandalous than my not having read the first Critique), that I couldn't bear to invite fellow philosophy majors over to my dorm without prematurely promoting it to my shelf of read books, where of course it would torment me, like the beating of a telltale heart, as if I were in constant danger of someone following the sightline of my nervous glances, spotting the book, and asking, nightmarishly, 'Ah, I see you've read the first Critique—how about those antinomies, eh?' So when for months I mastered the Critique by diligent lucubration, I did so not for the present pleasure of the text, but for what I just now referred to as teleological motives, with an eye toward the self I might be at seventy: my to-read shelf barren, my banter well stocked and alluding wittily to Kant, the great project of my education completed.

Were all my motives so petty, designed merely to elevate my self-image, rather than my intellect or my spirit? No, I read, too, in the pursuit of things that seemed in inspired moments ineffable and vast, and noble in their vastness.[1] But for the most part reading was just a joyless war of attrition with my to-read

---

[1] For instance, when Rachel and I first moved in together, I read the books that lined her shelves, because I thought that these would give me special access to her, teach me a little about her, just as eating her favorite brand of cereal (Special-K bran flakes littered with dehydrated strawberry shavings, little tart discs of bloodred that puckered my mouth to suck on them) taught me of her tongue, taught me the taste of her mornings and some midnights. I would study her copy of *Lolita* and try fervently to imagine her reading it—under what skies, in what seasons, with what things on her mind—as if all these granular traces of her could be scraped from the page by my reading, like breadcrumbs from a tablecloth, into the eager maw of my heart. This particular project tapered off gradually as we lived together, as she began to seem less inscrutable and more human and as I began to feel less pressured to solve the mystery of her loveliness. But even now it gives me pleasure, flipping casually through one of her novels, to see her pleasure on the page. To see which passages she has underlined or, as if they were correct answers, scrawled checkmarks next to. Even when I was reading my own copies of books, I strove to read them somewhat with Rachel's eye. Whenever I came across a passage that reminded me strongly of ones that she had underlined; or that called to mind an anecdote or key term or in-joke that we shared; or that contained some visual detail that, it struck me, she herself would be liable to notice, I wrote her name there in the margin: 'Rachel,' loveliest apostil. What was I doing? At the time, I conceived of it as a squirrel's project. I was burying her name in forgettable places so that, skimming through these books in a few years (perhaps after we had separated, perhaps after I had even forgotten her), my eye would be surprised by her name in the margin. Reading over the annotated passage, I would then be able to unearth from forgetfulness the day that I had marked it, as well as whatever memory of Rachel it had reminded me of in the first place (that scene she'd underlined in *Lolita*!, that anecdote!, our in-joke!—Rachel!), bringing on a remembering in my chest just charged with unbearable joy and suffering. And if, like the squirrel who forgets where half its acorns are buried and leaves them forever in the dirt, I happened never to skim through some of the books again, all the better, for her name would have time to take root and grow there, oak of unbearable joy and suffering.

list. Which, needless to say, was a war of attrition that the list easily won, marshalling in its favor factorial laws so ancient, so textbook hydracephalic, that they're almost clichéd: for every book I disposed of I acquired three. Nor was I even able to read these books with great rigor or systematicity, feverish as I was to be finished. If I organized any kind of Henry Bemis-ish summer syllabus for myself, linking texts and authors together in what seemed like illuminating combinations, I lasted through maybe two books of my master class before, distracted, I directed my energies elsewhere. How to commit myself to one line of texts when there was so much else to read, when time lavished on Russian Formalism was time lost in phenomenology, philosophy of language, critical theory? And so my to-read list layered itself in this way, with upper and lower crusts of priority, undergoing the most volatile upheavals and displacements. Certain entries from the bottom strata, books I hadn't planned on reading for months, would with an unexpected shift in interest be extruded above all others, as if to be read immediately, until I visited a bookstore and buried them beneath new purchases, themselves to be sifted and sunk; I would carry Shklovsky in my backpack, his essay collection just at the surface of my reading program, and then suddenly other authors—because they had been mentioned in conversation, because I had read an interesting *London Review of Books* article about them, because I had otherwise been made to feel remiss for not having read them (as if the mere mention of an unread author's name were some cloud of dust that I'd been left behind in, kicked up by a competitor I was compelled to catch up with)—would become my number-one priority, such that Heidegger or Wittgenstein or Agamben would all irrupt before him (i.e., Shklovsky), each promoted to the top of my reading program and abandoned in turn with equal fitfulness and inattention.

In a manner of speaking, my only goal in reading was to outlive my to-read list, to finish it before time and mortality finished me. And I was willing to make the appropriate sacrifices (a robust social life, for instance) to see this project through. What ultimately sustained and what alone could have sustained me were my teloi, specifically the illusion of progress that attended them, whereby I convinced myself that I was closer to my goal at twenty-four than I had been at twenty.[1] I cleaved to this illusion not only down the ranks of my to-read list, but also through the pages of a single book. And in fact there was nothing more immediately or visibly satisfying to me, nothing more addictive or compulsive, than the physical progress that my reading made through a single book. How the completed pages thickened beneath the thumb that pinned them down, and how the unread pages thinned! How the dog-ear—the creased page corner that served to mark my place and that, when the book was closed, appeared as a single black fissure in the otherwise white field of the fore-edge—how each day that dark line went deeper and deeper in, rightward through the white, bearing down on the creamy pages between it and the back cover like some snowplow's prow, shoveling all the snow of my ignorance! How when I pinned fifty or so pages between my thumb and

---

[1] I never could have read if I knew, really understood and *knew*, that there was no such thing as true progress: that I was trapped on an Eleatic treadmill, a Zeno-esque hamster wheel. Deep down I had to convince myself, delusionally or not, that I was nearing a definite end to my scholarship. Whereas the moment I accepted the futility of my task, I would have had to quit. 'For then,' Nietzsche writes in *The Birth of Tragedy*, I 'would have felt like those who wished to dig a hole straight through the earth: each one of them perceives that with his utmost lifelong efforts he can excavate but a very small portion of the enormous depth, and this is filled up again before his eyes by the labor of his successor, so that a third man seems to be doing a sensible thing in selecting a new spot for his attempts at tunneling. Now suppose some one shows conclusively that the antipodal goal cannot be attained thus directly. Who then will still care to toil on in the old depths, unless in the meantime he has learned to content himself with finding precious stones…?'

forefinger and scaled my thumb back along their edges, letting them siffle down swiftly like the pages of a flipbook, I could watch all my marginalia and ink in motion, as if animated, this blue-black cartoon of exclamation points and scrawled words and 'Rachel' popping instantaneously into frame! It was little visible rewards like these that made me feel as if I were accomplishing something. They quantified my efforts. They were, if not the fruits of my labor, then the rinds of those fruits. And it was that much easier to stay home nights and read when I could track my dog-ear's movement through the book, congratulating myself before going to sleep: 'I'm a hundred pages smarter tonight.' Or to finish the volume and slide it into place on my shelf, thinking, 'I'm one book smarter tonight.'

Such was the nature of this illusion of progress that it often felt as if I were just within reach of finishing the list, even as the list tripled beneath me. One more year of reading, two at most, graduate school, and then the list would be done with. So even if Mazoch's mention of a book that I hadn't yet read—or, worse, that I had never heard of—induced in me real impulses of panic, panic that announced mortality in my worry as the graying of hair or a heart surgery might have in another man, then, still, that panic was simply enough put aside, mollified, forgotten, by reading another book. Even if I was easily discouraged by counting up my books' spines and, assuming an average of thirty pages an hour, tabulating how much time I had spent reading them;[1] even if I earnestly considered shunting myself off the track of my reading and onto that of some

---

[1] Hundreds of hours, it turned out, thousands, a statistic of near-astronomical scale that had the power, in the shock of its high number and in its vertiginous mathematical sublimity, to wake me momentarily from my dazed reading and force me to consider all of the activities I might have been pursuing in that time instead: lovemaking, windsailing, preparing elaborate meals, all glimpsed in breathless montage, like the life I hadn't lived flashing before my eyes.

more vigorous hobby… still I recognized that such a path was by now closed off to me. Windsailing while unread books lay in my apartment would only make me anxious, and, besides, could be postponed, I consoled myself, until once the reading was done. For after all, didn't the books get read, sometimes as many as two in an afternoon? Didn't my bookshelf fatten like a leech? It seemed possible to finish the to-read list, not only within my lifetime, but within just a dedicated decade, giving over the rest of my life to vacation and illiterate ease. Was this merely a pipe dream? Was reading, as a worried professor once warned me it was, a race that I was always simultaneously winning and losing?[1] I couldn't be bothered, other than in bleak moments, to ask.

Benighted by bibliophily! And yet you couldn't even call it 'phily,' a 'love' of books, because I was mastered by meaner demons. Of insecurity, of anxiety, of self-abnegation, of anything but a pleasurable, healthy love-relation. It was as if what I suffered from was bibliophobia, a fear of books that I exorcised precisely by reading them, as if the very act of turning their pages—like switching on the light in a darkened room or throwing back the shower curtain behind which you are certain some murderer lurks—sanitized at once all the mystery of my ignorance of them, and defused their awful power over my imagination. But at any rate benighted by something.

---

[1] Strange that my visual representation of this metaphor, the image that came suddenly to mind when he spoke it, was not the 'Eleatic treadmill,' those nightmare legs that carry you no farther down the hallway than where you stand, running terribly in place, but rather (no doubt influenced by my memory of that Nietzsche passage) the childhood futility of trying to dig a hole in the beach, how the sand always spills back in faster than you can trowel it out. When now I imagine combining these two images—in order to generate a sandy version of the race that is always simultaneously being won and lost—what I come up with is the exacerbatory torsions of a man shin-deep in quicksand, how the churning of his legs only sinks him deeper where he stands.

Could anything have dissolved so thoroughly the illusion of progress, so bluntly given the lie to my 'antipodal goal,' as an outbreak of the walking dead? My reading was always oriented toward some future, in which I was educated and articulate and admired in high societies. And could anything have shattered so completely one's hopes for the future, one's life plans and social ambitions (to say nothing of society itself), as an undead apocalypse? When I am in my worst and most pessimistic moods, I assume that the epidemic can promise only a few outcomes, none of which involve the self I might be at seventy, reclining in a leather chair in my personal library, with winter light and wisdom redounding upon my gray head. In a matter of months, I sometimes assume, I will be fed upon, or all my loved ones will be fed upon, or I will take my own life, or, unable to bring myself to do this even after state and social institutions have collapsed entirely, I will grub among garbage bins behind abandoned grocery stores, defending myself from nomadic, malnourished, and desperate humans as much as from the undead.

I would no sooner read Kant in this world than I would on a desert island. And in fact I haven't read Kant, or anyone else for that matter, since that first week of panicked news reports. If I were to become more sensitive to the present pleasure of the text, as Mazoch and Rachel seem to be, if I learned to 'content myself with the discovery of precious stones,' then perhaps there would remain hope yet for Mazoch to make a Mr. Bemis of me. Until then, my books will remain boxed up beneath the bed, where I cannot see them.

Lately I have been trying to convince myself that it's safe enough to read again: that outbreaks and attacks are becoming ever rarer, and that there's nothing to worry about anymore. Even so, I lack the motivation to unbox my books. My only substantial reading material these past couple of months has been *FIGHT THE BITE*, plus research articles about the infection. The fact is—and as sad as it makes me to admit this—literature has begun to feel hollow to me. Nothing that I read helps me understand the undead. Philosophy, which was supposed to teach me how to die, to prepare me for death, has left me utterly unprepared to meet undeath. I am no better equipped to understand it, after all the Heidegger and David Chalmers and Kant I've read, than Mazoch is, who merely has Milosz in his quiver. So whenever I flip through my undergrad copy of the first Critique, for old time's sake, it is with a kind of sad apathy: Kant's awe-inspiring blueprints of the human mind (his architectonic tables of our reasoning faculties, categories, and intuitions) tell me nothing about the undead mind. After five or so pages, fidgety with impatience, I have to put Kant aside. Whether I will be able to read next week, once the search is over, I still don't know.

But I can predict that I will not be reading anything this morning, on my day off. What will I do instead? Make breakfast for Rachel. Make love to Rachel. Maybe take a walk to the LSU Lakes.

IT'S MID-AFTERNOON, AND RACHEL AND I HAVE found a nice patch of grass by the water. We've spread out a blanket on the northern shoreline, right beneath the shade of a live oak, where we've both been trying to clear our heads of thoughts of the infection.

I'm sitting with my back to the broad oak bole, legs spread out so that Rachel can nestle between them. She's reclining into me, her own legs straight before her and her head resting on my chest. My arms are crossed over her waist, her arms are on my arms. Ahead of Rachel's feet the muddy shallows lap at some agapanthus stems, and farther out, in the middle distance, the lake is bisected by an overpass of I-10, its concrete support columns grown mossy where they meet their reflections in the water. Beyond the freeway is the southern shore, its gravel strip shimmering in the sun like a beach. The cypresses along the side banks, emerging from the shallows, stoop over the brown water, and their branches are bare except for where ibises roost in them. When they flap their wings in the branches, the ibises resemble pale hearts in empty ribcages. Bordering the right shoreline, Park Boulevard is busy even now: traffic steady in both directions.[1] But the tarmac jogging path circling the lake is empty, and there is only one car visible on the opposite shore's

---

[1] The LSU Lakes have always been high-traffic. Because they're manmade, plopped as an afterthought into the middle of an already-developed neighborhood with already-developed traffic patterns, there's no cline of dwindling trees to intervene between the city and the natural space, no margin of carless quiet… simply an abrupt break where the two zones meet, such that each lake seems like an aside of water, cupped in the parentheses that the pavement makes around it. A wet digression interpolated into the city.

parking strip. The only vehicles on the overpass are eighteen-wheelers. Their passing trailers are rectangular and blank. The car on the opposite shore, I see, is a police cruiser. Atop its glinting roof, against the bright air behind it, there is the winking of its lights—blue-red, blue-red—as they strobe sirenlessly. It's a quiet day. The people who would be here normally (the sorority girls jogging along the path, the grizzled black fishermen fishing the fishless water) appear to be avoiding the lake, even though it isn't technically closed to the public. Standing a few yards ahead of the police cruiser is a single undead silhouette, staring in our direction. It has been standing like that without moving or making a sound since we got here. The officers in the cruiser appear to be supervising the creature, ensuring that it stays put until an LCDC van arrives to detain it. Other than this watcher across the water, Rachel and I have had the area more or less to ourselves.

'What are you thinking?' she asks me now, interrupting for the first time in several minutes our pleasant quiet. The goal we had set for the day was to avoid mulling on the infection. Rachel wanted for us to get outside in fine weather and 'think good things,' as alive to loveliness and light as if we were on a hike at Tunica. But the truth is that I haven't been able to stop thinking about the corpse across the water. Even when I try to focus on good things, my thoughts are brought ineluctably back to it; it alone is the final, dispiriting link in every chain of associations. As an example: for a while I had my head cocked back, so that I could look up at the parasol of oak leaves above us. The sunlight was glaring on the backs of the leaves, which—singularly waxy and heavy and dark-green—received this light in a blinding sheen. The sheen reminded me of nothing more than erased paper, that tanline-like whiteness that you can scrub paper down to if you erase in one place too many times. Because the leaves overhead were so similarly white (as white as nothing at all), it seemed as if someone had taken an eraser to them, worn them thin, leaving where their green was these patches of attrited whiteness. That was all pleasant and fine to notice. But then the glare of sunlight on the leaves started to remind me of nothing more than nothing, than erasure and absence, a leaf's Being being scrubbed away by an ontic eraser. And once my mind made the relevant connections between sheeny light and nullness, the game was up: I imagined that the oak leaves, glazed with erasure-colored sun, were absences that had actually *leafed into* the world, lobate blanknesses that had budded through the air and there unfolded, immaculately white, like magnolias of lack. This seemed as apt a representation as any for the infection (which, too, is an absence of sorts, which too has flowered whitely into the world, bite mark by bite mark), so there I was thinking about the infection and undeath and all the other unpleasant things that gazing at the oak leaves was supposed to be taking my mind off of. Not least the silhouette on the opposite shore, which for obvious reasons I found it impossible, then, not to look at. And the sight of it—awful even at this distance! That pale shape still stationed there, that corpse standing sentinel over us all afternoon… could my chain of associations have been tethered to any better death's head than this? Could I have hauled in my chain of associations, link by submerged link, and found any more horrific a memento mori attached as its anchor? The eyes white as erased paper, the cadaver a carapace of lack—*that's* where my chain of associations led!

Naturally, the longer I stared at it—and I did keep staring at it—the more morbid my thoughts grew. Not only was it undead, I realized, but it was Mazoch. His height, his shape, why not? Why couldn't Mazoch (who had called off the search under mysterious circumstances and who wasn't answering his phone and who it seemed less and less plausible was sitting in his room reading Milosz) have been bitten and killed, have reanimated and followed us here? Of course it was absurd, a paranoid fantasy. There was no way Mazoch could have died. Yet there were so many ways in which Mazoch could have died! At least a hundred ways! Dead in the ditch he swerved into when, driving home late last night, he nodded off at the wheel: if he wasn't killed on impact, if he was simply knocked unconscious and trapped, then roadside infected could have come to inspect the wreck and fed with ease upon his flesh. Or—if he made it home safe last night after all—say that he was bitten in bed in his sleep, having forgotten, from distraction or exhaustion or whatever else, to bolt the front door. Or—if in fact he slept soundly and without incident—say that, rather than read Milosz this morning, he decided to conduct one day's search without me, returning to Citiplace to inspect the empty theaters. Why not *this* morning, after months of daily exposure to the epidemic, for the probabilistically obvious to happen? Why not the one day that I wasn't there for a stray to catch him at his ankle and infect him?

Though what struck me as likelier still—likelier even than any of these scenarios—and likelier every minute that I compared the silhouette with Mazoch's likeness, was that Mazoch had infected himself. That he was sick, perverse, that finally he had snapped and that this was the hellish price he had to pay for devoting himself so crazily to the chase of his father. That 'taking the day off to read' was a euphemism for 'killing myself,' that what 'reading Milosz' meant was that Mazoch would stir into a glass of water a single drop of contaminated blood (milked like venom from a nail some infected had stepped on) and drain it down as resolutely as he would a protein shake. All week, I realized, he'd been trying to get himself infected: with Highland Road Park, with the chicken breast, with every nail rusted and jutting from his dad's doorjamb. He'd been playing Russian roulette with the infection. But time after time he'd escaped unscathed, and so today, I realized, he had decided to finish the job himself.

Nothing seemed more lucid or inevitable to me than this. For what if *not* this—precisely to become infected and to reanimate—had Mazoch this whole time been planning? What better way to intercept an undead father than by carrying out an Orphic strategy, by descending into the underworld after him? Undead, Mazoch could exceed the limits that as a mortal he's been bringing himself to the edges of. He could shuffle from Denham to Louie's and back again *without stopping*, could actually keep pace with the father he was pursuing. What he would lose in speed (the undead can't drive) he would gain in stamina (the undead need not rest), such that his body would finally be equal to this monomaniacal task. The only trick would be to ensure that his reanimated body did indeed wander to Denham and Louie's and back, to *Mr. Mazoch's* haunts, rather than to Matt's idiosyncratic own. Hence this hopeless search, designed less as an actual manhunt for Mr. Mazoch than as a training module for Matt's undead corpse. So that his reanimated body would wander to his father's haunts, Mazoch wandered to his father's haunts. Daily he drove to them, investing each with all the associative energies necessary to compel his corpse to return to it. Yes, Mazoch knew exactly what he was doing. If those two officers hadn't arrived this afternoon to arrest it, his reanimated body, memory-possessed, would have visited Denham and Louie's no less diligently than Mazoch had, no less routinely and methodically and obsessively than Mazoch had, when, himself memory-possessed, he drove to these sites every morning like some pilgrim of remembering.

How clear to me it all was! Mazoch, self-consciously blazing a trail for his reanimated body, laying down a track for it to travel! Mazoch, engraining in himself muscle memories, habits, kernels of place, plotting for himself a mnemocartographic itinerary, all to guide his reanimated body! What else had I taken him to be doing? Obviously his final effort of will was to tighten this spring within himself (as if each day's repetition of the routine—that mind-numbing drive out to Denham and back—were just another twist of the dorsal key of his inner tin soldier) so that his automatous corpse, like a wind-up toy whose 'winding up' Mazoch's last few weeks on Earth were, would wobble forward to exactly those places that Mazoch wanted it to. No wonder he had set the deadline at a month: that was probably how much time he thought the engraining would take. And no wonder he had been in such a rush to visit extra sites this week, then to search another week: he had to squeeze these sites into his itinerary. Highland Road Park. Citiplace. This lake that he stands right now on the southern shore of.

That *was* him, wasn't it, staring hungrily out over the water at us... thank God for that patrol car. It was only here, at the thought 'thank God for the patrol car,' that I truly comprehended what mortal danger I'd been in, here that the scales fell from my eyes (and, with them, any compunctions I'd had about abandoning myself altogether to 'bad thoughts'). For where else (it occurred to me) did Mazoch visit diligently every morning? Where besides Denham would his reanimated body, in inertial thrall to habit and reflex, have eventually been made to wander? Our very apartment! The home in which we slept! Oh, he would have headed straight there one morning, as if to pick me up for a day of work! This he didn't take into account, this he didn't plan for. He needed me to keep him company while for months he drilled a route into his body, he needed me to 'help him not to think' and to be a pleasant phatic presence in his passenger seat. But what he didn't take into account was that my apartment, first stop every morning, would have been as much a component of 'the route' for his reanimated body as any other site. One morning he would have done what he did every morning: he would have gone to Mustard Castle, taken the stairs to our apartment, and knocked three times at our door. There would have come in the middle of some morning Mazoch's familiar hearty knock at the door! And this time he wouldn't quit until it splintered. They never quit until it splinters, not if they know you're inside. Mazoch would have brought all his huge strength to bear on the battering down of our door, as if the only purpose he had ever had in mind, while working out, was splintering doors, as if for this and nothing else he exercised. To splinter my door and eat me alive he did his military pushups every morning! To keep himself well fed in the underworld he chinned himself on the pull-up bar in his threshold! To endow his corpse with what muscles it'd need to pry my life open like a crawfish shell, the better to suck my brains out, he curled his barbells before the mirror! That vain bastard would have eaten me alive—staring at his smug silhouette across the lake I felt sure of it!—if only those two officers hadn't been here to stop him.

So when Rachel asks me right now what I'm thinking, I'm thinking of the undead corpse across the water, imagining that it's Mazoch, and ideating its eating us alive in our sleep. But what I answer her is, 'Nothing in particular,' since this is, strictly speaking, true: I am thinking about 'nothing' *in particular*, particularly the nothingness of undeath, which I'm worried that Mazoch in particular may have infected himself with. And I am thinking, too, about the somethingness of that nothing. Staring at the undead silhouette, I can't help wondering what's going on inside its body, or what Mazoch—if indeed it is Mazoch—must be experiencing: no doubt an order of being inconceivable to me. Part of me yearns for a pair of binoculars right now, not only to confirm that the silhouette is his, but also to look him in the eye. For if he truly did infect himself, then he would be seeing everything he claimed they could not see. All the things that I (still on the mortal side of life) can barely understand. One of the living dead now, he would be living the very limit to my knowledge: he would *be* the nothing that can be known about undeath.[1] So it is this—the nothings that must be massing in

---

[1] For instance, the irresolvable question of undead vision—whether they are blind or all-sighted, whether they see a blackness or a Holbein blur—would be being resolved, right now, in Mazoch's eyeballs. And his skin,

Mazoch's mind—that I myself have in mind, when I tell Rachel that I am thinking about nothing.

To forestall any follow-up questions, I ask her reciprocally, 'But what about you? What were *you* thinking, just a minute ago, before you thought to ask me?' And how my mood lightens when she begins! For it turns out that Rachel has, somehow, avoided thinking about undeath and the silhouette all day. She's succeeded brilliantly in distracting herself and has thankfully thought enough good things for the both of us. Gesturing to the water, she enumerates all the good things there that have been holding her interest since we got here: (1) because the freeway bridges the lake, all the cars overhead get reflected, and the eighteen-wheelers especially have been enjoyable to watch (that is, not the actual vehicles speeding along the overpass, but their reflections in the lake below, streaking rectangles of distortion that shudder through the muddy water: they look so monstrous, she says, these gray shapes skimming beneath the surface, that whenever one passes she can't help thinking, 'A Leviathan! A Loch Ness!'); (2) when ducks kick off the shore and glide out across the water, their wakes ripple back in lunular trails—like this:)))—such that each duck seems to be opening up a string of parentheses, nesting digressions that manage to hold the entire lake (the reflected clouds and reflected eighteen-wheelers, and the floating litter, too) in their aside of water,[1] which can be

---

spritzed by a breeze blowing in off the water, would settle at last the issue of sensation: whether it is only numbness that the undead feel, or else a buried-alive tingling. Just so if he were given a boarded door or some mortal tool, to exercise either spatial hatred or a habituated muscle memory: his hand would answer all of our questions about the undead hand. Standing across the lake from me, Mazoch would have been initiated into that sublimity. He would have finally come to learn what for weeks, it would seem, he had been looking for his father to teach him.

[1] I was moved to see that Rachel, in her own way, was also thinking of parentheses this afternoon. After she explained the duck association to

closed only when another duck drifts by in the opposite direction, unleashing a terminating series of brackish brackets;[1] (3) she can't tell whether the white blob in the branches of that cypress, jutting out from the righthand bank, is a trash bag or an ibis, since the tree is far enough off that her eyes are unable to register any of the blob's smaller movements—whether the whipping of windblown plastic or the wing-shuffling of a bird readjusting—and she has waffled for so long regarding which it is (sure one moment that it enjoys a heartbeat, and a gullet and guts, full of all the thrumming life that living birds are stuffed with; then equally certain an instant later that it's just a pale plastic bag, puffed up and empty with air) that by now the white blob seems positively anamorphic, a smear of ambiguity that resolves from one angle into a bird and from another into a bag, as if Rachel, merely by tilting her head and following the spectrum along which these two images merged, could watch

---

me, I shared my pavement association from earlier, the way that the streets seemed like parentheses cupping the lake. Rachel was no less moved than I was. She smiled and tapped my temple with her finger, implying that I'd broadcast the thought of parentheses to her. (And is not the parenthesis the punctuation mark of telepathy? Aren't all graphic representations of telepathy, in comic books I mean, just trails of parentheses? Readers know that one telepath is broadcasting thoughts to another when lunular mind waves—like this:)))—emanate from her forehead. So if I did in fact transmit the thought of parentheses to Rachel today, the thought would have been projected from my forehead parenthetically, rippling through the air like a duck's wake.)

[1] 'Brackish brackets' is Rachel's phrase. What I didn't point out to her is that the LSU Lakes are freshwater, such that the brackets aren't likely to be brackish. But of course the ducks in *Lake Charles* would emit brackish brackets, since the water is saltier there, so her image still stands.

the smooth plastic begin to feather, begin to grow a beak and black eyes, as the bag graded into the ibis.[1]

'Well,' she concludes, 'I guess that's it—that's pretty much what I've been thinking this whole time.' *That's it.* What pleasant things to be thinking! Reflections, ducks, ibis-bags, not one of them referring to the silhouette. I wish I could think such pleasant things. Maybe once the search is finally over, I'll be able to. Maybe next week we can walk back here, and I can make it a point to admire the eighteen-wheelers. For a moment I consider confessing to Rachel how badly I've betrayed the spirit of our day's goal. I consider telling her what's been weighing on my mind lately, every hitch in the search I've kept hidden from her, and then sharing all of my suspicions about the silhouette as well. I imagine the two of us laughing it off together: 'It looks nothing like Mazoch!' we would laugh. What made me think that that silhouette was Mazoch?

But just then my cell phone vibrates once against my thigh, and a nightmarish ice-water feeling floods my chest: I am certain that I am being notified of Mazoch's undeath. As I dig into my pocket and withdraw the phone, I brace myself for the sight of the display screen... only to see, however, that Mazoch himself has texted me. Same time tomorrow, he wants to know? There

---

[1] *This* is the painting technique responsible for Holbein blurs: anamorphosis! I never did remember to ask Rachel about it, but today I didn't have to. She simply intuited, as if telepathically, that I was curious, and used the term herself. I had to squeeze her hand when she said it. And as I tilted my head with her and studied the anamorphic metamorphoses of the trash bag, marveling at its mimicry of an ibis, I wondered for the first time whether I might have been falling victim to an identical illusion. Namely, whether the white blobs of the undead's eyeballs, similarly anamorphic, might contain none of the mystery that I keep straining to see in them, but are rather like this trash bag: just blurry garbage—puffed-up, hollow, empty. (A 'phallic ghost,' in Lacan's phrase for Holbein's skull: a 'trap for the gaze,' which 'reflects our own nothingness.')

on my cell phone is his name and his number, the message stamped at this very minute. But is it really possible? Mazoch, delivered like that from undeath? Suddenly becoming *not* that silhouette—as irrevocably *not it* as the ibis that's just launched from the cypress branch is not a plastic bag?

I text back—not 'Thank God you're alive'—but the letter 'Y.' And when Rachel asks me who it was, I simply say, 'Mazoch,' as if this weren't in itself a miracle to be savored.

FRIDAY

IT'S FIVE P.M., THE END OF A LONG DAY. AFTER waiting all morning in Denham, we've spent the past several hours—as on other Fridays—visiting quarantines. Now we're at the last on our list: the levee.[1] There is nowhere else to look. At

---

[1] On the drive over Matt explained that his parents, high-school sweethearts, went on their first date here, kissing on the bank of the brown river. Would the area have looked much different then? One of my favorite parts of the levee is where the city's name has been spelled out in oversized cast-iron letters: B-A-T-O-N R-O-U-G-E, affixed like refrigerator magnets to the sloping concrete. Each letter is big enough that you can actually recline inside its negative space. When Rachel and I still came out here, we liked to watch sunsets from within the cusp of the R. I find myself wondering whether the letters would have already been in place when Mr. and Mrs. Mazoch went on that first date, and if so, whether they nestled inside one, and if so, which. (To keep rainwater from pooling in the letters—e.g., in the triangle of the A, the cusp of the R, or the trough of the U—the sculptors installed sluiceways at an angle in the iron, PVC-lined passages through which the water could slant and drain. This is also how the letters are cleaned, since when rain washes down the concrete into the river, it carries the dirt off with it and purges the letters' enclosures. Something about this process has always fascinated me, as if the letters, and the words BATON ROUGE, were themselves being cleaned, semiotically as well as physically. So as if 'meaning' [so often referred to metaphorically as the 'sediment' of a sign, the rich associational crud that a word has accreted, and been encrusted over with, in the history of its usage] could be washed away alongside literal sediment. Every time that a storm's white spume gushes from the letters' downspouts, it looks as if the words are hemorrhaging meaning. [An image, incidentally, which seems to me like another good representation of the epidemic. For isn't this the effect that the infection has on language? Whenever the undead bite people, their victims' speech is soon reduced to moaning, as if undeath were a kind of contagious aphasia. By puncturing the skin with a bite of their

the base of the embankment, where the canted concrete yields to the yellow-grassed riverbank, Matt stands beside me with the binoculars, peering across the Mississippi. There are three barges moored on the opposite shore, each crammed to capacity with undead.[1]

The barges must be thirty yards away, but even from here I can distinguish the fence of chain-link that has been erected around each boat's perimeter, a barbwire barrier rising head-high and hazing the air with grayness. Standing behind the chain-link, boxed in on each bed, are what look to be two hundred undead silhouettes, packed shoulder to shoulder and wall to wall. Each barge resembles a little chunk of prison yard: the silver fence

---

dumb mouths, they might as well be puncturing the words themselves, so absolutely do these words hemorrhage their meanings. And once everyone is bitten, I often imagine, there will be no more spoken language: only this far dictionary of moaning. It's even almost tempting to think of the epidemic, of the undead in general, as having been sent to serve just that purpose, like some tidal wave of aphasia returning speechlessness to the earth: first to puncture words, installing sluiceways in the language, then to wash through them with the white spume of that moaning, rinsing the alluvia from their letters.])

[1] This is the LCDC's infamous flotilla of 'processing centers.' Until space can be made in the nursing homes or hospitals, the barges serve as auxiliary lazarettos, flat-bottom ferries on which the infected can float, waiting for some Charon to come quarantine them. Earlier this afternoon, as Matt and I were making the rounds of the real quarantines, he skimmed the thumbnail photos of their patient rosters, which LCDC still declines to post online (the logistics of such a database—a public registry of corpses' faces—have generally been too grisly to legislate): each Friday he has to sign in at front desks for access to the rosters, then flip through the clipboards for a mug shot of his father, and today this task felt more futile than ever (he had already checked the house in Denham a final time this morning. To my surprise, he didn't discover any muddy boot prints, or make any more mention of an extension). And now we're here, where no one has yet compiled a patient roster. The place is too makeshift for that. Mazoch just has to make do with the binoculars.

and the tense inmates. Presiding over these prison ships is a single police officer at the top of the levee, stationed in a glass guard booth on the slope directly behind us. The sun is hovering high overhead, spangling the muddy river water densely. That clouded current, purling south, is broad and brown, and where the light flecks it it looks nebular somehow, but fetid, like a diarrheal Milky Way. Indeed, so massive and cosmic is the Mississippi that the boats on it seem toylike. And at the sight of them it hits me—viscerally, as if for the first time—that obviously these infected cannot stay here: they will need to disembark before hurricane season.

Barging the undead, as LCDC and FEMA are now holding weekly press conferences to admit, is an untenable stopgap solution. Even if Baton Rouge is spared a direct collision in August or September, we can still expect storms heavy enough to demolish the fences, which is why LCDC's timeline requires decommissioning the ships in the next couple of weeks. Some pundits, still horrified at the thought of the infected being brought back ashore (especially if it means reinstating residential processing centers), have suggested that they simply be relocated a few yards downriver, aboard the USS *Kidd*, the *Fletcher*-class destroyer docked here as a war memorial. Easily capable of housing the few hundred bodies, the Navy vessel would then serve—from the pundits' point of view—as a kind of negative Noah's ark, preserving anti-creatures or demons from destruction by flood. But no one has seriously brought this suggestion before the Louisiana Naval War Memorial Commission, and it seems likelier that the city's surveyors will find some disused municipal building (a library, a prison, a dorm room) to be retrofitted as a quarantine. At any rate, they will have to find *something* before August. By then, any loose infected—any strays on the streets, who have not already been rounded up and quarantined, or else stumbled upon some reliable shelter to squat in—are going to be in for an interesting time: dashed by floods headfirst against telephone poles; brain-fried in electrified rainwater; crushed beneath fallen branches. Staring at the clear sky above us, I find it difficult to believe that there are already tropical storms forming over the Atlantic right now. But that is how it happens: one day you turn on the weather channel and see, in that satellite photo of the ocean far below, a cloudbank where the blue should be. It is vast, and white, with a spiral's pupil in its center, and it reminds you suddenly—as it couldn't have even a year ago—of an immense undead eyeball: milky, hundreds of miles wide, this blindness in the sky. You can monitor it daily, watching as it approaches the coast, but there is simply no way to tell: whether it will weaken once it hits land, or worsen as a hurricane; whether its winds will accelerate (ascending the pentatonic intensities of the Saffir-Simpson Scale: becoming a Category 3, then a 4, then a 5), or whether they will dissipate harmlessly. No way to tell till the week of. The day of. Those are the kinds of odds that Mr. Mazoch is looking at, if he's still on the streets come August. And though Mazoch has never spoken openly about this, it has to be some of what he's thinking right now as he chews the skin along the inside of his cheek, and scans the barges for his father's face.

'See anything?' I ask. He doesn't lower the binoculars. 'Matt?' '*Shh.*' I stare at him a moment longer, then turn to the silhouettes. Which one is it, I wonder? I hear Matt hiss 'Shit,' and when I glance back the binoculars are hanging at his chest. His face looks broken. 'What is it?' 'I thought it was him,' he says. 'It *was* him. But then it turned around.' 'Do you want to keep looking?' I ask. 'I can't make out any faces beyond the first rows.' Of course: as if the undead would have been arranged, as for a class photo, with tallest in the back. Our only option is to keep trying our luck from the levee. Disconsolate relatives are typically advised (as we were ten minutes ago, by the guard in his booth) to wait a week or so until the present load of infected has been relocated, then to make the rounds of the other quarantines ('Go back again,' Matt had sighed, exhausted).

'You want to take a look?' he asks, offering me the binoculars. I squint at the dim figures across the water, which together resemble some flash-mob mirage of the single lakeside silhouette from yesterday. He is asking whether I want to study them, on this our last day. But I shake my head. I do not need to see hundreds of undead eyes today. Rachel was right: the search is making me morbid. I need to think better thoughts. If there were only one out there, or even a handful, I might accept Matt's offer. I might try to satisfy my curiosity, or else—if I could never satisfy my curiosity—come to terms with the radical insatiability of my curiosity. But a whole crowd of them? To be overwhelmed by that wide wall of white eyes, hundreds, all bearing down on and boring through me... to have *that* be my last memory of the search? It would be too much.

After I decline the binoculars, Matt lifts his chin at something over my shoulder, then asks: 'You see that?' When I turn around all I see is the Mississippi Bridge: its great latticework of girders is gridded against the southern horizon like a waffle iron, filled with blue sky as with batter. Then, far above the bridge, I spot what must have caught Matt's attention: a high airplane, trailing a bright contrail behind it. The line of vapor has silvered brilliantly from within, and the jet, itself glinting like a knife tip, seems to be cutting into the sky to reveal it, carving a gash for this bright light to seep through. Like an incision being made in a lit lampshade. This is the first time since the travel ban has been enforced that I've seen a contrail in the sky. It's a species of cloud I'd thought had gone extinct, and watching this one now is strangely thrilling, the way that finding the first coelocanth must have been, or seeing the dove come back from the flood, olive leaf in beak. When Matt sees that I can see the jet, he asks, 'How many passengers do you think are infected on that plane?' 'Christ,' I say, 'I don't know.' Probably any passengers would be military personnel and FEMA agents, well screened by virologists before boarding. Nevertheless, I try to think of how many people would be inside the glint above us, and what the chances are that at least two or three of them could have made it through the screening process undetected: latent carriers, bearing the infection with them wherever the plane is bearing them. I say, 'Maybe zero.'

'I'm beginning to suspect my dad isn't even in Baton Rouge anymore,' Mazoch says. 'As in he's boarded a plane somewhere?' I ask. I try to imagine Mr. Mazoch making a getaway flight that first night, hours after he was bitten. Fleeing to Italy, and renting a hotel room to reanimate in.[1] But this is not what Mazoch has in mind. 'No,' he says, 'not necessarily. Just that he might have driven off, before… Or else crossed the border on foot.'

I have a difficult time telling how serious he is. Not only are there border guards stationed to keep the epidemic within state lines, but Mr. Mazoch, who seems never to have left southern Louisiana, would have too provincial a memory system to be compelled abroad anyway.[2] Mr. Mazoch, the prince recluse of Denham Springs, not only contracts an uncharacteristic wanderlust but also actually bypasses every border guard instructed to

---

[1] I've never considered the traveling undead before. What would happen if you reanimated while abroad? How would your undead body, discombobulated in this unfamiliar space, ever orient itself? If you were on vacation in Venice when the epidemic hit, and ended up getting infected, your body would just have to spend its undeath in Venice, wandering to your most recent haunts: the beach, the gondolas, the hotel restaurant.

[2] From the LCDC's point of view, provincialism like this is a blessing. The fewer undead there are trying to pass from city to city and state to state, the easier it is to staunch the epidemic at local levels. Like Mr. Mazoch, I'd be one of the more manageable undead. Shuffling within my hundred-mile nostalgic radius, I would pose no threat to Floridians or Texans and do nothing to help spread the infection. Let this, then, be my gift to the human race: that I've never left this place.

stop him? Those are a lot of what-ifs for Mazoch to be broaching now, on this our last day. But maybe that's simply what he needs to believe, in order to be able to quit: that his father won't be in Baton Rouge when the first hurricane hits. That he is too far abroad to be found. In order to absolve himself of the responsibility to go looking, Matt might be expanding the parameters of the search beyond feasibility, forking bales and bales of square miles onto the haystack that Mr. Mazoch is already the proverbial needle lost within.

Unless he has no intention of quitting. Unless what he is really doing—by placing Mr. Mazoch abroad in his mind—is precisely the opposite: extending the search indefinitely, devising a task that he could never satisfy himself as having finished. This way, after having scoured every inch of Baton Rouge, Matt would still have Texas, Florida, and Arkansas to check. Then he could move on to Montana, Mexico, the Mariana Trench. There would always be one more corner of the globe for Matt to search for his father in. And supposing that Matt survived beyond the year or so it would take Mr. Mazoch (in most climates) to decay, he might still feel obliged to check Alaska, or the North Pole while he was at it, or any other place where his father's body might have been frozen. If that is what Matt wants, I realize, I cannot help him: if he would prefer to spend the rest of his life holding out this last North Pole hope (laying away a little nest egg to buy a snowmobile with, so that he can go hunting for his popsicle father), then closure will be impossible. And maybe that has *always* been what Matt wanted. Not to find Mr. Mazoch, but to never find Mr. Mazoch: to forever have this desideratum dangling just out of reach, leading him day after day deeper into the calendar, like his own Bethlehem star to follow.

'Listen,' I say, and I want to ask Matt what it is that's driving him to find his father anyway, whether he wants to put the man down, out of his misery—whether *he* wants to be the one to do it, rather than a thunderstorm or a riot guard with an assault rifle—or whether he just wants to see for himself that the man is infected, and escort him safely to a quarantine. What it is he'd be unable to do or driven to the ends of the earth to do, if Mr. Mazoch actually were abroad. What I ask instead is, 'Do you really think that he's abroad?' 'No,' he says, 'or—I don't know.' He raises the binoculars again to peer across the water: 'But he's probably not on these barges.'

I look along with him, straining my eyes to distinguish the shapes of some of the undead. They're too far off even to tell how tall they are. Watching Matt as he watches, I see that he is no longer chewing his cheek: his square jaw is grim and set as he scans those rows of decaying faces. Somewhere among them is the Mr. Mazoch look-alike. I picture a hulking frame in a blue plaid shirt, its back to the binoculars. An undead ringer from behind. And what if he had never turned around? We would have had to call Rachel to cancel our celebration dinner and wait here, until finally the guard made us leave. Then we would have had to return here tomorrow, and the next day, and the next, until finally the barges were emptied, never able to find the doppelganger again in the crowd. Then we would have had to revisit all of the quarantines, skimming through the mug shots in the rosters, until finally Matt found the face that isn't his father's, the face that *could* have been his father's.

If Matt's hopefulness had been dragged out like that—if the close call had taken a week to resolve—I doubt that this search would be finished. As it stands, I can barely believe that it *is* finished. All day, as Matt has been taking his leave of Mr. Mazoch's sites, there have been very few leave-taking gestures: he did not lock the door in Denham, or even bother casing the antiques mall; he did not try returning to Citiplace, or to Highland Road Park. With silent unceremoniousness he drove us from one site to the next, then on to the quarantines, without the least degree of anxiety or panic. As methodical as on any other day this month. He didn't behave as if the search was over, because for part of him—I realize—it wasn't yet: the search wasn't finished until the day was. At each site there was still the next site to check, and after the quarantines, the barges. It was as if some part of him kept believing—up to the very last minute, until the doppelganger turned around—that his father might be found.

FOR DINNER, RACHEL MADE A RICH ORANGE curry that she had me slice potatoes for, and I threw together a very basic salad: greens, cheese, balsamic. Mazoch thoughtfully brought a bottle of wine, a Gewürztraminer[1] that I had to drink Rachel's glass of because she complained, smacking her mouth and her face, that it was too sweet. She polished off a glass of Syrah instead, and now we're all pleasantly drunk at the table. Although the ostensible occasion for this dinner is the end of the search, none of us have dared discuss it. Nor has Rachel interrogated Matt about his motives. The furthest she has gone is to ask him how our day went, and the two of them have been going back and forth about quarantines. To distract myself in the meanwhile, I've been watching the candle flames gutter in their sockets.[2] And on my salad plate there is a leftover film of balsamic and olive oil, a viscid, deep-brown emulsion, which— when I incline the plate left and right—rolls darkly down to the edges, like a storm cloud on a dish. Neither Rachel nor Matt seems to notice me.

'If you ask me,' Matt continues, 'LCDC are being big softies. Tremendous softies. The infected need to be burned or buried,

---

[1] Mazoch: 'I picked this one out because it sounded like a tank.'

[2] When Rachel first lit the wicks, there was still a good bit of wax built up around the bases of the brass candlesticks: the white runoff had congealed somehow anthropomorphically, in these knotted strands, such that it looked as if a congregation of gnarled ghosts was kneeling in prayer before the flame. They reminded me of the nightgown-clad and spectral infected that I had seen standing in the pasture that one morning. Midway through dinner, though, they all began to soften from the flame and melt, pooling in haunted puddles on the tablecloth.

not barged. Not treated to a cruise on the Mississippi.' Rachel looks horrified, and I know she's struggling not to bring up Mr. Mazoch: 'That's so... *callous*. You can't be serious.' 'Do you know what Baton Rouge's current ratio is? Of the undead to the living? Something like one to twenty. So about forty thousand undead. That's as if every LSU student were infected. And you're telling me that you want to keep them on barges and in quarantines?' 'Well, we couldn't keep them there forever. But we can't just kill them all either. They're people, they have families. Imagine—' 'Families they wouldn't blink at eating.' '—imagine if every coma victim in the nation were euthanized at once, or everyone with Alzheimer's. That would be so tragic. Whatever this infection is, we've known about it for less than a year. We've had less than a year to study it. Why not just be patient, wait for a cure?' 'Because there's no cure for death!' Mazoch says, laughing. 'You don't rub Neosporin on a dead body—you burn it or you bury it.' 'You're talking about genocide.' 'No, absolutely not, it is misguided, boneheaded, and dangerous to talk about genocide. There could be nothing less relevant or helpful right now than mapping human models of violence over what's happening. This talk about *euthanizing* the undead or *murdering* the undead. Committing *genocide*. The only vocabulary commensurate with the epidemic is an epidemiological one, one that calls a virus a virus. Each undead body is a viral agent, programmed only to spread a disease, and I could no more murder one than I could murder HIV.' 'The problem with that analogy—' 'You want to personalize them, I understand that. They wander back to their homes, as if they remember, as if they're still people. You hear pundits say, "They need to be burned," and you bristle. You learned about the Holocaust like everyone else in elementary school, so you think we're on the verge of some equivalent evil: the systematic cremation of millions of people. But these aren't people. This is nothing like Europe's so-called Jewish problem. If anything, this is a dybbuk problem. And if we don't put a bullet in the head of every one of them, sooner or later it's going to be a problem of apocalyptic proportions.' 'You can't believe that. You sound like a movie trailer.' 'I really do believe it. There are forty thousand contagious cannibals—and think about that for a moment. *Contagious* cannibals. You get bitten and you become one, you are what you're eaten by. Nothing could proliferate more factorially, more fatally, than a virus like that. And there are forty thousand of these killing machines being kept in, what, libraries? Dorm rooms? Barges? What happens when they break free? What happens when a hurricane hits and causes another "spill," or when the virus mutates and becomes airborne?' 'So that's your final solution: a bullet in the head of every infected citizen. Don't bother building a more secure quarantine, or housing them on some kind of land preserve. Don't study them and try to understand the infection. Just burn them or bury them. Never mind the fact that there's clearly something still left in there, some residue of who they used to be. Memories of certain neighborhoods, motor skills. When you see a little infected girl picking up her violin, or when you see those lab experiments: how smart they still are, their aptitude for problem solving—' 'Problem solving! Let me tell you about problem solving. The only problem they'll solve is how to get past your barricades and eat you alive. Problem solving of the octopus prying open the oyster. Problem solving of the polar bear unzipping the zipper of the tent. *Those* are the problems they know how to solve.' 'But that's just it. We have no reason to believe they can't be domesticated. What if they can be trained, tamed, taught not to attack people?' 'Rotting corpses as household pets, or in the zoos. A plague straight out of Revelations, an army of walking dead, and you'll picket for their domestication.' 'I'll "picket" so that innocent people aren't killed. These *are* people, Matt. People with a disease. Do you know what I heard on the news the other week? There was a sound bite of an infected man moaning. A speech pathologist had taught him to say "Barbara." He drew it out in a moan, it was breathy, but it was clear as day: "Barbara." Barbara, his daughter, was in the studio when they played the sound bite, and after she heard him say her name, she buried her face in her hands and wept.' 'That's very heartwarming. You could teach a parrot to say "Barbara." You could teach a Furby to say "Barbara"! This is echolalia and nothing else, this is sophism and wishful thinking. Here's a sound bite for Barbara: have a speech pathologist teach one to moan, "We are going to eat you." We are going to eat you! That's all their moaning means. Teach one to say that, and then we'll see whether little Barbara bursts into tears.' 'She was forty.' 'Who?' 'Barbara. You called her "little Barbara." But she was forty years old.'

It is at this point that Matt turns to me. 'Well, you've been especially quiet this evening. What do you think about all this?'

What have I been thinking? That Matt's vehemence in this debate comes as a shock, even to me. I can't help wondering how much of it is the Gewürztraminer talking. The disappointment talking. Whether it is perhaps just the pointlessness of the barges—his anger at his missing father—that is fueling his resentment of the undead race right now. Or whether he is simply being provocative, contrarian, baiting Rachel with this eradication rhetoric. Whatever the explanation, he can't possibly believe the things he's been saying tonight. And even if he does believe them tonight, he couldn't possibly have believed them *this entire time*, every day this past month. Could he? The crestfallen son I saw at Citiplace was not on the lookout for a 'contagious cannibal' or 'killing machine' to kill: he was searching for his father. So if Matt really does propose mass extermination, then he has to be making some exception in his heart for Mr. Mazoch. Doesn't he? Not that he would shelter him and keep him alive, necessarily, just that he would be horrified if he found a lynch mob dismembering him. That at some level Matt must recognize the residual humanity of Mr. Mazoch—his ineliminable

Mr. Mazochness—since at some level Matt must feel that only he, Mr. Mazoch's son, bears the right or the responsibility to murder the man (if, indeed, he plans to murder the man). Otherwise, why search like this? Why race against what clock? Why not let the exterminators take care of him, or the armed guard, or the hurricane? Is more or less what I've been thinking.

I've also been thinking about Rachel, whose face has been growing increasingly distraught, and who has surely been imagining Matt putting a 'bullet in the head' of Mr. Mazoch. If she had heard him going on like this any earlier, there would have been no question of her condoning the search. And it's been valiant of her—in light of the search's failure, when all this rhetoric is empty and inconsequential—to refrain from bringing up his father. To keep the argument abstract.

I, too, would like to keep the argument abstract, and the final thing I've been thinking is how to explain Rachel's point of view to Matt. Put it in terms he'd understand. I want to try to communicate her empathy for the undead—her respect for creation[1]—without any more recourse to infected fathers or little Barbaras. So when he asks what I've been thinking, I ask in turn, 'Have you read *Homo Sacer*?' 'No,' he says, 'but I've played bisexual baseball.' 'No, like—' 'I'm kidding. Of course I've read *Homo Sacer*.'

---

[1] Because of course her respect for creation would encompass the undead. When for breakfast she eats a grapefruit on the landing, holding closed her bathrobe and watching the sunrise over the apartment complex's courtyard, and announces, 'It's a perfect morning,' she means all of it, nothing escapes her, not the sweet pink of the grapefruit, or the warm breeze, nor the bare light that collects in the glisten in her spoon, nothing, and if there happened to be an infected in the courtyard that morning, not that either. Her heart is like the sweep of a radar screen, this white line revolving a green field. Missing nothing and loving every blip. This is probably not something that Matt would understand. *I* barely understand. Which is why I've been trying to think of other terms to put it in.

But Rachel, as it turns out, hasn't, so for her benefit I find myself drunkenly reconstructing Agamben's argument[1] before making my own point, which is that, basically, Rachel's ethical unease regarding the reduction of the undead to something like bare life may after all be justified. 'Because you can imagine exactly the kind of argument that Agamben would make: the undead occupy a "zone of indistinction," a cloudy biological interstice, and it would be all too easy to dehumanize them, justifying anything from forced labor to genocide. Even if you reject the term "genocide," you're still talking about extinction. You'd be wiping out a new form of life in less than a year of its inception. Think of what scientists still have to learn from them: organisms of dead cells, creatures that persist *beyond* cell death. For all we know this could be a net evolutionary gain, the human race's phylogenetic solution to mortality. So I think what Rachel's saying is, "Hold on, let's wait a minute—before we do anything rash why don't we study this some more."' 'And what I'm saying is that we don't have a minute. We have approximately until hurricane season.' 'Yes, Matt, you've made it abundantly clear

---

[1] Which I think I do an okay job of. The book is bound up with the 'zones of indistinction' between life and death, namely what happens when political life is stripped from biological life (e.g., when a citizen is deprived of human rights), such that someone is biologically alive while legally dead. Agamben's eponymous mascot for this mode of 'bare life' is *homo sacer*, a figure in classical Roman law who could be murdered with impunity— without its being considered criminal homicide—but who couldn't be sacrificed. (Agamben, for this reason, refers to *homo sacer* as a 'living dead man.') Other examples abound, all of them politically disquieting: refugees who are afforded no rights in their host countries, German Jews who were fastidiously denaturalized before being murdered in the concentration camps, coma victims who are declared clinically dead before being euthanized, et al. In each case the divestment of political life from the biological body authorizes the murder, torture, or mistreatment of the living-dead man in question—a point that, in however slurred or garbled a fashion, I think I'm able to convey to Rachel.

already that that's what you're saying.' 'The insane thing isn't that walking corpses might be divested of their legal rights, Michael. That's not the insane thing. The insane thing is that they haven't been *yet*, that it's been two months now and legal rights still adhere to them—walking corpses!—even as they decay on their feet. You don't find that insane? True, the police aren't going to conduct any murder investigations, if they find a slain undead in the streets. But by letter of the law you could be arrested for homicide. "Man"slaughter. That's what's insane!' 'The only people who have been or are going to be arrested for homicide are the sadists who lynch the infected. And you probably feel even as strongly as I do that lynch mobs shouldn't be allowed to string stray infected up in trees. I hate to invoke families again—you seem to think it's rhetorically illegitimate—but imagine if "little Barbara" walked outside and saw her undead father hanged, ten drunk men beating at him like a piñata. Or saw them pouring gasoline over him in the yard, setting him ablaze. These are the people who are and who will be arrested, not the families who quietly decide to put an undead relative to sleep.' 'What you—'

Rachel expresses her desire to be talking about something else, and in response we all stop talking. The room becomes sauna-like with silence, the quiet as thick and conspicuous as heat. I'm still thinking about what I was just on the brink of saying: I wanted to ask Matt how *he* would react, if it were Mr. Mazoch who had been taught to moan 'Matt,' or if it were Mr. Mazoch strung up in a tree. As for Matt, he's probably still on his own brink.

Eventually he is the one to break the silence. Clearing his throat, he addresses me: 'Mike,' he says. 'Matt,' I say. 'Listen,' he says. 'About my dad's windows.' I do some throat-clearing of my own. So he's finally ready to confess about the windows: either to claim responsibility for them, or to admit that he never truly suspected his father. To spare him the awkwardness—and to keep him from divulging any need-to-know information that Rachel does not need to know—I try to cut him off. 'Matt, I—'

'I need to know who broke them,' he says. Rachel sits up at this. 'What?' she asks. 'Someone broke your dad's windows?' He wipes his palm in the air before him, as if washing a windowpane: 'Right in the front of his house. First thing we saw Wednesday morning.' 'Oh, my God,' she says. 'I'm so sorry. I had no idea.' 'Mike didn't tell you?' 'No,' she says, looking confused. 'It must have slipped his mind.' Matt turns to me: 'You didn't run it by her?' 'Run what?' I ask. 'The extension. You said you'd run it by her.' 'You'd run *what* by me?' Rachel asks. Before Matt can spill the entire miserable business to her, I interrupt him: 'Matt, I thought you knew. This was our last day. This *dinner.*' 'No,' he says, shaking his head. 'No, I can't quit now. Not yet. I need to give it more time. Just in Denham, just another week or so. You don't have to come—' Here he stops himself, for we both know this isn't true. I *do* have to go with him. I can't let him go alone. That's the only reason he's sharing this absurd plan with me: he knows I'll insist on going with him.

'"Extension"?' Rachel repeats, narrowing her eyes at me. I wince. After everything Matt has said tonight, I realize how this must look to her. She must think that I have known all along about Matt's violence (his genocidal rants, the volatility of his emotions, his clear and present capacity for patricide): that I have known about it but ignored it, turned a blind eye to it, even done my part to conceal it from her. She must think that I have been hiding the windows and the extension for the same reason. In short, that I have been Matt's willing accomplice, accompanying him on a manhunt while downplaying all of its dangers. In a sense, of course, she's right. That is exactly what I've been doing. There are things that I've been hiding from her: Matt's violence, my doubts. And if he weren't here right now, I'm sure I could explain it. Make her understand why I had to keep silent. But that's not going to happen while he's sitting there listening.

For now, I try to soft-pedal the extension: 'It was just an idea Matt was floating,' I tell her. 'Hypothetically.' I look to Matt for confirmation, but he is still shaking his head: 'Mike, I told you. I need to know who broke them.' '*You* broke them!' I almost shout, biting my lip just in time. He continues: 'You don't believe me about the windows. I know that. And it's fine.' 'Matt, it's not a matter of whether—' 'That's fine,' he repeats. 'Because I can just go alone.' 'Alone?' 'I've been thinking about it,' he says. 'And I can't quit now, even if you do. Not two days after the break-in, not with two weeks left till hurricane season. I'm going to Denham tomorrow. I told you, you don't have to come—' Again he stops himself, providing me an opportunity to rush in to his rescue. I look to Rachel for assistance, or permission, but now she is the one shaking her head. 'Michael?' she says. 'You're going?'

After a moment of strained silence, I splay my hands in helplessness. 'Of course,' I tell her. 'You didn't think I'd let him drive out there alone?' I try to keep my tone breezy, smoothing over any hints of tension for Mazoch's sake. 'What's a few more days?' I ask. Rachel smiles weakly. 'No, no,' she says, like a gracious hostess, 'a few more days. It's nothing.' 'Really,' Matt protests, 'you don't have—' But Rachel cuts him off: 'Michael's right,' she says. 'You can't go alone. It's too dangerous.' I can tell by her voice that she and I do not have the same danger in mind. It's not Matt's safety she's worried about: it's Mr. Mazoch's.

Matt beams at us both, as if genuinely oblivious, and lifts his wineglass over the table. With the last remaining sip of Gewürztraminer, he raises a toast to 'one more week.' We all clink drinks, and Rachel shoots me a withering glance over the rim of her glass. Matt doesn't notice this either. Later in the night, when he finally rises to leave, he even hugs Rachel good-bye, and at the door he squeezes my hand hard, gripping my bones like a barbell. 'See you tomorrow?' he asks. 'Same time?'

'Same time,' I say.

'Same time?' Rachel repeats, the moment I've closed the door, without any regard for her volume or for how far down the walkway Matt could have possibly gotten. She's standing behind the couch, arms crossed over her chest: 'You have to stop him.' 'I'll talk to him tomorrow,' I promise. 'Not good enough,' she says. 'Don't "talk to" him, Michael. *Stop* him. You heard him tonight. He's a murderer. He's a homicide waiting to happen. If he keeps on like this, he'll—' 'What am I supposed to tell him? Tell me what to tell him, what *you* would tell him, and I'll tell him.' 'Tell him he's a maniac, Michael! That he's driving himself insane!' 'Rachel, I can't tell him that.' 'Why not? Because it will hurt his feelings?' 'Mazoch? I'd be more afraid of his feelings hurting me. I'd be more afraid of Mazoch flexing his feelings, and a button popping off his shirt and hitting me in the eye.' 'Tell him he needs to quit the search. Tell him that if he kills his father, if he kills a *fly*, you're calling the police. Tell him you'll have him locked up for "man"slaughter, if it comes down to that. I don't care what you tell him. But don't come home and tell me that you've set him loose for another week.' She stops herself here, taking a deep breath. And although she doesn't say as much, I can sense the ultimatum lurking beneath her final sentence: that it's the search or her. That if I continue to accompany Matt now—aiding and abetting him in what certainly seems like murder—she couldn't bear to live with me. Yet staying home isn't an option either: if I call it quits without trying to intervene—if I simply dust my hands of Matt and Mr. Mazoch, looking the other way on a potential patricide—she will hold me partially to blame for whatever happens. I shake my head in disbelief: 'You make it sound like I want him out there. Like I approve of all this. What, do you think I'd help him hide the body?' 'Like you hid the extension, you mean? And the windows? And God knows what else?' 'I didn't want to frighten you, is all. I assumed a hooligan had vandalized the house.' I pause to assess the truth value of this (Matt qualifies, probably, as a hooligan), then press on: 'And since the search was almost over anyway—' Rachel rolls her eyes at the lameness of this explanation, leaving me no option but to double down on it. 'It was an error in judgment,' I say, 'and now you can't forgive me. I'm not just a liar apparently, but a killer too. You hear Matt spouting off for one night about the Holocaust and dybbuk problems, and suddenly I'm his Eichmann. Honey, you can trust me. You don't have to worry about Mr. Mazoch.' 'Let's not talk about Mr. Mazoch, Michael.' 'Why not?' 'Just, let's not talk about him. Okay?' 'Why? What is it this time?' 'Drop it.' 'You think I'm insufficiently sensitive to discuss Matt's father?' '*Drop* it.' 'You think I'm too callous and fanatical, like Matt?' 'You really want me to tell you?' 'Yes! Please!' 'I know how you see them. Mr. Mazoch is no more human to you than he is to Matt: just a weird new life form. You'd sooner strap him to an EEG than get him to a quarantine. You'd rather hand him over to Oliver Sacks than to LCDC. No, Michael, I "trust" you. I know you would never let Matt kill him. You're too obsessed. Sometimes I think what you really want—' 'What? Say it.' 'Is to be infected yourself.' 'Jesus Christ.' 'Just so you can see what it's like.'

As Rachel and I continue to argue (while doing dishes, cleaning the kitchen, brushing our teeth), I try not to let on how much her accusation has shaken me. But I can't stop thinking about what she's said. I know that it's preposterous, of course: *I* know—even if Rachel doesn't—that I'm not some overzealous Jekyll, ready to inject myself with a sample. Yet it's still disturbing that that is how she sees me. When I review the few risks I've been exposing myself to lately (for instance, hiking into an overgrown field), I can hardly imagine the mountains she must be making of them: treating each as an attempt at self-destruction, a way of flirting with infection. As if, in her eyes, I'm just as bad as Matt. As if there is some subconscious part of me—a hidden undeath drive—that *desires* being bitten. Is that why she thinks I'm accompanying him tomorrow?

In the end, I promise her I will find some way of 'stopping' him. This is as we're lying in bed, that I promise her this. She has her back to mine, in the addorsed posture of domestic discord, and I think I can feel her nod in the dark. We pass the rest of the night in silence. For my part, I have not been able to fall asleep. I doubt that Rachel has either. As I've been lying here, my back to hers, I dread the things she must be thinking. How I've betrayed her. How she doesn't know me. 'Who is this person?' she must be asking herself. 'This stranger? What is he doing in my bed?'

SATURDAY

ON THE DRIVE INTO DENHAM THIS MORNING, NOT long after we cross the bridge, Matt and I hit a roadblock. Fifty yards from Mr. Mazoch's, there is a checkpoint barring the way: sputtering flares, orange barricades, riot guards. 'What's this?' Matt asks, slowing to a stop. He starts to cut the wheel left, and I assume that he's about to turn around. Take us home. Instead, he drives us down a side street, circumventing the barriers, and after a series of back alleys and shortcuts that I do not recognize, we emerge on the other side of the roadblock, pulling into Mr. Mazoch's driveway.

From here, it's immediately clear what the commotion is. At the Freedom Fuel down the street, there are four police cruisers in the parking lot, corralling a crowd of what looks like fifteen infected silhouettes. These can't be strays—there must have been a 'spill' at one of the nearby quarantines. Matt and I turn to watch the scene through the back window: the cruisers are parked hood to hood in a quadrilateral formation, penning in the silhouettes, which shuffle back and forth restlessly. Until an LCDC van can arrive, they are evidently going to have to be wrangled this way. Indeed, even as I am thinking this, I hear a siren somewhere behind us, a single far-off *whoop-whoop*. I glance back to the windshield, expecting to see the LCDC van coasting up the road, but what I see is another orange barricade, which has since been dragged into the street we used to get here. Trapping us in. I laugh to myself. Of course we're trapped here. Of course this is happening. The one day that we overstep the deadline—on our *first* supernumerary day—Mazoch drives us into a maelstrom of moaning corpses. At least I'm here with him, I console myself. I was right to come, just as I told Rachel.

Because if Matt were alone right now, he would surely be sprinting into that parking lot, trying to wrestle his way past the riot guards.

As if reading my thoughts, Matt begins to unbuckle his seatbelt. 'Hey?' I ask. 'What's up?' Without answering he pushes the car door open and climbs out, and before I have a chance to stop him he is hurrying across the yard. But he does not sprint toward the Freedom Fuel, as I had expected. He goes jogging up the driveway and disappears into the house. It does not take me long to realize what he himself must have realized: that if Mr. Mazoch *is* one of those infected, then there may be signs of struggle in the living room. That is what he has raced inside to find. Shattered chairs, boot scuffs on the linoleum, claw marks in the walls. Any proof that his father has been dragged out bodily, kicking and moaning, by the riot guards now holding him at the gas station. I wait for what feels like much more than a minute—five, ten—before I finally stop counting. Probably he has taken up his post by one of the windows, peering through the binoculars at the parking lot. Scanning the crowd for his father's face.

I still have not tried talking to Matt this morning. We left my apartment in silence, with some vestigial tenseness from last night. My plan was to deliver my speech when we got here, but I was too infuriated. Now I'm stuck waiting in the car, killing time until he returns. It will have to be when he gets back. The moment he sits down in the driver's seat, I will have to talk to him. And so that is what I have been preparing to do while he's been inside: rehearsing what I will say to him. Drafting an apostrophic monologue in my mind. Telling him things in my head and telling myself that I'll tell them to him when he returns. What I've been telling him is this:

'No, listen. You're never going to find your father. Isn't it time you gave up this particular ghost? To have checked the number of sites that we have, the number of times that we have, for as long a time as we have, would have been enough to satisfy any reasonable person. Your father's obviously been hit by a car or shot dead, or else he's fallen off the map altogether. Wandered into a swamp and sunk. But you're not a reasonable person. You want to check each site more, even to check more sites. You ask me, "What if he isn't in Baton Rouge?" What if? You'll drive to New Orleans, Mississippi, Arkansas, is what if. And why? Because he's "a walking corpse!", "a rotting corpse!", "straight out of Revelations!" Because he has to be "burned or buried!" forthwith! Until you went off like a Neo-Nazi about the need to extinguish the infected, I thought that you might still want to protect the man. If your goal was to commit him to a quarantine before he got himself killed, if our search was conceived as a rescue mission, then indeed your indefatigability would be noble. But it's obvious that your only aim is patricide: not to avenge your father's murder, but to re-murder your murdered father. And so your indefatigability is insane. Three weeks ago, when there was a chance he could be found, even this—a mercy killing—might have seemed reasonable to me. But now? The odds are so high that he's already dead, yet still you need to find him. You're combing rubble, ground zero, for the man you want to kill. We're well beyond the dedication of a son who can't stand the thought of his undead father. This is the dedication of a warlord, a warlord ordering his enemy's head! And you'll go further even than that. You won't stop until you sever his head yourself! With your own hands! It's not enough for you to just assume that he's roadkill, you have to *see* him dead—best if beaten to death by you of course—and you'll search full-time to do it. Where is all this energy and anger coming from? What has been sustaining you every day for the past month? Whom or what would you even be avenging by killing your father? Certainly not your father. Are you mad at him for letting himself get bitten? Did those unboarded windows, that unlocked door, seem as careless to you, as selfish, as the cigarettes and fast food that he gave himself a heart attack with? Do you think that he has neglected his obligations to you as a father, that he should have fought harder for your sake to survive? That, if he really loved you, he would have come to Citiplace? What shit! You don't need me to tell you what shit that is, Matt. Because blaming a man for dying is what's selfish. And clocking eight-hour days to hunt the object of your mourning, so that you can vent your rage on it with a baseball bat. For that matter, enlisting your friend to accompany you on this manhunt, endangering that friend by driving him through infected neighborhoods, without being forthright with him about your motives; but enlisting him anyway because his presence "helps you not to think"—i.e., helps you not to get locked into the obsessive and embittered track of indictments against your father, memories of your father, thoughts of your father that would eat you alive as surely as your father would if only you were left alone with them—is what's selfish. To say nothing of shattering windows like some madman, so as to fabricate evidence, and feeding me a line about how we've been "closing in"... all so that you could spring this extra week on me at the last minute. And what happens then? Am I supposed to ride sidecar like this for another month? A year? How long do you need to keep looking, before you finally accept that there's nothing to find? No. I can't let you keep on like this. Not for another week. Not for another *day*. Whatever it is that I'm complicit in by accompanying you in this, it isn't healthy for you or right. Call this the intervention of a concerned friend, consider this my official unsolicited advice to you: quit when I do. Forget the search. Try volunteering or something else instead. Defer to the hurricane and count your dad among the victims. But don't spend another week gnawing at this wound. Because I won't be gnawing at it with you.'

Is more or less what I've been thinking at Matt this morning. Now I twist around in my seat again, to check on the progress at the Freedom Fuel. In the time that I've been waiting, additional infected have arrived: either attracted on their own by the commotion, or else rounded up in the vicinity. Wherever they came from, six new silhouettes have converged on the nearest cruiser, clumping around its sides. If the police are concerned about this, they don't show it. As I watch, a single infected (a stick figure, at this distance) detaches itself from the hood and starts wandering across the parking lot. The cruiser merely flashes its sirens—they glint blue-red, blue-red for three revolutions above its roof—and the infected comes shuffling back.

At the thought of Mazoch watching this from the window, through his binoculars, I become strangely enraged. I can actually feel the monologue welling up in my mouth, like spit before the vomit, and I unbuckle my seatbelt as violently as I can before flinging open the car door.

But when I jog up the driveway and up the porch steps and barge into the living room, I don't find Matt standing at any of the windows. He's slumped on the sofa: elbows on knees, head in hands. The binoculars are lying on the cushion beside him. He looks up at me. 'Any news out there?' 'No,' I say, 'not yet.'

I take a moment to survey the living room. For the most part it's as I suspected: no signs of struggle, no traces. But this is the first I've been inside since beginning the search, and I'm surprised by the degree of dilapidation. The place looks even more miserable than I remembered. In the short time that the windowpanes have been shattered, the interior appears to have been exposed to catastrophic elements: the carpet where I stand is sodden from dew and rain, and the July air is heavy and hot and hard to inhale, exactly as humid in here as outside. Along the walls, the outlets are nicotine brown around the sockets (power surge?), and in the corner of the room, all three bulbs of the brass floor lamp (whose central pole branches out into three adjustable eyestalks, forming an ommatophorous torchiere, each stalk capped with a miniature trumpet shade of jade-green glass) are blown, charred black from poppage. Elsewhere the unchecked humidity seems to have had effects that I associate only with serious flood damage, for instance in post-Katrina photos of abandoned buildings: the five faux-mahogany particleboard blades of Mr. Mazoch's ceiling fan all droop downward now, curling together in a tarantula of warped wood; and the walls' navy paint seems to be, like, *bubbling* in places, trapped air (I guess) swelling it upward in convex blobs. The place is falling apart. Plus random animals appear to have taken advantage of the shattered windows as well. Dotting the gray carpet are the dried fecal pellets of free-ranging rodents and cats, which fauna are probably also responsible for the shredded paper strewn around the coffee table.

This coffee table—actually an old treasure chest, wooden, with a vaulted top and rusted hinges—is currently serving Matt as a footrest. I wonder whether he has been sitting there this whole time, kicking up his feet while I waited alone in the car. Or, for that matter, whether he has been sitting like that all week, every morning after his inspections. This is the room that he has had to see each day. He looks up at me again, head still in hands, and sees me staring: 'What?'

'Listen,' I say, on the verge of launching into my monologue. But I find that I'm unable to. I snap at him instead: 'Well, what are you waiting for? Aren't you going to come look out the window? You've got a straight shot with the binoculars.' He shakes his head. 'I looked earlier,' he says, and there is immense futility and tiredness in his voice. I wonder whether he knows about the new arrivals, the six additional infected to buoy his hope, but I have no intention of telling him. 'I'm sorry, you know,' he says. 'For driving you out here like this. Into the middle of a lockdown. You were right the other day, what you said: about the risks I've been taking. What we're doing is dangerous, and you didn't have to do it. So thanks.' 'Well thanks, Matt. I appreciate that.' 'And I just wanted to tell you that you don't have to worry about it. About me—' 'Really, it's—' '—because I'm finished.'

I study his face for some clue, but it's inscrutable. 'Finished?' 'This, the search, it's over. You were right. It's been over, and today's the last day I'm going to ask you to do this. So I wanted to let you know. You know. How much I've appreciated...' 'The help.' 'Everything.' Somewhere behind me, another far-off siren sounds outside, and Matt lifts his chin at the window: 'How are things looking at the Freedom Fuel?' I turn to the frame and make a show of peering through it (I even arch all ten fingers over my brow, forming a glare-reducing testudo with my hands, such that I am the very image of flamboyant voyeurism), but in truth I'm too distracted by what Matt's just said to concentrate, and anyway there don't appear to be any new details to discern: the six new infected are still absorbed by the cruiser; the LCDC van is still nowhere to be seen. 'Well?' he asks. 'No sign,' I say.

I continue looking out the window all the same, fingers steepled at my forehead, rather than turn to face him. I can barely process what he's said. If it's really true that he's finished, then that would at least absolve me from the obligation of delivering my monologue. Reasonable, realistic, and resigned, he would not need to be talked out of anything. But on the other hand, this is the same Mazoch whom I had imagined—just yesterday—driving himself to the ends of the earth, his deepest desire precisely never to be finished. It's possible that he's only telling me what he thinks I need to hear. If he has a bad conscience about putting me in danger or endangering my relationship—if he regrets having invited me along in the first place—then he might be trying to get me to quit. He did declare this the last day of *our* search, after all, not his. His exact words were, 'Today's the last day I'm going to ask you to do this.' Maybe Mazoch, in his own way, was trying to insinuate or admit that he has every intention of carrying on with the search without me.

'So what are you going to do?' I ask him. I keep my voice casual: 'Now that you're finished.' 'I'm not sure, to be honest. Maybe volunteer. Take a look at one of the shelters.' 'That's good. I was going to say something about that.' Mazoch doesn't respond. If he's planning to continue the search on his own, he evidently isn't going to tell me. But if he wants to keep his search a secret, let him. Let him drive alone to this dilapidated house, and sit on that waterlogged sofa, every morning for the rest of the summer, if that's the form his mourning takes. When Rachel and I invite him over for dinner, we'll just talk about other things. And when he and I meet up to play chess, we'll studiously avoid the subject. We'll all pretend he isn't waiting still.

'What about you?' he asks. 'You and Rachel?' 'Oh,' I say, 'I don't know. She'll just be happy that I'm home.' Or vice versa. On my way out this morning, Rachel stopped me at the door, placing her hands on my shoulders. She made me promise that today would be the last day. I nodded, said 'I promise,' and gave her a covenantal kiss on the cheek. If I had decided to go out again tomorrow, there's no guarantee that she would have been home when I got back. And even with the search over, it will take longer than next week for us to normalize. Worry for Matt will continue to be the explicit subject or tacit subtext of our every waking moment. Whenever he doesn't answer his phone, Rachel will assume that he's snuck off to Denham. And whenever I go out to buy milk, she'll assume that I've snuck off with him. I doubt that Matt fully appreciates this—the extent of the dust cloud that he has left behind him, domestically—and I'm tempted to let him know. No, Matt, Rachel and I have not made plans. We haven't been able to think too far beyond your manhunt.

'Plus there are projects,' I say. 'Things to do around the apartment, hurricane-wise.' In the silence I feel Mazoch nodding behind me. It may have just occurred to him—as it's occurred to me—that this house, too, is unprepared, hurricane-wise. If no FEMA crews get here first, it'll probably be demolished come August. A single week of mild storms would be enough to reduce the living room to a ruin: for rain to lash in through the broken windows; for mud and mold, for water rot, to claim everything; and for the creeping tendrils and vines, which cling already to the window frames, to spill over into the space of the house, covering the floors with lush overgrowth. Followed by whatever havoc would be wrought by the rodents and cats, driven inside by the wind. So even if Mazoch *wants* to keep coming here—sitting vigil among his father's things; basking in the memories of the man that they catalyze—soon enough that won't be an option. There won't be any 'here' here to speak of. By September, whatever of his father's things remain will be utterly defaced: the antiques and trinkets strewn across the room will be rusted over, and the furniture all moth-eaten and murling. Sunlight will puncture the staved-in roof, birds roost in the rafters. Every surface will be maculated with mold. Eventually the space, arrogated by nature in this way, won't even remind Matt of his father at all. Its signifiers of 'Mr. Mazoch' will gradually be overcoded by signifiers of ruin, anonymized by them, until 'Mr. Mazoch's house' has grown indistinguishable from any other disaster site: just generically derelict, and therefore unrecognizable. Whether or not Matt gives up looking for his father, I have to imagine he'll give up coming here.

I turn back to look at him. He's still got his elbows on his knees, head in hands, and though his shoulders flex beneath the thin white cotton of his t-shirt, he looks small somehow. Hunched into himself like that. He even looks—sitting alone on his dad's sofa, in the middle of his dad's wrecked and ransacked living room, surrounded by all the dead man's antiques—like a little kid. His dad died here. This is the place he died. And the sofa, the wooden chest, the brass floor lamp: these are his dead dad's things. In any other era, Matt might have inherited them. Now he sits among them, in the house where his dead dad came back, and where for a month Mazoch has waited, daily, for his dead dad to come back. He won't be coming back. Not here, not if he hasn't already. And not only that, but who knows where he even is by now. Matt knows that. Something in his hunched posture suggests to me he's accepted this: the windows, the missing shirt, the closing in. He'll never see his dad again. In this moment, he really does look finished. Leaning forward, fingers buried in his hair, he's staring beyond the far wall without blinking. He looks like a statue of something: one of those bronzed embodiments of abstract concepts. He looks like the perfect sculpture of having come to terms—with loss, with death, his dad's absence—he looks like a Rodin of resignation. Printed across the plinth the treasure chest makes beneath his feet should be the title, 'I'm Finished.'

I feel a newfound respect for him swell inside me. What strength it must have taken for him to be finished! Seeing me staring, he makes a quizzical expression. Then he reaches for the binoculars. 'You want to take a look?' he asks, holding them out. 'Sure,' I say, and cross the room to accept them.

Back at the window I face the Freedom Fuel, raising the binoculars and bracing myself for whatever it is I might see: a rotting face, two white eyes. But by chance what the lenses alight on is the besieged cruiser, its passenger side, and all I have a view of is the backs of two infected as they beat their hands against the window. Their shirts are all I see. A black polo on the left, a blue work shirt on the right. I try panning the binoculars between their shoulders, to clear a sightline through the window, and eventually I get a bead on the officer inside. He's looking out the windshield, head in profile. He can't be much older than we are: a scrawny kid with a blond buzz cut and a strong square jaw like Matt's, gripping the steering wheel and looking bored. He stares stoically ahead, presumably at the three infected pounding on the hood, and I wonder whether the expression on his face (phlegmatic, contemptuous) is what the scuba mask conceals in the shark cage: they want nothing more than to destroy him, but they can't get at him. He can go on sitting there, baiting them, until the van arrives to detain them. Like Matt, this officer is probably fantasizing about putting a bullet in the head of every infected surrounding his car. And perhaps, in the very near future, he'll be authorized to. If quarantines nationwide keep overflowing and no medical solutions are forthcoming, the government might decide to unknot the Gordian hordes by sanctioning mass extermination. Of course, the executions would have to be handled humanely, conducted by whitecoats with syringes. But this kid might still get his chance to take a few potshots. I imagine him and a partner parked in the bayou at night, hunting for strays, one swinging the beam of a roof-mounted searchlight, while the other hangs out of the passenger-side window with a scoped hunting rifle (just like the bored sniper teams who are occasionally dispatched to neutralize nutria rats, prowling the swamps late at night in a wildlife-control jeep, and searching the bright plate of their spotlight for any hollow eyeshine [e.g., in bushes or in lakewater, where two jacklit tapeta, flaring out momentarily, will yield a brief Geminian glimmer]). I imagine the kid and his partner searching the darkness for those milky-green cataracts, and taking a swig of bourbon for every pair that they extinguish. A pull of Bulleit for every bullet they put in the head of an infected.

Stepping back from the window, I manage to get a better angle on the righthand infected. His upper torso is completely visible now, and I can see that his blue work shirt is ratty, scuffed with mud and ripped in places, as if he's been wandering in a swamp himself. No bloodstains, though. The back of his head looks human: a shaggy mane of gray hair, jagging unkemptly to his shoulders. His shoulders slope massively into his torso, which is barrel-shaped and obese. Clearly this infected used to be—is—a tower of a man, huge in height and bulk. He's still leaning against the passenger side of the car, pounding on the window, so it's difficult to tell how tall he really is. But tall, at any rate. Tall enough to carry his excess weight. From his silver head of hair and (literally) blue collar, I try to make inferences about his age, his station. From his shoulders I make inferences about his physical dimensions. What I come up with is that the infected looks about sixty, about six feet, about three hundred pounds. Working class. When I look more closely at his shirt, I notice that it's plaid. The same generic pattern as the scrap in Highland Road Park.

No. That is insane. That is exactly the kind of thought you can't let yourself think, I tell myself. For one thing, you don't even know that he was wearing that plaid shirt when he reanimated. And secondly, *any* infected could be wearing a plaid shirt. You said so yourself. You're making the same mistake Mazoch made, yesterday at the barges. Making a false positive. Treating that torn blue plaid like some boar's tusk scar. No, that infected isn't Mr. Mazoch. It couldn't be.

And yet, on the other hand, it could be. His height, his shape, why not? All that would be required is that his undead body tried returning here today, either for the first time in a month or for the third time this week. Before he could reach his house, he would have been diverted into the Freedom Fuel parking lot, either attracted there himself, or corralled by the police officers. And that could be him pounding on the window of the cruiser, trying to get inside, reaching for the blond-haired square-jawed boy whom he could very well have mistaken for Matt.

I center the infected's head in my binoculars, magnifying its mop of unruly tousles. That way, when it turns around to the house (*its* house?), I'll have its face in frame. Absurdly, I feel this need to see its face, as if everything would be settled then. As if I'd be able to recognize Mr. Mazoch, whose photo I've still never seen, or discern some family resemblance.

But the infected does not turn around. It keeps beating its gray fist against the windowpane. It certainly does look as if it has had a lot of practice punching windowpanes. Indefatigably it beats, showing no sign of stopping, and I know now that nothing is going to catch its attention from behind. In the shatterproof glass, it has found the perfect opponent. Pounding away, it is free to indulge its breaching instinct indefinitely. Nothing will distract it from this task, not until it's too late: not until the LCDC van arrives to detain it. If I want to determine whether it's Mr. Mazoch, I'll have to call Matt over to the window. I'll have to tell him, casually, that some new infected have arrived, and hand him the binoculars to check.

Except I can't just call Matt to the window. Now? Now that he is finally 'finished'? Calling him to the window after he has finally let his father go, and given up the search for good, would be to risk relapse in the worst way. If I made him lock his binoculars on the back of this so-called 'Mr. Mazoch' (but in fact just another false positive, some evilly conceived Mr. Mazoch doppelganger), Matt would be ruined. He would again be filled with wishful thinking about his father: that the man was waiting for him somewhere, that he still existed to be found. Even when the infected did turn around, and Matt confirmed for himself that it was just another false positive, the damage would already be done. The search's embers would be rekindled in Matt: if not this infected, he would tell himself, in this parking lot, then some other infected, somewhere else. The trick was just not to give up.

And even that reaction would be a best-case scenario. Because Matt might not bother waiting for it to turn around. Instead of seeing 'his father' out there, he might simply see the monster he had condemned so mercilessly last night: a 'killing machine' and 'contagious cannibal,' trying to 'solve the problem' of the cop cruiser, beating against the window so that it could get at that officer (that Matt doppelganger) inside. So that it could eat what it thought was its son alive. The moment Matt saw that, he might be crazed with the need to kill it. I'd have to hold him back by main strength, just to keep him from sprinting with his bat to the parking lot, where he'd be sure to get himself arrested, if not shot, if not bitten. Yes. That could happen, too, if I called

Matt over. Then I would have all that blood and horror and heartbreak on my hands.

I think back to the day when Rachel and I visited her father's grave. If I had actually heard something suspicious then (a far rustle underground, a scratching sound), what would I have done? Would I have told her, leaving her no option—psychologically—but to dig down through six feet of earth and splinter her dad's casket? Or would I have let it go, dismissing it as the nothing that it probably was? Sparing her that misery.

I pan the binocular lenses over the infected's shoulder, looking into the car again. This time, the officer's back is to me. With his right hand on the wheel, he's gesturing with the left above his head, whipping his index finger around in a frantic circle, as if miming lasso motions. He appears to be signaling someone. Dropping the binoculars from my eyes, I squint through the sudden sunlight and see whom he must have been signaling: at the edge of the parking lot is the white LCDC van, its sliding side door already open, and two officers in riot gear standing beside it. Their silhouettes are black, a complete and Kevlar dark. When they arrived I have no idea. While I was watching the doppelganger, the LCDC van must have pulled quietly into the parking lot. 'Vermaelen,' I hear Matt say behind me. 'What's the word?' 'Van,' I say. 'Give it a few minutes.'

I steeple my fingers over my brow again, shading my eyes. On the passenger side of the cruiser, Mr. Mazoch (or his doppelganger) is still standing in place. But his companion in the black polo has already begun to wander toward the van, having abandoned the officer at the wheel for the freestanding riot guards. The dark silhouette shuffles slowly, heading across the parking lot's stark white concrete. One of the guards has his arms extended before him, locked stiff like a fisherman's, and as I watch he begins to swivel in place, turning his torso from the cruiser to the van. Suddenly the infected swerves, staggering in that direction, moving in a rigid line toward the van's opened side door. Wherever the guard turns, the infected follows. It takes me a moment to understand what is happening, but then I remember these high-tech shepherd's staffs from the news: they're the standard wildlife handlers, an aluminum pole of pool-cleaning length, with a steel collar attached at its end. Clamping the collar around an infected's neck, an officer can wrench its body in the desired direction, controlling its movements from ten safe feet away. A handler such as this must be what the riot guard is commanding. Invisible in the distance, its thin pole is what's responsible for this optical illusion, in which the guard appears to have telekinetic powers: how he seems to just Jedi the infected forward with his gesturing hands. Sure enough, the second guard now extends his own arms before him, and the infected begins writhing violently, in sudden protest. Meanwhile a third guard is sprawled like a marksman across the van's hood, presumably aiming an assault rifle or something at the entire scene. Providing the others cover as they corral the infected. Everything else is deathly still and quiet.

I raise the binoculars again and zero in on the Mr. Mazoch doppelganger. He is still leaning against the cruiser, but he's motionless, no longer pounding its window with his fist. He stands at attention, all six feet of him ramrod straight with his arms at his sides, his head slightly inclined to peer over the roof. At any moment, I know, he will be unable to resist his curiosity any longer. Following suit with his companion, he will shuffle into the parking lot, to investigate these strange new humans who have arrived on the scene. Then, before he understands what is happening, those mandibular pincers will come clamping around his neck from behind, and an unknown power start wrenching at his spine, until he is dragged into the van.

Even as I am thinking this, Mr. Mazoch—if indeed it is Mr. Mazoch—begins to move. He sidesteps rightward, crabwise, along the length of the cruiser. I follow him with the binoculars, trying to keep his gray head in frame. In seconds he clears the cruiser's hood, and with nothing to separate him from the LCDC van, he begins to stride forward. Soon he has put sufficient distance between himself and the binoculars for me to be able to see, not just his torso, but his entire body. He takes long diagonal lunges across the parking lot, heading for one of the riot guards. He leaves his arms at his sides, where they swing languidly. His gray hands. Over his shoulder, a few yards away, I can just make out the riot guard. He is aiming the wildlife handler at Mr. Mazoch, and he is outfitted (as I'd figured) in the full exoskeletal regalia: the gleaming visored helmet and Kevlar vest and glossy greaves and gloves, all pitch dark in the morning sunlight. He has his combat boots posted firmly on the ground, hunching himself down into a tense stance, preparatory to wrestling with the infected. The aluminum pole is held outright, the collar's clamps opened wide and ready to seize their prey. The thing looks like a praying-mantis face. Mr. Mazoch pauses, as if evaluating the situation. He angles his body leftward slightly, blocking my view of the riot guard, and I can't see what's going on with the pole. Only the familiar close-up of his gray hair and blue plaid shirt. He stands confused, deliberating. He's just a yard out of the mandibles' range. Any moment now—the second he resumes shuffling forward—he is going to walk into that trap. I keep the binoculars trained on the back of his head, too scared to look away. Except then, just when I think that he is about to take a step, something must finally catch his attention from behind. For in a slow, graceless motion he is turning, shifting his body around to face the house.

At the sight of his face in the binoculars, I stop breathing. But it is just a stranger's face. No different from a funeral corpse: the gray skin drawn tight around the mouth, the expression slack and placid. The pallor. At first it is impossible to determine anything by his features. I could easily convince myself that this is Mr. Mazoch's face; I could just as easily convince myself that it isn't. After a second or two I think to close my eyes, and I try—as during the second defamiliarization exercise—to build a mental image of Matt's own face. I clear my head of all interfering thoughts and images, and really try to *see* his face, to see it as it would be in old age. At Mr. Mazoch's age. Beginning with the wire-frame template of Matt's head, I fill it in with flesh and craft the finer details: the strong square jaw, the blunt nose, the cleft chin. Meditating unbrokenly on this face for several moments, I finally snap my eyelids open. And there it is: its afterimage shimmers briefly beyond the binocular lenses, slipping over the infected's face like a mask. It fits the infected's face perfectly. Mapping onto all his contours. The jaw. The blunt nose. Even the cleft chin. Yes. There's no denying it. That is Mazoch's face. Mr. Mazoch's face.

Now would be the time to call Matt to the window, if that were a thing I was going to do. But I can't. As Mr. Mazoch stares back at his house—back at this room where he reanimated, the grave that he crawled out of—I stare mesmerized into his eyes, which are wide open and white, and which seem to be peering into my own eyes, directly through the binocular lenses. I know that this is impossible. That he cannot see me. That at most I would appear as a silhouette in the window, a dim shape beyond the frame. Yet his eyes never blink, and I feel seen. Magnified, they look exactly as I have always imagined: each is as bone-pale and opaque as the Holbein blur. I could swear that they are seeing something. I try to imagine what it must have been like for him, those first few seconds after reanimation. To have to come to in this room, mere moments after bleeding to death. The opening of his eyes one more morning: sunlight on the ceiling, these memories again. Whatever it was he saw then—whether the skull's side of his life, or all the paths of the underworld, or the beacon of a Bethlehem star—it must have led him wandering into the past. For that is the world he belongs to now. That is probably what he's seeing—what he's peering into—at this very moment: memories of this house. Visions of Matt as a kid in this house. The long nights spent cataloguing antiques. As for the house itself—its dilapidated exterior, the dingy siding and shattered windows—he probably can't see it at all. It must appear to him as it appeared to me, in the streaky rearview mirror at the beginning of the week: vague, whorled, amorphous. Which is just as well. The building is not what he came back here to see. This house is not his home, anymore. Even though he has returned to it, he is looking through it—beyond it—to his true home. He cannot see it, but he knows it's here. He is transfixed by something else, his eyes wide open and opiated, lost in an enraptured staring. His gaze is glazed with satiety. Whatever it is he sees, he obviously can't tear his eyes from it. He needs to get his fill of it, before turning his back on it, and facing the riot guard behind him.

Watching him, I realize that Rachel was right: part of me really does desire this. To see for myself. See what it would be like. Of course, I could study the undead for the rest of my life, I know, and still not comprehend what they're experiencing. The only way to see for myself would be to get bitten. That is clearer to me now than ever, confronted with the inscrutable whiteness of Mr. Mazoch's eyes. They are clouded with mystery, giving nothing away. Admonishing me from that other world.

Was Rachel right about that too? Would I actually let myself get bitten? If given the choice, is the infection how I would prefer to go? After all, it is an entirely new form of dying: different from cancer, or car wrecks, or heart attacks. Different from anything any of us grew up expecting. Instead of the certain nothingness of death—the complete cessation of consciousness—there is this strange and ineffable something. And although we can't know what it will be like, we can assume that it is more than nothing. So if someone offered me a bite wound on my deathbed, I might be tempted to take it. When it came time to relinquish being, I might be unwilling—or unable—to let go: of my self, of my memories, of this world. I might try to keep one foot on earth (my phantom foot), while the other tested out Lethe.

Maybe that is the source of Matt's anger: not that Mr. Mazoch let go—let himself get bitten, let himself die—but that he *didn't* let go. That, at the critical moment, he clung to somethingness, rather than pass over into nothingness. I look into his face through the binoculars: his eyes are still wide and white; his mouth hangs open slightly, breathless, in the labored gape of sleep apnea. He may not have let go, but Matt has let him go. As far as Matt's concerned, his father is dead. And once the riot guards clamp him down and wrestle him into the van, Matt won't be responsible for him. Quarantined, Mr. Mazoch will be free to pace back and forth in his room for the rest of his 'life,' walking the treadmill of its floor in the direction of his memories.

I let the binoculars drop to my chest. Instantaneously Mr. Mazoch—if indeed it is Mr. Mazoch—vanishes. His face is replaced by the glacial brightness of the day. Squinting in the sunlight, I can barely even make out the parking lot, where everything has become frozen and small again. It takes me a moment to relocate the doppelganger and the riot guard: I see a bluish silhouette and a blackish silhouette, standing together in a static diorama. A few yards behind them, the other guard is busy with his wildlife handler, tugging an infected forward. As for Mr. Mazoch, he still seems free, for the moment. It's possible that he has already turned around, away from the house, and is about to advance on the riot guard. Or else that the guard has taken a step forward himself, and is about to clamp his neck from behind. They're too far off to know for sure. Whatever the case, it will only be a matter of time. In twenty minutes, half an hour, all of the infected will have been rounded up, and the van will pull as quietly out of the parking lot as it pulled into it. Then the distant *whoop-whoop* of a siren will signal the end of the lockdown, and the barriers will be dragged out of the streets. Matt and I will leave this house. Matt will drive me home.

I turn my back on the window, and have to blink blindly at the dimness of the living room. Matt, a dark shape on the sofa, clears his throat. It has been several minutes since either of us has spoken. 'Vermaelen,' he says. 'See anything out there?' I can't tell whether he's looking at me, but I shake my head. I mean to tell him no. There's nothing to see.

ACKNOWLEDGMENTS

My thanks to the following institutions for their generosity and hospitality: the Iowa Writers' Workshop, especially Connie Brothers, Deb West, and Jan Zenisek; the Speakeasy, especially Jackqueline Frost and Andrew Meyer; and the Corporation of Yaddo, especially Sean Marshall and Candace Wait.

Thanks as well to the following readers for their insight and support: Jin Auh, Adam Eaglin, Aaron Kunin, Eric Obenauf, Emily Pullen, Arden Reed, Ed Skoog, Caroline Thomas, Rachel Van Pelt, and Eliza Jane Wood. Special thanks to Ben Mauk.

Finally, this book is not for or to Sam Chang, but by and with her. Thank you.

COMING SEPTEMBER 2013!

"It's fine work in its manic pacing and its summoning of certain cultural emblems. Present tense with a vengeance. *I hope the book finds the serious readers who are out there waiting for this kind of fiction to hit them in the face*."
—DON DELILLO

MIRA CORPORA IS THE DEBUT NOVEL FROM ACCLAIMED PLAYWRIGHT Jeff Jackson, an inspired, dreamlike adventure by a distinctive new talent.

LITERARY AND INVENTIVE, BUT ALSO FAST-PACED AND GRIPPING, *Mira Corpora* charts the journey of a young runaway. A coming-of-age story for people who hate coming-of-age stories, featuring a colony of outcast children, teenage oracles, amusement parks haunted by gibbons, mysterious cassette tapes, and a reclusive underground rockstar.

WITH ASTOUNDING PRECISION, JACKSON WEAVES A MOVING TALE of discovery and self-preservation across a startling, vibrant landscape.

Pre-order now for $16 at <u>TwoDollarRadio.com!</u>

Also published by **TWO DOLLAR RADIO**

HOW TO GET INTO THE TWIN PALMS
A NOVEL BY KAROLINA WACLAWIAK

"One of my favorite books this year." —*The Rumpus*

"Waclawiak's novel reinvents the immigration story."
—*New York Times Book Review*, Editors' Choice

RADIO IRIS
A NOVEL BY ANNE-MARIE KINNEY

"Kinney is a Southern California Camus." —*Los Angeles Magazine*

"[*Radio Iris*] has a dramatic otherworldly payoff that is unexpected and
triumphant." —*New York Times Book Review*, Editors' Choice

THE PEOPLE WHO WATCHED HER PASS BY
A NOVEL BY SCOTT BRADFIELD

"Challenging [and] original... A billowy adventure of a book. In a book
that supplies few answers, Bradfield's lavish eloquence is the presiding
constant." —*New York Times Book Review*

I'M TRYING TO REACH YOU
A NOVEL BY BARBARA BROWNING

✱ *The Believer* Book Award Finalist.

"I think I love this book so much because it contains intimations
of the potential of what books can be in the future, and also
because it's hilarious." —Emily Gould, *BuzzFeed*

THE ORANGE EATS CREEPS
A NOVEL BY GRACE KRILANOVICH

✱ National Book Foundation 2010 '5 Under 35' Selection.
✱ *NPR* Best Books of 2010.
✱ *The Believer* Book Award Finalist.

"Krilanovich's work will make you believe that new ways of storytelling
are still emerging from the margins." —*NPR*